BORROWED BRIDE

A FAKE MARRIAGE, SECRET BABY, DARK, MAFIA ROMANCE

AJME WILLIAMS

Copyright © 2025 by Ajme Williams

All rights reserved.

No part of this book may be reproduced in any form or by any electronic or mechanical means, including information storage and retrieval systems, without written permission from the author, except for the use of brief quotations in a book review.

This is a work of fiction. Names, characters, businesses, places, events and incidents are either the products of authors imagination or used in a fictitious manner. Any resemblance to actual persons, living or dead, or actual events is purely coincidental. The following story contains mature themes, strong language and sexual situations. It is intended for mature readers only.

All characters are 18+ years of age and all sexual acts are consensual.

ABOUT THE AUTHOR

Ajme Williams writes emotional, angsty contemporary romance. All her books can be enjoyed as full length, standalone romances and are FREE to read in Kindle Unlimited.

Mafia Mysteries (this series)
Tangled Loyalties | Savage Devotion | Bulletproof Baby | Cursed Confessions | Borrowed Bride

Dynasty of Deception
Merciless King | Ice Princess | Lost Prince | Stolen Queen | Triplets for the Mafia Prince | The Godfather's Christmas Twins

Shadows of Redemption Series
Soldier of Death | Queen of Misfortune | Prince of Darkness | Angel of Mercy

The Why Choose Haremland
Protecting Their Princess | Protecting Her Secret | Unwrapping their Christmas Present | Cupid Strikes... 3 Times | Their Easter Bunny |

SEAL Daddies Next Door | Naughty Lessons | See Me After Class | Blurred Lines | Nanny for the Firefighters | Snowy Secrets

High Stakes
Bet On It | A Friendly Wager | Triple or Nothing | Press Your Luck

Heart of Hope Series
Our Last Chance | An Irish Affair | So Wrong | Imperfect Love | Eight Long Years | Friends to Lovers | The One and Only | Best Friend's Brother | Maybe It's Fate | Gone Too Far | Christmas with Brother's Best Friend | Fighting for US | Against All Odds | Hoping to Score | Thankful for Us | The Vegas Bluff | 365 Days | Meant to Be | Mile High Baby | Silver Fox's Secret Baby | Snowed In with Best Friend's Dad | Secret Triplets for Christmas | Off-Limits Daddy

Billionaire Secrets
Twin Secrets | Just A Sham | Let's Start Over | The Baby Contract | Too Complicated

Dominant Bosses
His Rules | His Desires | His Needs | His Punishments | His Secret

Strong Brothers
Say Yes to Love | Giving In to Love | Wrong to Love You | Hate to Love You

Fake Marriage Series
Accidental Love | Accidental Baby | Accidental Affair | Accidental Meeting

Irresistible Billionaires
Admit You Miss Me | Admit You Love Me | Admit You Want Me | Admit You Need Me

Check out Ajme's full Amazon catalogue here.

Join her VIP NL here.

DESCRIPTION

I picked the pocket of New York's most dangerous man.
I never planned to see him again...
Until he claimed me as his wife.
Now I'm carrying his child – and his secrets.

Rule number one: Never steal from a mobster.
Rule number two: If you break rule one, don't agree to be his fake wife.
And the golden rule? Don't fall for the ruthless, irresistible mafia king who now calls you his.

Because when you break all these rules, you're left with a shattered heart, a secret child, and years of hiding from the man who thinks you're buried six feet under.

Self-preservation was never my strong suit.
Marco Barrone wasn't just another mark.
He was a predator in Armani, with eyes like winter steel and a smile that promised ruin.
Dangerous. Magnetic. Lethal.

I thought I was smart, lifting his wallet in a sea of New York faces. I've never been more wrong.

When his hand clamped on my wrist, I expected a bullet. Instead, I got a ring, a fake marriage, and a night that left me with more than just memories.

Now I'm hiding a secret bigger than both of us – a little girl with his eyes and my smile.
A daughter he doesn't know exists.

Six years later, just when I thought fate was done toying with me... Two pink lines tell me I'm about to double down on my mistakes.

Marco is about to be a father again.
This time... to twins!

1

GIANNA

A distant rumble of thunder through the stone-gray clouds above sends shivers down my spine.

There's a storm coming.

The subtle rumble adds a note of haste to the stream of people around me who flow, unhindered by my stationary presence, like a river flowing around a rock. No one notices me. No one stops to ask if I'm okay or if I need help.

Every New Yorker is in their own world, floating in a bubble that instantly becomes more secluded with the threat of rain hanging overhead.

I sip the coffee I bargained from the cart a few blocks over, watching men tuck their coats tighter around their necks and women clutch their bags a little closer as they pick up the pace. Traffic flows like the rapids, stopping for no one until the red light acts like a damn and forces a halt to the flow. Horns screech loudly as if the red light is a strange anomaly and a never-before-seen phenomenon. The river of people around me wanes slightly as groups hurry to the other side of the street, and then it starts up again.

This works in my favor. When people are distracted, they're more interested in getting back to their cozy homes, safe from the rain.

They don't notice someone like me.

The homeless don't exist.

I scan the crowd as the last hot dregs of my coffee slip down my throat and pick a target.

I'm not fussy about who, but the man I spot looks like he's got some cash to spare. I'm cold, and with a storm coming, I definitely don't want to spend another night on the street.

Topping up my funds is as easy as slipping my fingers into unsuspecting pockets, but in order to get something that secures me a few nights in a decent hotel, I need to steal from someone so careless they won't think to cancel their missing card until at least a few days later.

From the way my target is barking at the poor girl behind the pretzel cart, he looks exactly like the type. He's tall and rotund, with a cream coat dragging behind him as the long fingers of the wind whip through the streets. A stronger gust knocks the porkpie hat from his head, and of course, he takes that out on the pretzel girl too.

She keeps her head down, busy with salting the twisted dough in her hand.

I crush my paper cup against my palm and stride forward with my head held high. Weaving around the people of New York is second nature to me now; I've been doing this for almost as long as I can remember. It's as easy as breathing, and in a single blink, I slip into character.

My smile becomes easy, and my auburn locks dance about my shoulders, thick enough to withstand the next rushing gust of wind.

A few inches away from the man, I stumble hard with a soft cry and launch myself into his arms. His tirade abruptly ends as he has no choice but to catch me.

"What the bloody hell do you think you're doing?" he barks at me in a deep voice. He's so angry that his plump cheeks ripple when he snaps his mouth shut. "Watch where you are—"

There it is.

The moment we lock eyes, this man instantly stumbles over his words and a crimson flush rises in his cheeks. His anger dissipates because a beautiful woman has just fallen into his arms.

"Oh, sir, thank you so much!" I gasp, putting my whole heart into sounding distressed and grateful. "I just got so dizzy all of a sudden and lost my footing."

"My—it's ... it's quite alright," the man mumbles. He grips my arm and uses his body to steady me—just as my fingers slip into his pocket and locate the heavy leather of his wallet.

Within three seconds, it's stuffed deep into the pocket of my leather jacket.

"I'm so sorry," I say again, leaning heavily against the man as I pretend to be uncertain of my stability.

"Are you okay? Do you need me to call someone?"

Our eyes meet and the truth of his questions is clear in his eyes. He wants me to be okay. He wants me to be so thankful that he stopped me falling that I throw myself at him and fulfill his wildest dreams. That deep hunger is so apparent that it sickens me.

Men are too easy to read.

"No need," I say, finally steadying myself and placing a hand over my bust, drawing his eye to my visible cleavage. "I think it was just a dizzy spell. Thank you, thank you so much."

I step around him, sliding my hand slowly over his forearm. He's so distracted that he only nods and smiles at me, his eyes still firmly on my chest. I glance at the girl behind the cart, who stands with eyes wide, holding the pretzel up. I wink at her and make a note to send a tip from this guy's wallet. Then I melt into the crowd with my prize.

I don't open his wallet until I'm two blocks away. Inside are a couple of credit cards, his ID, and a generous wad of cash. His useless club cards end up in the trash alongside my discarded cup, and I pocket the wallet and credit cards. Counting the cash, my heart sinks. It's a thick lump, but it's all small bills totaling seventy-five dollars.

He won't notice his wallet is missing because he has no plans to pay for that pretzel. And when he eventually does notice, he won't remember enough about me to call the cops. But, at most, I have two days with his cards.

I need to find a hotel that will let me withdraw cash. Given how untraceable it can be, it's my preferred method of payment, but given his lack of on-hand cash, I doubt it will be enough.

I need another mark.

The sky grows darker, and the people around me are more aggressive in their movements. I wander down the street with my hands in my pockets, dodging men and women seeking shelter from the faint drizzle of rain that appears in the air.

Suddenly, a sharp scream cuts above the noise of the traffic and my heart leaps into my throat. No one else around me reacts. I scan the crowd, searching multiple faces for the source of the scream just in case someone is in need of real help.

I locate the source thirty seconds later, and what I feared was a scream of terror turns out to be a scream of excitement from a child bouncing up and down on the balls of his feet. He's pressed against the window of a toy store, breathing heavily against the glass and pointing furiously at something inside. His parents stand around him with affectionate smiles on their faces, and I watch as they scoop him up, kiss his cheek, and carry him inside.

A bitter flurry of resentment rises inside me.

Life on the streets is rough, but seeing happy families just makes it even rougher. Seeing what I never had brings out my bitter, jealous side. It's pathetic, being jealous of a child. But I can't help it. Most of my family are dead or dead to me. There's no love there. No comfort.

Certainly no loving kisses and toy shopping.

I kick the ground as I walk, trying to shake out the bitterness.

I have to refocus. I need more money. Something decent that will get me a score big enough so I don't need to worry about food for at least a week.

The streets thin out as the rain turns from a faint drizzle in the air to something slightly more substantial. Those impatient with the weather seek out taxis to carry them home. Maybe I'd be doing the same if I had somewhere to go.

Then I see him. Out of the crowd melts someone who just *screams* arrogant dick. They're a little more difficult to steal from, but it's always worth the risk.

This man strides tall through the street, utterly unfazed by the weather and seemingly blind to how those around him scurry out of the way. He must be someone important, or at least he thinks he is. Sometimes, all it takes is the right attitude to trick people.

I know that all too well.

He's tall, with black hair slicked away from his forehead save a single curl that sweeps down across a lined forehead. Dark brows pull together as he walks and talks, muttering close to the phone in his hand.

Surprisingly, he's quite handsome. More than handsome, actually. His chiseled features are straight out of a magazine, with an angular nose and a square jaw so sharp it could cut straight through glass. A dusting of dark facial hair shadows his full, pink lips.

And his eyes.

They're a striking ice blue, seemingly gleaming in this dark gray world. I can't stop staring at him as he strolls down the opposite street, moving like he's the only man in existence.

He's the perfect mark. I move from where I've been hugging a wall and take a few steps toward the crossing, but as I do, I spot something else.

This man isn't alone. At first, I think he's being followed, given how these other men blend into the crowd and would be missed by anyone unskilled. But I see them as clear as day. Usually, I'm on the lookout for other people sneaking so I don't move in on someone else's mark, but this time it brings these men to my attention.

They're dressed in dark jeans and sweaters, much more casual compared to the handsome man's pristine suit. I can tell at a glance he's got an Armani shirt on, and those can go for fifteen hundred dollars alone. It's not until one of the men quickens their steps and takes the phone from the handsome man that I realize what they are.

He's not being followed. He's being protected.

This should warn me away from him, but it doesn't. I press the button, bringing the river of traffic to a halt, and then I cross the road to his side.

I like a challenge. I can already picture what it will be like to soak in a gold tub on this man's dime, knowing I swiped his gold right from under his nose and the nose of his guards.

The little voice in my mind that warns me not to be stupid slowly fades away, smothered by the sudden increase in my heart rate. Adrenaline sweeps through me and my fingertips tingle. He favors his left side as he walks. It's subtle but his left arm doesn't swing out as wide, which means that's where he keeps his valuables.

I straighten my posture and fluff my hair, using the dampness from the light rain to my advantage and quickly curling my bangs. I'll use the old stumble trick here because I'm confident this man will be far too annoyed at my presence to care.

People step aside as he strides closer, and suddenly, there's no one between him and me.

Then he looks me in the eyes.

It's so unexpected that I nearly overbalance. People in New York don't look me in the eye. They can sense my homelessness just by being in my vicinity so they never, ever look me in the eye.

He does, and for a brief second I'm completely entranced by the gemstone-like shimmer in his icy eyes. Just as quickly as he looks at me, he looks away.

Shit.

Get it together, Gianna.

Shaking the strange, entranced feeling away, I tilt my head down and pretend not to see him. As soon as I'm close enough, I stumble into him with a surprise cry.

"Oh my God, I'm so sorry! These shoes are killer, I swear." My hands subtly grasp his coat for balance and I push into him, trying to throw him off-balance. The man is like a rock and a wall of solid muscle presses against my body as I fake my loss of balance.

Within three seconds, his slim wallet is in my grasp and tucked into my shirt as I straighten up.

"Sorry!" I don't glance up at him, not wanting to be caught in that icy stare once more, and then continue down the street as if nothing happened.

The weight of his wallet rests against my collarbone, safety tucked under a strap.

Suddenly, a large, rough palm grabs my bare forearm and jerks me backward. My heart leaps into my throat as I spin around, and the tall, handsome stranger bears down on me.

Shit!

He throws me backward, and I hit the brick wall hard enough to knock all of the air out of my lungs. I gasp hoarsely. The man gives me no space. He presses right up against me with his hands firmly gripping my waist and pinning me to the wall. The rough brick scraps against my lower back as my T-shirt rides up.

My heart races.

"Not so fast," growls a deep voice so gravelly that a strange, warm shiver curls up my spine and skitters across my shoulders. Muscles strain against his expensive white shirt, and as the fabric pulls at the buttons, I glimpse some dark ink underneath.

Hesitantly, I look up, and I'm instantly trapped in those icy eyes.

Around him, the men from earlier close in like shadows, blocking all possible escape routes.

"You picked the wrong man's pocket, sweetheart."

2

MARCO

A pickpocket. It's not unheard of, but this one is either stupid or damn suicidal.

"Was it worth it?" I demand, my voice low enough for only her to hear as my hands sweep up her waist. Where did she stash it? A pickpocket as fast as her surely didn't have to hide my wallet somewhere I couldn't reach. The fabric of her T-shirt rises with my fingers, briefly exposing her midriff.

"Worth it?" she hisses back. Her head jerks away from where my lips tease the shell of her ear and I'm faced with thick auburn curls.

"In some cultures, you'd lose a hand for what you've just done. Stealing like some filthy street rat."

She doesn't reply. Coward.

My knuckles brush against the weight in the left pocket of her jacket just as I find a firm bulge near her breast tucked just underneath her shirt. I'm not kind as I roughly seek out both items and pull them from her. Taking half a step back, I glance down.

Two wallets. One is brown, worn and frayed at the edges. It's heavier than my own sleek, black card holder. It seems this thief has an array of talents.

Traffic beeps behind us, and the air fills with the slick sound of tires on a road that's getting wetter by the second. I don't have time to delay, but I'm also not walking away from this just yet.

"Is it a death wish you have? The last person to steal from me was cut into tiny little pieces and fed, bit by bit, to the hippo at the zoo," I say, studying her from head to toe.

She's trembling.

Her knee shakes against my own despite the firm set line of her lips and the sharp edge in her gaze. She's not what I would expect from a pickpocket at all.

"That's twisted," the woman replies tightly.

"So is stealing," I snap, lifting my wallet. "This is not yours. I don't give a shit what little sad story brought you to the streets so I'll ask you again, do you have a fucking death wish?" I don't try to keep the anger out of my tone, but as she shakes before me while trying to look unaffected, I take her in fully.

The rain drizzling around us soaks into her hair, darkening the auburn and bringing out the red streaks hidden in the color. Her almond-shaped eyes, lined with black, are espresso-brown, though they almost look like pools of black ink in the low light. She has an oval face and full pink lips that turn pale with how she repeatedly presses them together. Dressed in tight jeans and a T-shirt that hugs her shapely figure, the leather jacket might be the most expensive thing she owns.

I wouldn't be surprised if that were stolen too.

Our eyes meet and a short, unexpected jolt of tension bolts through my chest. For a fraction of a second, she reminds me of someone. Someone long dead to me. The woman I once gave my entire heart and soul to.

Never again. She was cruelly taken from me, and that kind of pain never fades.

"Well?" I ask, tapping the wallets against one another. "Rat lost her voice?"

She lifts her chin slightly, exposing the golden length of her throat to my gaze. "I'm not a rat. You look like an asshole. Easy mark that doesn't keep an eye on his belongings." She smirks slightly and that right-slanted curl of her upper lip is so similar that tension forms in my chest once more.

Odd.

I open my wallet in front of her. "You read me so well, so tell me, where does the value lie? Is it the wallet itself? It's expensive leather; I'm sure you could pawn that to some disgusting broker for a pretty penny. Is it this?" My fingertips nudge against the sparkling platinum trinket that dangles from the corner of the wallet. It's the only thing that's out of place in my entire look—my entire world—but it's a dear gift from my sister, and I'd kill without hesitation if it were stolen.

"Is it the money?" I flip open my wallet and pull out the wad of cash. At a glance, it's maybe two grand in big bills. I toss them out and her gaze drops to watch them scatter around her worn boots, soaking into the puddles forming around us. "No, that can't be right. While money is traceable, these days most people don't carry cash. It's the cards, isn't it?"

She remains tense despite the trembling of her knee against my own. "Sure. Assholes like you have more money than sense. You wouldn't miss some fucking plastic."

Her attitude amuses me despite the anger that her little stunt has caused.

"And this." I open the other wallet. It's empty of cash but there's a single credit card and some ID. Sliding it out, I study the information. "David Garcia. A relation?"

"A dumbass."

"Strange name for a victim."

"You're both far from being that," she snaps.

"Really? You think theft is a victimless crime?"

"I know it is," she replies tightly. "People like him. You. You don't know shit about suffering. All that money, it's not something you deserve. Whatever. If you're gonna kill me then kill me."

My free hand attaches to her throat within half a second and I tighten my grip just enough for her eyes to flash with alarm.

"You think you can pretend that you're not scared to die?" I hiss closely, brushing our noses together. "You *stole* from me. But you think it's all about money because of your pathetic, narrow-minded view of value. I'm not pissed about the money, or the cards, but this?"

I hold up my wallet so the little butterfly dangles from the corner. Her dark eyes dart to it.

"I'd start *wars* over this, you rat."

I step back. She slouches down the wall, coughing sharply and touching her throat with her own palm. "You're crazy," she gasps wetly.

"And you, what are you? Just a street thief? Have prostitutes upgraded since I last went looking for tail?" There's no denying her beauty. In fact, she's quite stunning in a dirty sort of way. If she was cleaned up and appropriately dressed, she'd crush the hearts of a dozen men with one glance.

"Fuck you," the woman spits. "I'm not a whore."

"Boss." One of my guards steps forward before I can reply. He slides his hand over his gun and the woman's eyes dart down to it immediately. "You want me to take care of this? You've got places to be."

As he speaks, my attention never leaves her. She doesn't flinch at the sight of the gun. Maybe she really isn't scared to die.

Frederick is right. I have places to be. And yet, somehow, I can't bring myself to walk away because another idea is forming in my mind. A street rat with no family and no value outside of what she steals from others.

She may be the perfect solution to a pressing problem.

"Call and delay," I order Frederick. "You, girl, what's your name?"

"What, you don't want to call me 'rat' anymore?"

"Rat it is," I decide, having no patience to battle back and forth with her. "I will give you a chance to earn your life back."

Her brow lifts and her eyes narrow while she massages her throat. "How?"

Inside my wallet, I remove my American Express Centurion Card and hold it out to her. "If you can find the limit on this card by the end of the day, you can go free. If you can't, you have to face the consequences of stealing from me with no exceptions."

She reaches for the card immediately but I curl it back toward myself, forcing her to hesitate.

"Do you understand? If you fail, then I get to do *whatever* I want with you. I could kill you. Sell you. *Fuck* you."

Her lower lip curls into her mouth and her brows knit together, then she glances up and fixes me with a steady stare. "Do I get to keep what I buy?"

Not the response I was expecting. "Sure, why not."

She takes the card and studies it, turning it over in her hands. "My name is Gianna."

"Marco."

∼

THE SHOPPING SPREE starts exactly as you would expect. Gianna picks the most expensive-looking storefront on the street and strides inside, buying everything she can get her hands on. She snaps up whole floors of furniture, entire suites dedicated to decorating new rooms, and all sorts of decor—including wallpaper and flooring. Each time she selects something, the card clears the purchase, and she moves on.

For two hours, we move from store to store, and she buys everything—the local bookstore ends up with empty shelves and an empty storeroom, the furniture shop has to close because they have no stock left, and five jewelry stores try to give her discounts based on the amount she's buying. She refuses, paying full price for everything.

She doesn't reach the card limit.

Gianna changes tactics as the skies above finally crack and the downpour starts. She goes from hotel to hotel, not caring about the downpour even as my guards try to keep her dry under umbrellas. She buys out every single available room, complete with room service.

"What are you doing?" I ask as she pauses in the middle of the street and quickly texts someone.

The rain rattles hard against the umbrellas keeping us dry, and Gianna flashes her phone at me.

"I'm not calling for help if that's what you're asking. I'm posting on a few forums that can reach out to the homeless around here and let them know a room has been paid for. Those people can get shelter from the storm."

She talks as if it's the most obvious thing in the world, and then she strides forward and continues her trip. It's an odd choice. With a challenge like this, I would expect Gianna to buy as many cars and boats as she can think of, but her mind seems to stall on the concept of luxury. Instead, she buys furniture and books to donate. She scoops up hotel rooms for the homeless.

And then we buy out an entire grocery store that she then instructs to be handed out to any of the homeless still on the streets while keeping a bag for herself. The bag contains personal hygiene products, vitamins, and other necessities that really should be an afterthought, along with that kind of card in her hand.

Still the card swipes, and still each transaction ticks through.

By the time night falls, Gianna runs out of open shops to visit. Soaked to the bone from all her rushing around, my guards and I lightly guide her toward a private boutique that refuses to let her inside until they catch sight of me.

They fall over themselves apologizing but I ignore them. My focus is entirely on her.

For a thieving rat, she's not what I expect. Most of her kind that I've come across are greedy and only care for themselves. I've killed any that I haven't flipped to work for me. After all, a talented pickpocket can be invaluable at the right gatherings.

But Gianna is different. Her focus is on other people rather than her own well-being.

The clock strikes eight and Gianna stands on a small circular stage in the middle of the dressing room while an assistant helps her into a gorgeous deep blue silk gown. It flows over her curves like water, and the silver embroidery around her bust draws my eyes to the swell of her chest over and over.

I won't deny her attractiveness. The way she carries herself is admirable and the small plan in my mind, the one that's been growing since I met her, is almost complete.

"Are you going to kill me?" Gianna asks suddenly, causing the assistant to drop her box of pins in surprise.

"Why?" I ask from where I recline in one of the soft leather chairs, tilting a complimentary glass of scotch back and forth between my fingers. "Do you think I should?"

"The dress cleared on your card," Gianna says. "Every single dress cleared. Every single thing I bought today has cleared without issue. I can't even fathom the expense. That card has no limit."

"It does."

"I don't believe you." She turns away from me, admiring herself in the mirror.

The dress is backless. The beautiful blue fabric hugs her body and creates a deep V-shape right at the base of her spine. I stare at the expanse of visible bare skin, and my fingertips tingle with a sudden urge to touch.

"You tricked me with a new card," Gianna continues, then she turns back to me. "Admit it."

"Is it a trick if you're the one that stole it in the first place?" I shoot the assistant a glare and she abandons her job and flees from the room. "You forget that you stole from me. *You* are the criminal. I gave you an out. Maybe you just didn't want it enough."

I walk slowly toward the stage.

Gianna's chest lifts and the hollow of her neck deepens. "Giving me a card with no limit sets me up for failure."

"It has a limit." I tap my temple with two fingers. "Up here. You can't fault me for knowing how to take care of myself."

Gianna swallows a soft, audible gulp as I reach the stage. "So you are going to kill me."

"No," I reply. "Not while you're wearing that dress. Take it off."

Her eyes narrow and I tense slightly, waiting for her reaction.

Will she run? Will she fight? Will she try and talk her way out of it?

Gianna does neither.

She reaches for the halter strap of her dress and unclasps it. When the dress falls from her body, it runs down her like water and pools around her ankle like a droplet of moonlight. She stands there in her underwear and her lips apart.

Before she can speak, I grasp the side of her neck and jerk her toward me. Our mouths collide in a sudden, powerful kiss that sends a jolt of yearning through my entire body. Her hands land against my chest, bracing herself against me. When her fingertips curl and press into my shirt, I prepare for a bite of teeth or something more, but there's nothing.

Continuing to surprise me, Gianna kisses me back. My world narrows to the soft press of her lips as they weave against my own, following my path in the kiss. She smells faintly of vanilla and rainwater, and her skin is hot beneath my palm. The contact is almost too much, as if an electrical charge simmers beneath her skin, searing into my hand.

When I pull back, Gianna pants, and her warm breath ghosts over my cheek.

"Perfect." I step back. She will be more than satisfactory for what I need. "You almost made me believe you could stand to kiss me. Good. Because this is just the beginning of how you're going to pretend to be my wife."

3

GIANNA

His wife?

I should say no. Who the hell demands that kind of thing from a stranger?

He stands there with his broad shoulders and his stupid, handsome face, leaving my lips tingling from the sheer pressure of the kiss, and then tells me I will be his wife.

Who the hell is this guy? With his gaggle of armed men standing in each corner of the dressing room and the waiting room beyond the curtains, a limitless card, and such an inflated ego that he thinks he can snatch a woman from the street?

Sure, I stole from him. I started this, but most people called the cops. This whole song and dance are so out of my wheelhouse that I have no idea how to navigate it.

And yet, there's a bubble of excitement fizzing away just beneath my ribs. It's exciting in an alarming way. A challenge I've never navigated before and, perhaps, an opportunity. This man is clearly rich and very powerful.

Maybe, just maybe, I can play him.

It wouldn't be the first time I've faked my way into a man's life to get what I needed. If I treat him like a mark, just like all of the others, then maybe I can turn this to my advantage. At least until I find a window to escape.

Hopefully, with a bunch of money to boot.

My pulse thrums like a drum beneath my skin and I look up into his icy gaze. Each time we lock eyes, I feel utterly pinned. It's like I've lost all control of my body. It's as thrilling as it is intimidating but I know how to work men. At their core, they're all the same, and this guy clearly has a raging boner for control.

Playing around that will be too easy.

He thinks he's picked up just a regular street rat scraping for survival. He has no idea what I'm really capable of.

"Sure," I say, slipping into an old persona I've used countless times to trick rich, hard men. "Do I get to know why you need a wife so quickly? You strike me as a man who can get anything he wants at the snap of his fingers."

"I can," Marco replies and he steps away. "But where's the fun in that? Get dressed."

He strides away from me and I step out of the puddle of fabric at my feet. Before I can make it off the stage though, he snaps his fingers in my direction.

Irritation immediately heats my blood. How obnoxious can this guy get?

"Wear that dress," Marco says, pointing at the blue one I recently discarded. "It has a part to play too."

A part to play? This guy talks like he's in the middle of some gigantic puzzle that only he can see. As he leaves, the rest of his guards follow him, giving me a moment of privacy.

I force a few deep, calming breaths to try and ease the rabbit-fast patter of my heart. The dressing room is an enclosed oval; the only way in or out is through the curtains Marco just stepped through. I have no choice but to dress and head out to meet him.

"Breathe, Gianna," I whisper, trying to comfort myself. "You've got this. Just another mark. Just another setup."

Unfortunately, the sound of my own voice doesn't calm me as much as I hope, and my fingers tremble as I step back into that dress.

I've never felt something so soft and silky against my skin, but as lovely as it is, it disgusts me slightly. I haven't showered in days. Wearing something this luxurious just feels *wrong*. I pluck at the fabric, trying to make myself comfortable but it clings to me like a second skin.

A new skin for a new life.

The dress is beautiful though. I just hope I don't have to wear it for long.

"Miss?" The assistant from earlier pops her head through the curtain. Upon seeing me dressed, she hurries closer with a pair of silver, strappy heels in her hands. "Marco's requested you wear these."

"What about my boots?" I glance forlornly at my trusty brown boots set neatly beside my old, folded clothes.

"I'm sorry, Miss. He says you won't need them any longer."

There it is—that control he enjoys so much. He wants to control what I wear and what I do.

Do I play the part? Or do I push back?

"Thank you." Smiling warmly at the assistant, I take the shoes from her and she dips her head, then hurries away.

I have a plan.

After fluffing what I can of my messy hair, I carry the strappy shoes in one hand and my bag of necessities in the other. My own comfortable boots warm my feet as I stride out of the dressing room and into the front of the store.

Marco waits by the door, having a hushed conversation with one of his guards—Frederick, I think he's called? Marco's ice-cold eyes dart to me for a second, then his entire stance freezes like a board when he sees the shoes in my hand and not on my feet.

"What do you think you are doing?"

"Anyone with any knowledge of women knows you don't wear shoes like *these* to travel. What kind of husband would you be, wanting me to break my ankle wearing these in the street?" I drop the fancy shoes into his hands as I glide past him with my head held high. "Those are party shoes, *dear*, not traveling ones."

I expect him to grab me like he's done before—and I'll need hours of therapy to work out why him grabbing me by the throat got me so hot and bothered—but he doesn't. Instead, Frederick opens the door for me, seemingly at Marco's instruction, and we head outside. Umbrellas are immediately raised to keep the rain at bay and Marco strides out next to me.

The shoes stay in his hand.

Smiling to myself, I gather my dress around my knees and slide into the waiting limo when he opens the door for me. Inside, the seats are butter-soft white leather and I immediately sink into them with a soft groan.

Luxury feels so damn good.

The doors shut with a soft but ominous click behind Marco, sealing my fate.

The carpet is dark, and the ceiling is covered in multiple tiny lights that sparkle like stars. One side of the limo holds a small table filled with various glasses and bottles, all secured in place by rubber grips to prevent them from falling. Dark wooden paneling runs the length of the doors, and the faint smell of smoke lingers in the air.

"Do you smoke?" I ask as distaste curls in my gut. I didn't taste ash on him during that unexpected kiss.

"No," Marco replies shortly. "My father does."

His father. Another piece of the puzzle. The more I know about Marco, the more I can play this game to my advantage. I'm already taking the shoes as a win when Marco sits them on the seat between us.

"So, are you going to give me the rundown?" I ask as the car pulls forward. Despite the softness of the seat, I remain stiff and on my guard. "Snatching a random woman from the street kind of screams desperation."

"So does stealing wallets," Marco replies. "Making a living off the backs of hard-working people. How *honorable*."

I narrow my eyes. "And you made all this money by being honorable? Wealth is inherently *dis*honorable."

"I wasn't talking about me," Marco replies. "The other wallet you had."

"Oh." I shrug. "He was an asshole to the pretzel girl so he deserved it."

"Moral theft." Marco watches me intently. "Interesting."

His gaze suddenly feels heavy and the building warmth inside the limo quickly becomes smothering. I adjust myself against the cushion and press my knees together.

"Is Gianna your real name?" Marco asks suddenly.

I contemplate lying and giving him an alias, but there's a risk he'll catch me out, so I stick with it. "Yes."

"I'll keep it short. I need a woman on my arm to appease my father. He's continuously harping on me about providing an heir for the family and I'm tired of it. My focus needs to be elsewhere on business, so that's where you come in. You will be kind and polite, respectful to everyone you meet. And—" Marco locks eyes with me. "You will keep your nose out of things that don't concern you. Am I clear?"

I'm a little too stunned to respond, but Marco continues regardless.

"In return, I will keep a roof over your head and I will provide for you so you no longer have to steal American Express Centurion Cards to buy *toothpaste*."

My cheeks heat up immediately. "Clearly you've never had to worry about where your next meal comes from," I mutter.

"No." Marco lifts one dark brow. "And you won't either. This deal will last so long as you can persuade my father and anyone else that we are married. Your job will be to keep the prying to a minimum, understand?"

This man is so ... confusing. He's clearly a good deal older than me, which doesn't faze me. I've scammed men of all ages, and all it takes is knowing which buttons to press. But there's something different about Marco that I can't quite put my finger on. He's cold, and clearly full of himself, but there are other things that trip me up.

His father demands an heir? A secret business?

He's clearly not political because that *warm* personality isn't earning any votes. I can't picture him as royal either, not with his guards threatening to shoot me in the street. So what is he, a cocky asshole with a trust fund?

Or something more criminal?

It has to be. What other option is there for this amount of wealth?

"Am I expected to actually give you an heir?" I joke softly, trying to get a read on Marco. "Because that will cost more than decent toothpaste."

"We will try," Marco replies flatly, and it's impossible to tell if he's joking back.

My stomach suddenly twists itself into knots and I bite back a groan. I've talked my way into several beds over the years. When I was younger, it was the safest way to get a warm bed for the night, but I was always gone by morning.

This is different. Serious. He doesn't *actually* expect me to give him a baby, does he?

My mouth turns to cotton, and I slide my fingertips over the twisted silver piping lining the hem of my dress. This may be too much for me.

I can play a lot of acts, but I can't fake a baby.

Suddenly, there's a time limit on my escape.

The air thickens in the car as we fall silent, swaying slightly as the car weaves through the streets of New York, carrying me further and further away from my familiar stomping ground.

The longer we drive, the tighter my gut twists. I'm alone.

Utterly and completely.

The one thing that catches my eye as we drive is Marco. He's mostly a stoic rock, emotionless, with his attention down on his phone. He doesn't speak. He scarcely even appears to breathe, but there's one movement that I watch intently.

As he sits there, he toys with the butterfly charm that dangles from the edge of his wallet. He'd mentioned earlier that the charm is the only thing he considers to have value, and my curiosity rises.

"What is that?" I ask. "That charm? Is it important?"

Marco doesn't reply. He doesn't even look up, but he tucks the charm away from sight into his pocket.

So, we're not going to talk about that. Got it.

The silence lasts for the rest of the drive. When the limo pulls to a stop, Marco hands me the shoes with a stern look and climbs from the car.

I roll my eyes and accept. I won the earlier battle but here I will lose. I remove my boots, the last comfort of my old life, and slip my feet into the fancy shoes. They're so new that the straps bite into my ankle, and my heel slips slightly against the sole, but they're on.

I slide from the limo onto a gravel driveway, and Marco's arm is unexpectedly there for me to hold on to and balance with.

"Actually," I say as I quickly take in my surroundings. "If we're married, what's my new last name?"

It's too dark to make out much detail of the surrounding gardens, but the gigantic towering mansion is lit like a Christmas tree. With four floors and burnt-orange stonework emblazoned with black iron railings, the place is stunning. Smooth, white stone steps lead up to a gigantic black door flanked by two burly men holding assault rifles against their abdomens.

"Barrone," Marco replies.

His words hit me like a truck and my next step makes me stumble. Marco's hand catches my elbow, but there's no warmth in his touch.

Barrone.

I know that name.

Everyone on the streets knows that name. You can't breathe without coming into someone pushing drugs for that family and their associated gangs.

Barrone. *Mafia.* They're the stuff of nightmares.

Anytime anyone vanishes from the streets, the Barrone name is whispered in secret. They hunt, maul, and kill anyone that gets in their way. There's no forgiveness with late payment, no respite for anyone who works for them, and if you even think of going clean, they'll kill everyone even remotely related to you before they hunt you down.

I had one run-in with this family a long time ago when I was young and stupid, and I swore never to cross paths with them again.

I'm so far out of my league that I can't even see the shore anymore. A smothering sense of dread looms over me as we walk in the shadow of the mansion.

I'm walking right into the jaws of *death*.

4

MARCO

Gianna stumbles and I catch her, gripping her arm tightly. I remain possessive, but I find myself hoping she can garner some reassurance from me.

I don't need her scared. I need her alert and as sharp with my family as she was with me back on the street.

She flashes me a small smile and while her face remains calm, her gorgeous eyes betray her nervousness. I don't blame her.

I've been making this plan up as we go and it all hinges on how this introduction is about to go. While I plan on sticking to this decision, if Gianna crumbles then I will be responsible for breaking the psyche of an innocent woman.

I don't want that kind of blood on my hands.

We step over the threshold and a servant rushes forward to take my coat from me. He glances at Gianna with wide eyes, and as he's about to leave, I stop him with a single look.

"Take her to the washroom. Get her a brush for her hair and let her touch up her makeup. Then, bring her to the study. Three minutes, not a second longer."

"Yes, Sir." The servant nods quickly and then bows his head at Gianna. "This way, ma'am."

She shoots me an uncertain look, then slips from my grasp as she follows the servant toward the nearest washroom.

I need her to look perfect.

In her absence, I have time to check my phone, which has been flooded with missed calls and ignored texts ever since I ran into her. This isn't the time for me to fall off the map and as I read, I can see that most think I was assassinated or fell wounded somewhere in the city.

We're on the brink of war, so such assumptions are not too wild. This is where my focus should be. Protecting my family and my people. Instead, my father is constantly pushing me toward marriage and a damn baby. This better work.

Three minutes later, Gianna meets me outside the study looking much healthier. Her wild curls are tamed, and her makeup has been adjusted.

I take her arm and lead her inside the study.

A large table stretches out in the middle of the room. The roaring fireplace to the left is surrounded by chairs filled with men. Those not seated stand around with drinks in hand and whatever argument we walk in on falls immediately silent.

"Marco!" The concerned faces and voices of my lieutenants fill the air.

"Where the hell were you, man?"

"We thought you'd been killed!"

"Did you forget that you set this blasted meeting up?"

"You're lucky we didn't start a war on your behalf!"

Gianna's hand suddenly tightens against my forearm at the influx of noises and questions that flood our way.

Those loud demands slowly fade as each man, in turn, spots the beautiful woman on my arm, and a painfully deadly silence falls.

"Who is that?" one man pipes up, and he's immediately silenced by his counterpart's sharp elbow in his ribs.

"This is Gianna," I declare loudly and my heart clenches faintly. "She's my wife. I know we had a meeting today but I was busy getting married."

The air suddenly turns cold like a frozen winter breeze has snapped through the room. No one speaks. No one moves. Everyone is frozen, waiting for one reaction in particular.

My father.

He sits by the fire, puffing slowly on a cigar. The trail of smoke from his mouth abruptly ends at my revelation, and he stands slowly. The cigar dangles from his fingertips, and he turns, revealing his handsome salt-and-pepper features to Gianna.

There's a split second when his face is calm and I contemplate a favorable outcome.

Then he explodes.

"My son!" he bellows like a bull. "Are you trying to send me to an early grave?! What the hell were you thinking? Have you lost all the fucking sense I crammed into that thick skull of yours?"

His eyes widen, revealing the whites all around his irises and his pale skin purples in his fury.

"You?! My son?! Marrying a complete stranger?!"

His anger is explosive, and I shift a half step in front of Gianna as her nails dig painfully into the soft flesh of my wrist.

"Father—"

"Do you have any idea the shit you've just landed us in? You selfish bastard!" He rages on, oblivious to my attempts to talk. "Do you have any sense of how many families will be personally insulted to learn that Marco Barrone has overlooked their daughters and married a nobody?" My father turns and launches his smoldering cigar into the fire. "We'll be in all-out war with every family from here to the coast because you can't control your fucking dick!"

I sigh, bored as the rampage continues. Several lieutenants turn to their phones, likely beginning the damage control because my father is right. I can think of at least ten families that will be furious to hear I'm off the market, but I'm confident we can weather the storm.

"Your mother would be so ashamed," Father growls, and tension snaps up my spine.

"Well, she's dead," I reply coldly. "And if she was here, this situation wouldn't even be a damn requirement, would it?"

"You listen here—"

"You act like he just plucked me off the street," Gianna suddenly speaks, diverting attention to her. "Surely he has more sense than that."

Cutting my father off is a bold move but Gianna holds her head high as she walks around me, keeping our hands interlocked. "Most parents would be happy their son married for love."

I didn't expect her to hold up her end of the bargain immediately, but once she gets started, she's on a roll.

"From where I'm standing, it seems like Marco has followed his heart swift enough not to disrupt anything so that he can put his focus where it's really needed." She smiles sweetly and brushes her hair away from her shoulder.

"You don't understand," Father replies tightly. "Bringing this family to the brink of destruction because he didn't think beyond his dick is *immediately* disruptive."

"Are you telling me that the Barrones aren't as strong as we're led to believe?" Gianna tilts her head and touches two fingertips to her lips. Then she turns to me and pouts. "Baby, did you exaggerate?"

She's so quick that I almost burst out laughing at her smooth performance, but I hold it together.

"She knows little," I say to my father. "And yet she has more faith in me than you."

"Do you not remember how things were when your sister died?" my father spits out his words and drags one hand through his thick, silver hair. "The fallout was devastating when we were unable to secure a union with the Simone family. How do you see this ending, hm?"

My defenses rise immediately at the mention of my late sister. "That was an entirely different situation," I growl. "And a different time. I am in charge now, and if any measly Simone has an issue with this, then I will gladly grind them into the dirt like you should have done years ago!"

My father glares at me, then he turns to the gathered lieutenants. "What are you all still doing here? Get out there, make the damn calls, and if any of you fail to smooth over this situation, it will be your head that rolls, understand? The fucking damage control. Get out. Now!"

Each man hurries out of the room, intent on running damage control for whatever family they are assigned to until it's just me, Gianna, and my father.

"Gianna." I squeeze her hand. "My apologies but this is my father, Dante."

"It's a pleasure." Gianna's smile is as sweet as ever. "Quite the temper you have there."

"Don't speak on things you know nothing about," Dante snaps.

"Oh, you think?" Gianna remains unfazed. "Your attention has been split, correct? All this family business which I am sure is *so* important, plus securing a suitable wife for your son so that you can get the heir you greatly desire."

As my father returns to his seat, he hesitates at her words. "You told her?" he asks, glancing at me.

"You think I would marry someone who doesn't want a baby?" I snort. "I'm not as clueless as you think."

"I get it," Gianna smiles. "I mean, I can imagine that it's like one gorgeous dress that everyone wants, and if you pair it with the right person, then it's a match made in heaven. But then someone brings in a completely different dress and suddenly it's a betrayal." She laughs softly. "The key is to be confident in your decision."

To my surprise, Dante's whiskery mustache twitches. "Quite the analogy."

"Well, I can't pretend to know what you're talking about, but I picked up on a few things during your rather um ... explosive reaction."

"Well," Dante sighs. "I suppose the board has been laid out now."

I remain near the door, watching as my father and Gianna fall into a quick conversation. She describes herself as an entrepreneur between jobs, claiming I swept her off her feet a few months ago and we'd been dating in secret ever since.

This seems to appease my father slightly as it makes this marriage seem less spur of the moment. Gianna talks smoothly, with a practiced ease I wouldn't expect from a pickpocket.

There may be more to this woman than meets the eye.

I let them talk for ten minutes, and then I take Gianna by the hand and excuse us both, claiming that it'd been a long day. She remains upbeat as I take her up the grand staircase to the third floor.

As we reach my bedroom, I open the door and part my lips, ready to tell her that she can sleep in here until I get a room prepared for her, but Gianna has different thoughts.

She lurches forward and throws herself into my arms, clashing our mouths together in a heated kiss that takes me completely off guard. Her teeth sink into my lower lip, sparking the heat of pain while her hands clutch at my neck and slide into my dark hair.

"Enough talk," Gianna gasps. "Fuck me already!"

I don't need to be asked twice.

I kick the door close and wind one arm around her waist. We only make it as far as the wooden dresser before she's hoisting her dress up to her waist and biting my lip harder. I thrust my tongue into her mouth, grab a handful of her hair, and shove her against the dresser.

She moans deeply and rakes her nails across my neck, creating trails of heat over my skin.

My cock swells immediately and desire punches through my gut. Gianna pulls on my hair, then uses that grip to crash our mouths together once more.

I can't resist. I feel powerless in the best way.

Spinning her around the dresser, I push her down hard against it while pulling her dress higher with my other hand. She's already ahead of me with her underwear by her ankles. My cock is ready to burst right out of my pants.

Raising one hand, I slap the perfectly round bubble of her ass, and her moan pitches; then she lifts her head and glances back at me as I wrestle with my belt and zipper.

"Wait—condom," she gasps. "No condom, no pussy."

Snorting in amusement, I grant her the request just this once and locate a condom in the bedside drawer.

She turns to face me when I approach her, cock stiff in my hand. With deft fingers, she tears the foil and slides the condom on with one movement that makes my cock jump, and my balls ache.

"Fucking hell," I grunt, shoving Gianna back against the dresser. She lands with a thump. The drawers clatter, and all the items on top—cologne and a few porcelain decorations—jump in response.

"Easy," I growl, draping myself against her. Sliding one arm around her waist, I pull her close and Gianna moans. She rises up and tips her head back onto my shoulder, giving me an opening to kiss her again as I thrust my cock deep inside her soaked pussy.

Three thrusts and I'm fully sheathed inside her. She moans openly with each thrust, then whimpers when we're pressed firmly together.

I kiss her deeply, and our tongues dance together, weaving silent music between our breathy gasps and whimpers.

I fuck her hard and fast, pouring all my early frustration into each thrust. It works wonders, especially when each thrust punches a moan of delight out of Gianna. Her hot skin burns against my own, and sweat trickles down my back as my muscles tense. Each slam of my hips shoves her against the dresser. Bottles clatter to the ground, knocked clean off while Gianna's hands scramble over the dresser, seeking something to hold on to.

In the end, she grips my arm and her nails cut me as I fuck her harder and harder.

We come together, and Gianna screams out her pleasure, a sexy sound cut off by how hard her body trembles and shakes in my arms. I pump deep inside her and keep her against me as pleasure overtakes me in a wave.

Holy shit.

Today has been the most unexpected day, but I like this change.

If Gianna is this dedicated to the part, the next part of the plan will be a breeze.

5

GIANNA

The next few days are a whirlwind. As a girl used to her privacy and keeping to the shadows, I'm suddenly under the constant watchful eye of two guards who become my shadows at Marco's request.

"No wife of mine walks around without protection," he told me one morning while straightening his tie and looking impossibly smug. "Where you go, they go. Try to give them the slip, and I'll lock you in here."

His tone was clear, and I fully believe he will lock me up if I cause trouble. However, rather than taking his promise as a threat, I chose to take it as a challenge. What better way to learn the secrets of the Barrone family than to learn how to give them the slip?

So, I agreed to play along. He wasn't kidding when he told me they would be everywhere. I tried to talk to them, but they were stoic and silent. It took me two days to learn their names: Anton and Ben. They moved when I moved, walked through the manor in circles without complaint when I was testing their reaction time, and even stood like knights outside of the room Marco prepared for me.

I hadn't expected my own room but I am grateful. It reduces the risk of me giving in to such carnal temptations like I did my first night here.

There was something about how Marco spoke and the thrill of knowing my presence was going to throw the entire Mafia into turmoil that just turned me on so much. And Marco was right there. An attractive asshole. If I was trapped with him for now, putting his dick to use would entertain me.

In the first few days, I tried to ask questions, but Marco shut me down immediately. He dragged me into the corner of one room and fiercely scolded me, reminding me that part of our deal was to keep my nose out of Barrone business. He was rather scary when he was angry, but the stubbornness inside me just rose to the challenge once more.

I needed to know more. Once I knew how big the score could be from this asshole, I'd know exactly how to play him.

The only time I didn't have Anton and Ben shadowing me was when Marco himself took over. He didn't watch me with the intent of getting to know me, but I noticed whenever he entered the same room as me and stayed for a while, Anton and Ben would slip away and leave us to it. Marco wasn't interested in engaging in conversation with me, but there did seem to be an understanding amongst his guards that no one could protect me better than him.

I tucked that note away for later and after nearly a week at the manor, swamped in more luxury than I knew what to do with, I changed tactics.

"Eat with me," I say to the blonde maid who hurries through the dining room one early afternoon. She freezes in place, clutching the silver tray laden with cups between her hands.

"I'm sorry, ma'am. I don't think I can."

"Don't call me ma'am," I groan. "We look almost the same age. Please. I need someone to talk to who isn't some old man under orders to watch me like I'm a porcelain doll."

The woman glances over her shoulder to where Anton and Ben stand against the wall, framing a bay window that looks out onto the extensive gardens surrounding the manor.

"Don't worry about them," I assure her. "They won't do anything. Please." Stretching out a leg under the table, I nudge out one of the chairs opposite me. "Sit. Please."

"I—I," she stammers, and my heart skitters slightly in my chest.

Is she scared or just shy? I'm about to press her once more when Marco strides into the room. He doesn't even acknowledge the girl, but he takes a cup from her tray as he passes and continues through the room, heading toward the white double doors at the far end.

"Darling?"

Marco stops in his tracks and turns to me immediately. There's no affection in his eyes when we meet, but whenever he looks at me, I get the feeling all he's thinking about is when we fucked. "What?"

"Can she eat lunch with me?" I nod toward the woman. "I don't know your rules around servants but I want her to."

Marco's brow lifts as if finally noticing the shy woman standing there. As he looks at her, I notice something odd. The woman doesn't cower from him or even bow her head like the majority of the guards do. In fact, she doesn't seem scared of him at all.

"Whatever, I don't care," Marco says flatly. He steps away, then swivels back a second later. "Kiss me, *darling*."

The way he repeats the pet name back at me almost sounds like a threat, but I rise to it easily. Standing, I lean across the table and grab him by the tie. For such a tall, broad man, there's something so attractive about jerking him about by such a thin piece of fabric. He moves easily for me, and I suspect he's trying to sell our romance to any eyes that might be watching, but it thrills me nonetheless.

We kiss slowly, eyes open the entire time, which makes the contact of our lips infinitely more intense. His tongue licks briefly into my mouth and then I bite his lower lip, holding on even as we part. There's a flash of crimson over his lip before he swipes it away with his tongue and I release his tie.

"Have a nice lunch," Marco says, and then he's gone.

"See?" I turn back to the woman and puff out my cheeks. "It's as easy as that."

"Okay." The woman still seems hesitant as she sets the tray down on the table and slides into the chair I pushed out for her. "Thank you."

"What's your name?"

"Tara."

"I'm Gianna."

"I know," Tara replies, clasping her thin hands together. "I-I mean, they told us who you were the night Marco brought you home."

"I bet that was an amazing meeting," I chuckle, popping a grape into my mouth. "What did they tell you about me?"

"Nothing," Tara replies immediately. "Well—they said there was nothing to tell because no one knew you."

"Did they tell you to keep an eye on me?"

Tara shakes her head, but the flush that creeps up her cheeks tells me otherwise.

"Don't worry," I assure her. "I might not know the exact rules of this game, but I've played plenty in my time. This is just a richer version." My attention drops to the fruit and cheese plate in front of me. With a quick twist of the vine, I pull some of the grapes free and pass them over to Tara.

"I shouldn't," she says, shaking her head.

"Why?" I ask sharply. "Is there some weird rule where the help can't share food with the wife?"

"No, not at all!" Tara says quickly. "I'm allergic."

"Oh." A wave of foolishness washes over me and I retract the grapes. "I'm sorry. Like I said, I don't know the exact rules."

"There's no rules like that here," Tara says with a wide smile. It makes her narrow face light up. She's rather beautiful underneath all that shyness.

"Are you sure?" I glance pointedly at the black and white maid outfit she's wearing.

"Yes. It's a quiet job, really. It pays well. And I get the weekend off like any other job," Tara explains. "This is just the uniform, like the guards' suits."

I glance back at Anton and Ben who still haven't moved from

their statue positions. "Oh. What's um ..." I point at Anton. "The pin on their suit. What is that?"

Each guard wears a pin on their lapel but when I asked Anton about it, he glared at me.

"It's the family crest," Tara explains. "Everyone under Barrone employ has that pin, see?" Tara lifts the white frill of her shirt collar to show the same pin attached to her dress. "It's a symbol of what family you're loyal to. Every family has a different sigil and a different pin. You can only receive a pin from the don, which in this case is Marco. Each pin also has a secret symbol visible under certain conditions that only the don knows so that fakes can't be made."

"Wow." My brow lifts. "That's way more intense than I expected."

"People try so hard to be sneaky," Tara says. "Loyalty is very important to these people."

"So I've noticed. And business-wise—"

Anton suddenly loudly and abruptly clears his throat, making Tara flinch.

"I don't know anything about business," Tara says hurriedly, and the relaxation that was creeping onto her features vanishes immediately. "I'm just a maid."

"No one is *just* anything," I reply softly, ignoring Anton. "Plus, now you're my friend."

"Really?" My heart squeezes at the way Tara's face lights up.

"Of course! You're the first person I've had a real conversation with."

"It must be so strange coming here like you did," Tara says, and her head tilts. "What were you doing before you met Marco?"

"I was—"

Tara is so sweet that it suddenly feels strange to lie to her. Like I'm doing something awful by deceiving her after she was so nice to me. Our conversation almost made me forget I'm playing a role.

"I was working as a pretzel vendor," I lie smoothly. "I worked, I would take the cart back to the distributor and either go home or go to clubs. A simple life, really. You know how it is, just doing what you can to make sure the bills are paid. Marco stopped to buy a pretzel and, well, the rest is history as they say."

"How romantic," Tara sighs wistfully as if we're not talking about Marco, the asshole. "Don't you have anyone out there that you miss, though? Family or something?"

I know she's just asking regular questions, but my defenses dart up anyway, and I shake my head, smiling tightly. "Nope. Nothing."

"That's a shame," Tara sighs, seemingly blind to my abruptness. "Well, you have us now. I hope you will love it here."

Tara spends the rest of lunch with me until someone comes looking for her to take her back to her duties. It feels nice to have a friend, though, and she fills my thoughts as I resume my exploration of the manor. I've run into very few staff. In fact, this place is either really empty or it's just too big, and I keep missing the rest of the employees.

But Tara is now on my list of friends, and she taught me a little about how things work.

It almost sounded like Tara has more freedom than I do.

"Gianna." A hand grasps my arm, drawing me from my thoughts as I reach for the next door I've never been through. I glance up at Ben who briefly tightens his grip. "Marco has requested you stay out of the south wing."

"Why?"

"It's his orders. And … construction."

"His *orders*?" I sneer. "What's so important about the south wing?"

"Nothing," Ben replies. "But please honor his wishes."

"Fine." I draw my hand away from the door and stride away with Anton and Ben on my tail.

Why doesn't Marco want me in the south wing? I don't believe for a second that it's because of construction. This manor is massive but it's not so huge that I'd miss the renovation of an entire wing.

I suddenly have a new plan, and it takes me until early evening to put it into action. Feigning tiredness, I retire to my bedroom and then send Anton away to fetch my dinner. While he's away, I manage to persuade Ben to hurry away and find me some period products, making him turn pale as I explain in great detail the specifics of my *emergency*.

Men, for whatever reason, cower so quickly at the prospect of women's troubles. If Marco was smarter, he'd have female guards.

With my guards distracted, I sneak through the manor and make it all the way back to the south wing without incident. The door isn't locked.

"If he didn't want me in here," I murmur to myself as I slip into a dull room filled with musty air. "He should have locked the door."

The room is filled with furniture but it's all covered in dust sheets. The curtains are drawn shut with light sneaking in through a few gaps and streaking the opposite wall with the orange of the setting sun.

There's no sign of renovation.

I walk from this room to the next, and the next. Each is the same. The air is thick, dust coats every surface, and all the gorgeous ornate furniture is hidden away under dust sheets. The walls are graced with large paintings much like the ones that hang in the entrance hall. Great depictions of cities across the world, castles and rivers, and then one that catches my eye.

It hangs above an unused fireplace, hidden under a thick layer of dust, but the image is clear.

It's a family portrait. A man who resembles a younger Dante, a kindly woman smiling, and two children. A boy and a girl are wearing butterfly brooches that are similar to the charm Marco has on his wallet. That has to be Marco and his sister. My heart skips a beat.

Its importance suddenly becomes clear. Is it his last memory of her? It seems too sentimental for a man like Marco, though.

Is this his mother's wing? Is that why it's closed? Dante had revealed last night that both Marco's mother and sister had passed. A nervous chill sweeps up my spine, and I glance over my shoulder, struck by the sensation that I suddenly really shouldn't be here. If this place holds emotional importance to Marco, he may be extremely unforgiving to find me here.

I should turn back.

Instead, I press on, consequences be damned. The more I know about Marco, the easier he will be to manipulate.

My exploration takes me through several winding corridors and more abandoned rooms until I find a smaller corridor that's not like the others. It's tucked beside a fireplace and there's no door that I can see. Light flickers at the other end, and like a moth to a flame, I follow it.

The light steadily gets brighter the closer I get, even as the narrow corridor presses in around me. My breath quickens, suddenly fearing the walls closing in and trapping me forever. Thankfully, when I stumble out into the light, I find myself in a stunning place.

I'm surrounded by hundreds of plants of all shapes, sizes, and colors. A multitude of floral scents attack my nose as I breathe in, and the gleaming light is the setting sun bouncing off the glass room.

Is this a ... greenhouse? Why is there a hidden corridor leading to a greenhouse of all places?

Suddenly, deep laughter catches my attention and my heart punches up into my throat as a softer, more feminine laugh follows. Cautiously, I walk forward and peer around a leafy plant.

My heart stops dead in my chest.

Marco is here. He leans down low, embracing a woman in a chair who buries her face into his chest.

"Oh Marco," she croaks softly, emotion flooding her voice. "I wish you didn't have to leave me."

What the fuck?

I need to get out of here.

I step back—and my ankle catches on the edge of a metal pail sitting just around the corner. The clatter of the metal is deafening as Marco and the woman fly apart.

Marco's thunderous eyes land on me, and his face twists with fury as he charges toward me.

"What the hell are you doing here?" he roars, roughly grabbing my shoulders as terror surges up my throat. "You're not supposed to be here. Ever!"

6

MARCO

"What are you doing here?!" I bellow. Anger surges through me like fog, clouding out all my other senses. Only one fact remains in my mind; keeping Emi safe. Nothing and no one else matters.

They never will.

"I—I'm sorry!" Gianna stammers, trembling in my grip. "I was just walking and I—"

"You don't find this place by just walking. You were ordered to stay out of the south wing! You really do have a death wish."

I'm in the process of dragging Gianna back toward the wall when a sudden sharp pain flares across my side as Emilia pokes me with her walking stick.

"Marco Francis Barrone!" Emilia scolds sharply. "Stop being such a terror and leave her alone!"

I freeze in place with Gianna trembling in my grip. She looks past me, and her shining eyes widen further at the sight of the woman behind me. I turn.

Emilia is on her feet, pulling a knitted shawl around her frail shoulders. She adjusts it, then moves the fabric over her badly scarred arm and hides it from view.

"Emilia," I snap, softening my voice. "You know what this means." I glare back at Gianna. "You will forget ever coming here if you want to make it out of here *alive*."

"Marco!" Emilia scolds and her stick smacks into my thigh. "She's here. She's seen me. There's no point keeping this a secret."

"Emilia, if anyone finds out from her, then you—"

"I am quite aware," Emilia interrupts briskly. "Let go of your wife and introduce us before I use this again!" Despite her unsteady stance, she waves her cane up near my face and I relent.

My grip on Gianna relaxes and she instantly jerks herself away from me.

"Emilia, this is Gianna. My *wife*," I say tightly. "Gianna. This is Emilia. My sister."

Gianna pauses rubbing her arm and stares openly at Emilia. Her eyes are so wide it's a wonder they don't pop out of her skull.

"Your ... sister?" Gianna croaks. She sniffles, quickly wiping at her eyes. "I'm so sorry, I didn't mean to—"

"Nonsense." Emilia leans heavily onto her walking stick. "Ignore my idiot brother. He's at war all the time, and he forgets to be human. Please." Emilia nods to the seats around the small table. "Sit with us."

I want Gianna to say no. Every second we linger here is a second too long. The more she knows, the bigger the threat she is to my life, and Emilia's, and I have spent *decades* keeping Emilia safe.

"I should leave," Gianna says shakily, glancing at me.

"Nonsense," Emilia says. "Sit down." Suddenly, she erupts into a wheezing coughing fit, and all thoughts of reprimanding Gianna vanish from my mind. I'm by my sister's side instantly, helping her ease back down into her chair. She tries to wave me off but she's far too weak now. Once seated, I crouch beside her and check the lines to the oxygen tank that sits beside her. Everything looks good.

"Emilia, you can't exert yourself," I warn gently.

Emilia scoffs roughly, dabbing at her scarred lips with a tissue. "If you weren't such a pigheaded brute, I wouldn't have to," she snaps. Her pale eyes lock on to Gianna, who sits very cautiously beside her. "It's lovely to meet you, dear."

"I ..." Gianna keeps her hands in her lap. "I'm sorry, I'm not sure I understand."

"What don't you understand?" Emilia asks.

I take my seat next to Emilia, watching Gianna with a frown. I should have known a street rat like her wouldn't have listened to a few simple rules. Maybe making the south wing off-limits turned it into a beacon for a thief like her.

"You," Gianna says, and her eyes dart to me. "I thought Marco's sister was dead."

"Marco, pour the poor girl some tea," Emilia snaps at me.

I roll my eyes but oblige. Emilia is the only woman in the world who can demand things of me, and I will follow her every request. It's the least I can do.

"This must be quite a shock. Since Marco won't, I will apologize for his behavior. He is very protective and has spent a lot of time keeping me safe. I imagine you were never supposed to find out."

"She was supposed to stay out of the south wing," I mutter as I pour the tea into three porcelain cups. "A pretty fucking simple request."

"I'm sorry," Gianna says. She sits as stiff as a board. "I was curious. I was exploring and I shouldn't have."

I want to say more. I want to yell at her, scare her until she begs for mercy and never even dreams of breathing a word about this place. Anger simmers just under my skin and I repeatedly flex my hand to try and remain calm.

"Indeed," Emilia says. "There is nothing I can say or do that will stop you from telling people what you have seen here. After all, that is your choice."

"Emilia—" I start to warn her, but she raises her hand.

"But you are correct. The world thinks I am dead. Everyone thinks I am dead except Marco and my father, who I am sure you have met."

Gianna nods quickly.

"It is a carefully crafted lie that Marco has spent his life creating and keeping so I am able to live in peace."

I watch Gianna like a hawk and see her seeking out pieces of the puzzle. My sister's constant coughing and wheezing, the scars twisted across her beautiful face and limbs, the oxygen tank at her side, and her obvious fragility. All pieces of a painful puzzle that Gianna has no right to.

"Marco keeps me hidden here, in this closed wing but it is nothing sinister, I assure you. I love plants, you see. When I was younger, they were my passion. Now I simply exist with them, watching them thrive year after year and praying the same for myself. Science, it seems, has not yet reached that level."

She chuckles softly and slowly reaches for her tea.

"I won't tell anyone," Gianna says quickly. "I swear."

"I can't stop you," Emilia says. "But I hope you will take everything into account before you do."

Slumping back in my chair, I watch Emilia closely to ensure she doesn't spill hot water on herself. She takes a few sips of her tea and then speaks.

"When I was thirteen years old, the estate was attacked. Marco and I hid, as we were ordered to do. We'd spent years doing practice runs of such things, but it was never supposed to be a reality."

I grunt softly, fighting the acidic wave of guilt that rises as Emilia talks. I feel responsible for that night and it weighs on me daily.

"Details are fuzzy, you understand," Emilia says. "I was young and Marco was only sixteen. We weren't privy to the inner workings of the family. We just had to hide and survive. Unfortunately, we failed." Her voice trembles faintly. "They found our mother first. They tortured her, assaulted her, and killed her. Then they found me."

Gianna's face turns as white as a sheet and her hands tremble despite her tightly laced fingers.

"Marco did everything he could to protect me, but what can a sixteen-year-old kid do against five grown men?" Emilia looks at me, then reaches for my hand. I grip it as tightly as I dare. "They beat him. I thought for sure he was dead and then it was my turn. Our father's guards arrived just as they finished with me. Marco recovered from his wounds, but I was not so lucky."

Emilia indicates to her face with her free hand and as she does, her shawl slips down her arm revealing the twisted burn scars coating her forearm.

Gianna gasps softly, and then her cheeks flush red. "I'm so sorry."

Emilia waves her off with a warm smile. "It was a lifetime ago, my dear. I'm thirty-seven now and still going strong!" She laughs, then her grip becomes like iron as she coughs harshly. "Anyway, I wanted to die for a long time, but Marco kept me strong. He kept me hidden and to bring me peace, he told the world I was dead. Father went along with it because of guilt, I suspect. I didn't want to be a piece of meat married off at the next convenience. I'd been meat once. Never again,"

Gianna glances at me. Her expression is oddly soft, but I can't quite decipher it. Anger still fuzzes the edges of my mind and her very presence irritates me.

"That's the real reason I needed a wife," I say tightly. "My father is growing more and more desperate as the world around us changes. He's seeing threats everywhere and thinks we are weak. He wants to reveal Emilia and marry her off to a family he thinks will strengthen us, and I refuse to let that happen. So now, we are married, and I will raise our family on our own merit not through an archaic wedding."

"Is that the real reason he was so furious?" Gianna asks. "He wants a union and you took that from him?"

"My sister is not for sale," I mutter. "Perhaps. I can't say for sure. But I definitely fucked up his plans."

"I am sorry, dear," Emilia says. "When Marco told me what he had done, I was furious that he roped some poor girl into the mess of our lives."

"It was necessary," I snap at her, then quickly reel myself in.

"Is it?" Emilia looks at me with sad eyes. "For years, you have blamed yourself for that night when you were only a kid. Just like me. You have protected me with your entire life and now this? There could have been another way."

"There was none," I say softly. "If not Gianna then it would have been someone else. Someone less fucking nosy for sure."

"Oh stop." Emilia releases my hand to slap my wrist. "Gianna, my dear. Despite my brute brother's reaction, I hope you understand that his anger comes from a place of protectiveness, not malice."

Gianna shoots me a small glare, not looking like she believes that at all.

"I have a small team here that helps me, a trusted team. You're the first new person I've met in … oh, twenty years?" Emilia chuckles. "But I am glad we got to meet."

"I'm so sorry," Gianna says weakly. "I had … I had absolutely no idea. I swear I won't tell anyone. I will forget this place even exists!"

"Don't you dare," Emilia laughs. "I would very much like for us to have tea. Maybe without the ogre."

"Ha ha," I mutter, rolling my eyes.

"You will be looked after here," Emilia says and she leans forward, placing one frail hand on top of Gianna's. "I promise that you are safe. Not everything here is as it seems. You need to remember that."

Gianna nods silently and her eyes drop to the table. She looks stunned and pale. My anger calms slightly.

If there's more to say, we don't get a chance because my phone blares to life. I answer immediately and Anton's panicked voice floods my ear.

"Boss!" he yells. "Gianna is gone! We've looked everywhere but we can't find her and—"

I hang up immediately and stand. "They've finally noticed you're missing," I say flatly. "Time to go. Emilia." I lean down and gently kiss her forehead. "Take your medicine. I will come and visit again soon."

"Please do," she croaks. "And you, Gianna. Come and see me too."

"I'll see what I can do," I sigh tightly. "I love you."

"Love you too." Emilia settles back into her chair and I send the alert to her team to return. Gianna rises and smiles at Emilia.

"I will come back, if I can. Thank you, and again, I am so sorry."

"Don't worry, dear," Emilia says. "It's just like Marco to find someone as curious as him."

As soon as we walk around the plants, I grab Gianna by the arm and shove her up against the wall. Her eyes widen and she grips my wrist, staring into my eyes as the anger swells in my heart.

"If you breathe a word of this, or even a hint to anyone—*anyone*—or endanger my sister in any way, I will make you *wish* you were dead. Are we clear?"

7

GIANNA

"Can I get you anything?" Tara asks from her spot in the doorway. "You've been in here for two days just *cleaning*."

"It's therapeutic," I reply from my spot on the floor. "Marco said I could have this room for whatever I want, decorate it how I want and stuff. There's just a lot to clear out, but I like doing it."

Plus, as I clean, it gives me time to process everything I learned about Marco and his sister.

"Okay." Tara nods. "Well, I will bring your dinner here later."

"Thank you!"

With a wave, Tara is gone and I'm alone once more. Anton and Ben learned pretty quickly that I wanted to do this myself and have spent most of their time outside the door, guarding me against anyone who might want to disturb me.

I've cleaned out all the dressers, had all the seating removed because it's not to my taste, and relocated all the books from the shelves to be cleaned and brought back in later.

As I work, my mind runs on a constant loop.

Emilia, Marco's sister, is alive and living in secret in a closed wing of the house. The mysteries surrounding Marco deepen with each day, and I'm sure I'll eventually lose track.

What struck me most about meeting Emilia was how Marco was with her. The weight of the world seemed to lift from his shoulders when he was with her, and I couldn't help but notice the genuine affection between them.

He smiled at her. Touched her. Held such warmth in his eyes that I didn't think was possible.

There's more to him than meets the eye. And that, more than anything, makes me nervous.

Marco is much more complicated than I anticipated, which affects my own plans. Keeping your mark simple is the best way to an easy payday, but Marco is becoming anything but. Seeing that soft side of him also unlocked a strange yearning in my chest.

Could he ever be that soft with me? Do I ever want him to be? The sex was great and everything but this isn't real. It can't be. But the more I learn about him and his family, the deeper I sink into their net and it'll be harder to claw my way out.

Dusting my hands along my thighs, I stand and stretch my arms long above my head. Cleaning and thinking is a good combination but I'm getting tired. I make a mental note to ask Marco if I can have a computer and turn to the gigantic wall unit that's my next task. Marco told me many of the rooms in this manor have been in disuse for years because there's no family here anymore.

Just him and his father. Dante. An angry man who seemed amusing the first time I met him, but learning how he wants to send Emilia off to a stranger doesn't sit right with me. It's uncomfortable and I can't look him in the eye anymore.

Not yet, at least. In time, it will be easy.

I dust along the shelves and clean the glass the best I can until I come to a drawer that's thoroughly stuck in the unit. Using all my strength, I pull, jerk, and wiggle the drawer back and forth until finally it scrapes free with a screech of wood against wood.

A chilling shiver steals down my spine at the sound and I shudder. Inside, there are countless old receipts, a couple of dusty books, and other odds and ends like buttons, a box of matches and some clothing pins. Yanking the drawer free, I'm about to tip the contents into a trash bag when something silver catches my eye.

A silver teardrop pendant. The dust vanishes in a single blow, and I eye the jewelry, unsure of what to do with it. Does this belong to Emilia?

I pocket the jewelry and resume cleaning. I'll ask Marco about it.

Three hours later, I flop down onto my bed with a long, low groan.

"Ben tells me you've been busy," Marco says, striding into my bedroom.

I prop myself up onto my elbows and watch him as he leans against the dresser. "Yeah. The room you gave me has all sorts of junk in it. When you told me the rooms weren't in use, I didn't think it would be this bad."

"We're busy people," Marco replies. "I got your message. You want a laptop?"

"Mm-hmm. So I can look up interior inspiration."

Marco watches me with an unreadable expression, then he nods. "I'll get you one. Goodnight."

As he turns to leave, I surge upward. "Wait! I found this when I was cleaning. Did it belong to your sister?"

Pulling the pendant from my pocket, I hold it up for only a second before Marco is right in front of me, snatching it away.

"Where did you find this?" he barks.

I glare up at him as my fingertips throb from having the chain ripped from my hand. "Like I said, while I was cleaning. Is it hers?"

When I expect another explosion of anger, to my surprise, Marco's face softens and he drops down onto the bed next to me. The weight of his muscles against the mattress forces it to dip and I slide slightly against him.

"No. This belonged to Fawn. I never thought I would see this again."

"Who is Fawn?"

Another sister?

"She was the woman I was going to marry."

My heart stalls slightly in my chest and an odd curl of tension worms through my gut. "Huh?"

Marco sighs deeply. "I suppose there's no point keeping it from you. When I was eighteen, I fell in love with a brilliant, magnificent woman. I was angry back then. Angrier than I am now."

I lift my brow. It's hard to imagine him angrier than he is now.

"After what happened to my sister, I hated the world but Fawn was this beautiful soul who made everything better. She was the love of my life and I was going to marry her, but she ..." Marco's voice thickens. "She died. She was killed by her *asshole* ex who couldn't take no for an answer and leave her be. I failed her. Like I failed my sister."

Marco's fist curls around the pendant, and when he looks at me there's a flicker of something in his eyes. I can't tell if it's warmth or the lingering love for Fawn.

"So, Gianna. When I tell you this world is dangerous and that you should stay with your guards, and stay safe and not pry, I'm not being an asshole. I am trying to keep you safe. Do you understand?"

I do. More than I expect. I feel unexpectedly sympathetic. From Emilia's story, Marco did everything in his power to protect her; what happened wasn't his fault. It's hard to imagine anything different with Fawn. Whether Marco has been dealt a bad hand or it is because of this life, I can't tell, but it's the most sincere he's sounded since I met him.

"I understand," I say softly. "And I'm sorry for your loss."

"It was a long time ago," Marco replies and he stiffens against me. "I would appreciate it if you didn't tell anyone about this." He winds the pendant around his fingers and then slips it into his pocket.

"Of course."

I've learned so much about him these last few days, and a new side to him is appearing. Suddenly, his prickly demeanor makes sense. He's suffered the loss of two important people in his life—Fawn and his mother—and works daily to keep his sister safe and hidden. No wonder he's so angry all of the time.

"I have something similar," I say, unsure where the urge to share came from, but once I start, I can't stop. "This." I lift my hand and pluck at the faded thread bracelet around my wrist. "It was made by the first friend I ever made on the streets. She was a sex worker and she was so kind. A little bratty and harsh, but once you got to know her, she was an angel."

Marco's eyes dart between my face and my wrist. "It's pretty."

"You think?" I chuckle softly because he sounds utterly flat. "She vanished not long after she made it for me, but not before she taught me a thing or two about surviving on the streets. I always wanted to find her again but I never could."

"Why?" Marco locks eyes with me and I'm pinned in place. "Why were you on the streets? You're beautiful and charming. I find it difficult to place you there."

"That's because I'm smart," I tease. Marco makes a noise that could have been a laugh and my chest constricts.

I want him to laugh with me the same way he laughs with Emilia —though I'm not sure when that started to matter.

"I just got dealt a bad hand."

Marco nods and seemingly has no intent to press me. I'm not sure if it's because he doesn't care, or because he's trying to respect my privacy, but the urge to talk once again rises in me.

"I was pretty neglected as a child. My father used me and my brother as a punching bag almost daily, so I learned to be scrappy and fast y'know? My brother turned to alcohol and stopped protecting me, and once I became a teenager, the abuse turned sexual." My throat recoils at the word and I swallow hard. "I left pretty soon after that."

Marco's face is like thunder. "Your mother?" he bites out.

"She only cared about money and her man. I went to her for help, but in her opinion, I wasn't paying bills and had to earn my keep somehow." Saying it out loud to a man I've only known for just over a week leaves me feeling raw and exposed.

This isn't a cover or a story. This is my truth.

"Gianna." Marco's tone softens so much that he sounds completely different. His words are like a lullaby rather than the barking snippets I'm used to. "I am so sorry. They should have protected you and cared for you. And your brother ... he should have fought in your corner."

I shrug, straightening my back as if to escape the pain knotting in my stomach. "He was a kid. He dealt in his own way. I dealt with mine. I ran away, turned to a life of crime you could say. I did things to survive. Things I'm not proud of. But that's just the way it is, right?" I gaze up at him; his blue eyes are suddenly like the warm depths of the ocean. "We play the hand we're dealt."

"Indeed," Marco says softly. He gently takes my hand and his touch is the softest it has ever been.

"Last I heard, my father died from a dirty needle, so that's karma as far as I'm concerned."

"I am sorry," Marco says. "That I put my hands on you on the street and the greenhouse."

"Marco, that's not the same."

"No, but it was surely unpleasant for you, and for that, I apologize."

I don't know what to say. An apology for that didn't even cross my mind since his manhandling had left me hot and bothered. But here he was, suddenly apologizing for crossing a line he didn't even know existed.

"I promise you will be respected here. No one will touch you without your permission, and I swear no one will hurt you. You may not believe this promise, but time will show you that it's genuine."

"I ..." How do I respond to that? Marco is like a coin with two very different sides, and he's flipping back and forth so quickly that I can barely process it. This side of him is the side that was with Emilia in the greenhouse, and it almost feels like I shouldn't be seeing this kind of softness.

"Thank you," I say after a moment, and I pat the back of his hand with mine. "Would you believe me if I said I was fine because it was a long time ago?"

"I tell myself that about my sister," Marco says quietly. "Some things never ease with time."

I understand him. It pains me, but I understand.

My stomach twists and a rush of heat washes over me from head to toe. Never in a million years did I expect to be having a heart-to-heart with this man, but when he looks at me, there's a new warmth there that makes it worth it.

Marco stays with me. We talk long into the night about the past and the time he shared with Fawn, while I tell him a few truths and maybe tales about my time on the streets. He listens with careful intent and I grow so comfortable that when sleep comes and we fall into each other's arms, I don't question it.

But when morning comes, Marco is gone. I wake to a cold, empty bed and an absence of the warmth that was so comforting the night before.

As I sit up, my heart clenches painfully in my chest.

Why do I feel so oddly abandoned?

8

MARCO

"This is important," Dante says as he adjusts his bowtie in the mirror. "I need you to understand this."

Standing by the window, I stare out over the vast gardens of the Barrone estate and nod once. "I know."

"Do you?" Dante turns, and I catch him glaring at me out of the corner of my eye. "Do you really understand? This past week or two you've been so infatuated with that woman."

That woman.

Gianna.

My key to a plan and the most unexpected addition to my life. Just the thought of her sends a shiver curling down my spine. She makes me feel exposed. In her short time here, she's already stumbled onto my sister and learned about the single greatest love of my life. She was never meant to be privy to any of that.

She's learning. She's seeing me in a light that was never supposed to be turned on.

Yet, as exposed as I feel, there's an aura of excitement around the whole thing. Emilia hasn't had a new friend in decades, and I haven't been able to talk to anyone about her or Fawn. What are the chances Gianna will be that person?

Assuming she keeps her mouth shut. She knows a lot now. Enough to bring me to my knees and I don't think she even realizes.

That woman.

She holds my attention and I'm drawn in, despite trying to hold myself back. I can't get too close. If I do, I'll be signing her death sentence if I haven't already.

"*That woman* is your daughter-in-law," I reply lazily, taking a slow drink of my scotch. "You should be happy."

"Happy?" Dante scoffs sharply. "Are you blind, Marco? Do you not see what you've done?"

I drain my glass, watching the sun vanish beneath the horizon, and then I turn to my father. "I fixed our problem."

"You made it worse!" Dante hisses and he approaches me quickly. "I have done my best to calm our relations with the other families but the Simones? They are furious."

"Why?" I frown deeply. "They have no daughters for me to marry. Father, this archaic tradition does nothing but bind bad blood, and I for one don't want to be bound to the fucking Simones."

"You'd be lucky," Dante snaps. My father studies me, his expression unreadable. There's a hint of anger in the set of his mouth but disappointment lingers in his eyes.

"No, father. We would be terribly *un*lucky. And I am trying to break that streak."

"What is unlucky?" comes Gianna's voice.

My father steps back and reveals the absolute vision of Gianna as she walks into the study. My mouth drops open and I don't even try to hide it.

She pauses at the door and curls her hand on her hip, a light smile playing across her shining peach lips. She's dressed in a satin, white floor-length dress with a single thigh-high slit up one leg. As she poses, she stretches one long leg out to the side and the fabric pours around her like liquid. Each breath makes the fabric shimmer like the ripples of a rock pool. Sparkling blue beads decorate the neckline and the hem of the slit, and her thick, auburn curls flow around her gorgeous face like some kind of copper halo.

Her eyes, lined with black, lock on to mine, and her smile widens. "Since no one saw the wedding dress, I suppose this will have to do."

Oh. She's good.

Diamonds sparkle at her neck and dangle from her ears, a gift I left her earlier this afternoon when informing her of the dinner. I'm pleased to see she's wearing them.

"You look *amazing*." No word of a lie. I approach her, still aware that my father is watching and never have I been more excited to kiss her than in this moment. However, as I take her hand and lean in, she holds up one hand and presses her fingertips to my lips.

"Nu-uh. I *just* finished my makeup," she says with a sly smile. "Later."

Oh, she's killing me.

The muscles of my abdomen tighten and my cock twitches faintly in my suit. It takes every ounce of my control to smile and kiss against her fingertips instead.

"Of course, dear."

"Father." Gianna's eyes slide away from me and lock on to Dante. "You look devastatingly handsome."

Dante straightens up slightly at the unexpected compliment and clears his throat. "Yes, well. Tonight it is called for." With that, he strides out of the room and Gianna instantly relaxes slightly.

"Is tonight really that important?" she asks.

"Yes. Tonight we have to ensure peace with the other families. As you're aware, many were pretty unhappy when they learned I married out of the blue. Some took it as a personal insult against their daughters that I chose someone not from any of the top families."

"These people really value unions, huh?"

"It's how things are done," I say, unable to take my eyes off her. "Going against the norm is unheard of."

Gianna looks back at me, pinning me in place with those gorgeous eyes of hers. "But some people are worth it."

Emilia darts into my thoughts and I nod. "Exactly."

"It's better this way," she continues. "Maybe they will learn not to treat their daughters like livestock."

"If that was the case, I wouldn't need to go to such lengths," I murmur as she slides her hand around my elbow. "You ready?"

"As I'll ever be."

∼

THE DINNER STARTS WELL and to my relief, many of the family delegates love Gianna. Whether it's because of her upbringing or her ability to read people, she gets on like a house on fire with almost everyone. Those with something to say about my sudden wedding clam up the moment they see her and eat their words the moment they talk to her.

She's kind and courteous, humorous, and above all, respectful. She bows her head, shakes the hands of the right people, and delivers such tasteful compliments that any of the women jealous of her instantly become her friend. I stay by her side for an hour, but business pulls us apart. Anton and Ben follow her closely, and I watch her from across the room as talk of drug deals, territory, and a new shipment of fake guns from Mexico washes over me.

Gianna is a distraction I never want to lose.

I listen to one man detail the struggles of keeping one of his businesses afloat since ratting out a mole in his organization—turns out the man skimming off the top was also the man keeping things running. Another complaint is that the Triad are getting too bold in their deals and asking for too much money. They ask my opinion and I give it as abruptly as I can. We spend an hour talking back and forth about the benefits and consequences of welcoming the Triads into a serious deal—I think it would benefit us, but some Italians refuse to look beyond their own borders.

I refuse to care. I won't secure the Barrone legacy by relying on families that fall apart after rooting out traitors. The conversation bores me and I cast my attention back to the main room, seeking out Gianna.

I find her within a few seconds, then anger grips my heart. She's across the room, laughing alongside a man who puts his hand on her bare arm and leans in close as if they are sharing a private joke.

My world turns red.

She's not just with any man.

She's with Leonardo Simone.

The sleazy head of the Simone family. They were once the dream union for my family back when I was a child, but the death of my mother swiftly put an end to that. Seeing him near her is like someone reaching into my gut and dragging my balls through my ribcage.

That fucker.

I stride across the room and reach Gianna in just a few steps. She turns to me with a bright smile, but it fades the moment she locks eyes with me. I clearly haven't hidden my emotions very well.

"Back. Off," I snarl, shoving myself between Gianna and Leonardo.

Leo raises his hands and laughs like the bark of a fox. "Hey friend, we were just chatting."

"I know you and your 'just chatting,'" I snarl. "Back the fuck off and leave her alone."

"You're acting like I'm some kind of danger to her," Leo replies easily, then his eyes narrow like blades. "*We're* not the ones dealing in the skin trade."

"Keep spewing your lies like I give a shit. You're lucky we're even here, so I'll say it again, in case it's struggling to get through that thick skull of yours. Leave my *wife* alone."

"Is that wise?" Leo's eyes widen and he places one hand on his chest. "After all, isn't it *you* that women have such a habit of dying around? Your mother, your sister, your ex-whatever she was. Honestly, Gianna darling, you might be safer—"

He doesn't get to finish his sentence. I punch him so hard in the mouth that his teeth snap shut and his head whips back so fast that his sunglasses fly up in the air. My knuckles ache, but my anger finally has an outlet, and it's Leonardo Simone.

I tackle him to the ground and we land with a crash, two muscular bodies colliding with heated yells and furious fists. He punches me in the ribs, I elbow him in the kidney. We roll over, and he crashes his elbow down onto my collarbone. I switch our positions and punch him twice in the face. We brawl and snarl, delivering blow after blow until Anton and Ben surge forward and pry us apart.

They waited long enough for me to gain the upper hand.

With my shirt awry and blood pouring from a split lip, I'm hauled upward as Leonardo's own men pull him backward. My father strides between us and holds up his hand, his face contoured and purple.

"This restaurant is *neutral fucking territory*," he yells, bringing silence to the entire building. "There is no fighting. Not here. Do you understand? You both know better, yet you brawl like cats in heat!"

I may be in charge of the Barrone family, but my father shows how much power he still carries from the respect he's earned over the years. No one talks over him and no one interrupts.

"Were you not the head of your respective families I would order you both slaughtered outside for such a disgusting lack of respect!" Dante continues. "You apologize. Now. Whatever this is, it's over!"

He points at me, his eyes sharp like a bullet. Then he points to Leonardo who nods, wiping blood away from his nose and mouth. Anton and Ben release me when my father stalks away and a cautious rumble of noise rises once more around us. Anton hands me a napkin and starts to adjust my jacket but I shrug him off. I don't need help. I need Gianna.

I swivel on the spot, scanning the crowd expecting to see Gianna alarmed or even pissed off at my lack of control.

She stands nearby, but instead of looking alarmed, she looks oddly distracted as she stares past me. "Gianna?"

Her eyes flicker to me after a few long seconds, and then she frowns. "Oh, Marco."

"Are you alright?"

She doesn't have a chance to answer because Leonardo steps up behind me, his presence making my spine recoil.

"Marco," he says loudly, throwing himself into the display of apologizing. He clearly wants to look like the bigger man.

I turn to face him. "Leonardo."

"My apologies." Leo holds out one hand. A hundred curious eyes watch us from around the room. I can't have him look better than me, so I grip his hand and shake it.

"Accepted. Mine, too."

Leo smiles widely as if accepting my apology, then he suddenly jerks me close and embraces me.

"The real twist is that the women around you don't die. They just fake it to get away from you," Leo hisses in my ear. "After all, isn't that how your sister is alive?"

9

GIANNA

"It wasn't me."

The words are out of my mouth as soon as the door closes. The drive home was tense, with Marco mostly on the phone barking orders like his life depended on it. Even his father was oddly silent and he vanished when we arrived at the manor, presumably off to do whatever Marco was demanding of everyone else.

"It was *someone*," Marco replies tightly, pacing back and forth as he wrenches his tie away from his neck. "That weaselly little fucker!"

Marco's phone blares to life and he answers it, storming to the other end of the study. Alone, I sink down onto the nearest chair and carefully remove my shoes. My toes and heels ache but it was so worth it to feel this beautiful for the first night of my life. And yet, it's soured.

Leonardo claimed to know that Emilia was alive. Such a revelation clearly shook Marco to the core and Leonardo slipped away with such a smug smile on his face, it was a wonder Marco let him walk out at all.

It turns out he's trying to find a credible reason for Leo to make such a claim while clinging to the hope that it's just some weird shot in the dark to try and fuck with him. Leo seemed charming up until

Marco arrived, then he became rather snakelike. It was an abrupt wake-up call that everyone in this life has some kind of agenda.

But that's not what shook me the most. While Marco and Leo were brawling on the floor, I saw something. It was hard to be certain in the commotion of the fight, but I'm fairly certain I saw someone I recognized at the party. I have no friends and certainly no family. Running into anyone from any part of my life sets off alarm bells.

But I can't be sure. The person I saw shouldn't be at parties, never mind at a Mafia dinner. I mull her face over, trying to decide if she's real or if I'm just filling in the blanks because she was familiar. If there's a chance—any chance at all—that she's a part of this world, then I'm not safe—not in the slightest.

"I don't care what it takes!" Marco yells suddenly, making me jump as his voice slices through the silence of the room. "I want security doubled and I want eyes on Leo. He doesn't breathe or take a shit without me knowing about it, understand?"

While my mind wandered, Marco had discarded his suit jacket and belt, leaving him in just a crisp white shirt that threatens to burst at the seams each time he heaved a deep breath.

Would he protect me?

If I told him the truth, would he even care? Or would he decide I'm no longer worth the hassle and just do away with me?

Marco grunts sharply. "No. I'll do it. I'll reach out to him once I've made sure we have no holes to plug. The guy's bragging about my deceased sister, of course I'm fucking concerned."

He ends the call and slams his hand down on the desk. I rise slowly and pad barefoot toward him.

"Marco?"

He's glaring down at the wood, panting harshly and his muscles are so tight that each line is defined even through his shirt.

"Is there anything I can do?"

"No one knows," he murmurs tightly. "I make sure of it. All these years, I've made sure of it. No one knows. And yet he says these things..."

"Maybe he's lying?" I offer softly. "I don't know how he works but maybe he's lying to get a rise out of you? Throw you off your game while he plans something bigger?"

Marco lifts his head and his eyes lock on to mine. "You're right. You don't know how he works." He straightens up further and sighs with a rasp. "I need to find out if he knows anything. If he doesn't then he can rot. If he does, then I will kill him. Fastest way to keep him quiet."

"That would start a war, son, and you know it." Dante appears at the door, back from wherever he rushed off to. "The Simone family is bigger than ours, Marco. Stronger too."

"They're bigger sure, but not stronger. They're like chickens scattered in the wind, lost and headless. They use their numbers to swarm but how many times have we pushed them back, hm? They mean nothing."

"Don't underestimate them," Dante says.

"What would you have me do?" Marco bellows suddenly and I flinch, my heart racing. "You know exactly why I have to stamp this out. I will not have these past decades mean nothing because Leonardo fucking Simone thinks he has all the information!"

Dante doesn't reply. He looks between us and shakes his head. "Then let us hope that Gianna is right and he is merely trying to mess with your head."

∼

WHAT A NIGHT. Exhaustion weighs down my limbs as I climb the stairs and my mind races. Emilia's survival might no longer be a secret, and a ghost from my past haunts me. Could things get any worse?

A few steps from the top, Marco suddenly scoops me up into his arms and I don't have the energy to be indignant. I wind my arms around his neck and cling to him with a soft noise of appreciation. He carries me the rest of the way, all the way to my bedroom, where he then sets me down on the bed.

Being apart from him after such a whirlwind night isn't something I'm ready for so when he tries to step away with a grunt, I catch his wrist.

He turns to look at me, clearly as tired as I feel, but there's something so insanely attractive about his half-open shirt dotted with blood and the rough mess of his hair.

I don't speak. Honestly, I'm not even sure what I want from him other than his presence. He holds my gaze for what feels like an eternity, then suddenly surges forward and our mouths collide. He kisses me like he's trying to consume me, and I am *here* for it.

My mind goes quiet, and nothing exists but the plush press of his lips, the rough scratch of his facial hair, and his large, hot hand on the side of my neck.

Right now, I am his.

Marco breaks the kiss and shoves me back down onto the bed, then he disappears down between my legs. My dress flashes up and Marco is completely out of sight.

But I can feel him. His rough hands as he caresses up my legs, his hot mouth as he presses open-mouthed, biting kisses up the inside of my thigh, the rough prickle of his stubble against my sensitive thighs, and then the wet drag of his tongue. He moves up between my legs and his broad shoulders force my thighs apart around his bulk.

He breathes hot against my panties, sending a curl of heat through my core and every muscle clenches in anticipation. Marco growls softly and a flush of tingles like pinpricks dance over my limbs, sending a shiver through my spine.

He pulls my panties to the side, then buries his face against my pussy like some kind of animal.

I squeal and immediately melt into moans as Marco utterly devours me. He grips my thighs tightly to stop me rocking away from him and presses his face deep between my folds. His tongue licks from my oversensitive, aching clit, down to my hole that throbs for anything and everything he can give me.

Marco licks with purpose and his tongue weaves through me like he's writing music. No part of me is untouched and just like a musician, he seems to quickly learn exactly how to play me. I'm more sensitive on the right side of my clit, and each time he favors his attention there, my moans pitch.

Then he doesn't leave me alone. He lavishes attention inside and out, moaning and growling faintly against me as he drags me closer and closer to orgasm.

My whole body is on fire, stoked by the flames of his enticing tongue and I clutch at the soft fabric of my dress. Suddenly, it's too soft and smothering. I want to feel Marco everywhere. I want to taste him, to run my fingers through his hair, and trace the scars on his body. I want to feel the safety of his thick arms.

That desire, along with his constant attention throws me over the cliff and I come with a long, loud scream. My shoulders and torso jerk upward from the bed with each powerful pulse of pleasure that draws through me and Marco doesn't move. He eats me out like a man possessed and doesn't stop until my orgasm has passed and I'm left a whimpering puddle on the bed.

Only then does he pull back and kiss the inside of my thigh.

"Get some rest, Gianna," he says.

I lazily stare up at him and for a moment, it feels like he might stay. I want him to offer as much as I try to will myself to ask but the words never come.

Instead, Marco leaves and I fall asleep the moment I slip out of my dress.

Marco's attention wasn't enough to keep my dreams trouble free, and I woke groggily. It's too early for anyone to be awake, but that woman is on my mind, and I can't stand it.

Turning on the bedside light, I stretch across the bed and locate my laptop from the floor where I left it. Hauling it up, I create a nest with my pillows and yawn so widely that my eyes water.

"Fuck," I croak, regretting not brushing my teeth before falling asleep. As I shift to get comfort, my pussy throbs from contact and I bite back a whimper. Marco well and truly left his mark.

Laptop on, I immediately google a case from four years ago. Multiple news articles pop up onto my screen, and my heart begins to pound.

Four years ago, two con artists were arrested for a theft that resulted in someone dying. Both culprits were sent to prison based on the statement of a third person present that night.

I was that third person.

My picture was kept out of the paper as part of the deal I struck with the police. I was young and stupid, and the other two were juicier arrests, so no one cared about me. I had to provide information, and I got my life back—not that it was much of a life.

Those two responsible for that man's death should still be in prison but seeing her face again in these articles only makes me certain that I saw one of the women at the dinner tonight.

"Shit," I murmur, dragging one hand down my face.

If she's out of prison, that means she definitely knows who put her away.

Me.

And if she's with Leonardo, it can only mean one thing: she's coming for revenge.

10

MARCO

Gianna's nails claw down my back, leaving red hot trails in their wake. I arch away from her writhing body with a growl and roll my shoulders, chasing the tingling sensations. Her pussy clamps tight around my cock, interrupting the flow of my thrusts inside her and as I move, her hands slide down my chest.

"Fuck," she moans, tossing her head back and forth. "Don't stop. Keep *going*."

She's so insistent and I have no desire to disappoint her. I resume my rapid pace of thrusts, tightening the arm I have around her waist that forces her body to curve, her hips to tilt and my thrusts to reach deeper.

Gianna whines and throws her arms above her head, spreading them wide and curling her fingers into the sheets below. Her breasts sway with each thrust, sweat gleams against her skin and each deep thrust makes her abdomen visibly clench.

I am in awe of her beauty. Dressed up, naked; it doesn't matter. There's just something about Gianna that's under my skin and I never expected it. I could stay here forever, buried balls deep inside her, and just watch the pleasure dance across her body like an orchestra of twitches and movements.

My thighs ache and my left knee complains slightly but I ignore it and continue pounding into her. She was quick to correct me when I changed pace too much and I learned that she needs a specific constant once she's found her pleasure.

Today it's me fucking her as hard as I can with her back bowed to hit her G-spot with each movement.

She's drinking it up like a parched woman. Her head tosses back and forth once more and her hands move to her own body, cupping and squeezing her breasts. I'd do the same, but my free hand is keeping one of her legs up parallel against my chest, allowing me to thrust even deeper inside her.

I never want to leave.

"Yes," Gianna chants breathlessly. "Just like that. Just like that. Don't you dare stop."

There's a sudden teasing temptation to halt my movements and force Gianna to lose her focus just so I can stay here longer. A delayed orgasm is always worthwhile, but I don't have the heart to see the disappointment on her face so I resist.

This time.

"Fuck." I turn my face into her knee, kissing the soft, tender skin there as the walls of her pussy ripple around my cock. It's taking all my restraint not to come right this second, but I'm determined to make her come first.

It's always sweeter that way.

Gianna cries out and both her hands shoot to her flushed face, then they drop back to her nipples. She twists them sharply, and her entire body bows into a deep curve as she comes with a loud cry.

"Marco!"

The sound of my name on her lips, wrapped in deep, lustful tones, is all I need to tip over the edge as I crash into my own orgasm with a deep moan. I bite her thigh, growling softly as my core clenches repeatedly and I pump my load deep inside her—well, deep into the condom wrapped around my dick.

But the illusion is hot enough.

Her body clenches and bows, writhing back and forth as pleasure overtakes her. By the time it's over, we're both panting and sweaty. I let her leg fall down to the bed, and Gianna groans, then she reaches for me, and I lean down on command.

We kiss lazily, and only for a few seconds until the chill in the air forces me to retreat and I pull out of her. I remove the condom with a snap of latex and toss it into the trash, then move to the dresser in my room in search of clothes. Giving Gianna her own bedroom works in terms of trust but with her lying naked on my bed, I oddly miss not seeing her things in the drawers next to mine.

Maybe one day.

Is that wrong of me to think about? That this could become a real thing? Something more than a deal and sexual stress relief?

Picking out a towel, I turn back to Gianna on the bed but she's moved. She has one hand between her legs and the other in the trash can.

"What are you doing?"

"I'm sticky," she murmurs. "I'm never this sticky." A moment later, she locates the condom and after a quick inspection, thrusts her finger through a tear in the latex. "Shit. Condom broke."

"Fuck," I snort, handing her the towel. "My father's demands for an heir might finally come true."

Gianna slumps back onto the bed with a groan. "Doubt it. I had a pretty bad case of mumps as a child. I doubt I can even get pregnant."

Something about that sends my heart south in my chest and I'm not sure why. Am I ... disappointed to hear that? Gianna must be confident in her words because she doesn't appear that panicked at the broken condom, but I will respect her wishes.

"I'll get you the morning-after pill," I say. "Just don't let Dante find out because he might end up spiking your drinks or some shit."

"He'd do that?" Gianna asks, her cheeks draining of their red flush as she cleans herself up.

"Fuck knows. But if he finds out there's a chance you're pregnant, he won't leave you alone."

"Hm." After a few passes of the towel, Gianna drapes herself back against my pillows and it's killer that I have to get dressed rather than return to bed with her.

"I will honor my promise," I assure her. "We will deal with the heir issue later. Right now, Leonardo is my focus."

"And the snitch," Gianna replies softly. She fixes me with a soft gaze. "You believe me, don't you? That it's not me."

"Yes." I nod, buttoning up my shirt. "You accepted my deal because you didn't want to die. It would be counterproductive for you to reveal a secret and earn a quick way to a painful grave." Dressed, I lean over her naked body and gently kiss her collarbone. "Have a good day."

"You too." She waves lazily at me and my chest squeezes at the sight. What I would give to return to her warm body and tender arms.

Instead, I have business to attend to. For the past few days, Leonardo Simone has been blowing up my phone with pictures of random women, along with the tagline *Is this your sister?* Each time I get a ping, my heart punches up into my throat as I fear he will send me a picture of the real Emilia.

So far, it's been no one of note and I know he's just fucking with me. He's enjoying feeling like he has something on me, so I need to get to the bottom of it. I need to find out who betrayed that Emilia is alive. I questioned her entire team, and none of them had any phones beyond the ones I had given them, with no evidence of calls outside the home.

Emilia understood my concern, but I could tell she was pissed I spent hours interrogating the four people that have spent the past twenty years keeping her alive and safe.

Trust is hard to come by, and someone here has broken it. Whoever it is, I will crush them to fucking dust.

Striding through the estate, I'm on my way to the kitchen when another notification pops on my phone. Expecting it to be from Leonardo, I almost ignore it. Knowing I can't, I check my phone and my gut clenches. It's a message from one of the men I have tailing

Leonardo who confirms Leo has stopped off at one of his warehouses and hasn't moved for an hour.

Do I confront him? Do I end this game right now, head-on?

Yes, I do.

I send orders to Anton and Ben to keep Gianna safe, and head for the garage. Leonardo's games end now.

∽

When I arrive, there's already a tense stand-off between my men and Leonardo's men. I'm quickly informed that Leo was in the process of leaving so my guys stepped in to stop him since I was already en route. I thank them and stride into the building. The sharp scent of wrought iron, lead paint, and something acidic assaults my nose as I walk deeper into the building, passing countless wooden crates and forklifts on pause since the arrival of my men.

I walk around the corner and find several of my men with their rifles up and aimed at Leonardo and his men, of which they lack numbers. Odd considering this is Leonardo's territory, but clearly he's shoddy at running it.

"Oh," Leo snorts, rolling his eyes the moment he sees me. "It's you."

"What a greeting. Are you always such a charmer, Leo?"

"It just comes naturally," he mutters. "The hell are you playing at, Barrone? It's like you're *begging* for a war."

"You think? We're just having a friendly conversation," I say, striding in front of my men until Leo and I are face-to-face. "I'm not the one playing fucking mind games here."

"Oh, you got my text then?" Leo smirks. "You could have just called. You didn't have to come all the way down here."

I glance around, noting the numerous crates that are open and cast to one side, and the number that are still awaiting retrieval. A single spark and this place would burn faster than a bonfire.

"Stop with the games, Leo. You wanted my attention, you fucking have it. So out with it. What is it you think you know?"

"Do you think it will be that easy?" Leo rolls his eyes and crosses his large arms over his chest. "I know you, Marco. I know the sick and twisted games your family are involved in. There's no way I'm giving this up easily without making you *suffer* for it first."

"So you have nothing," I sigh, trying to force him out of his bluff. "I should have known. Simones are nothing but empty threats and hot air, I should have known. But toying with my dead sister? You have a death wish and I'll *gladly* oblige."

"Ah-ah!" Leonardo holds up one hand, pausing my step forward and he reaches for something in his pocket. "You don't want to do that because the second you spill a drop of my blood, this goes public to all of the other families. You're strong, Marco, sure, but even you can't take on everyone."

I eye the white paper in his hand as the back of my neck prickles. He's right, in a sense. We can't take on every family in the state. At the moment, we can barely handle Leo thanks to my father's poor planning. Gritting my teeth, I remain silent. I want Leo to think he has me, so that he will keep talking.

I know it's worked the moment he smirks.

"I saw you at that party. People talking to you about guns and drugs as if they don't know the truth."

"The truth?" I prompt.

"Everyone knows the real Barrone meal ticket is sex trafficking," Leo spits in disgust. "Everyone knows your currency is *people*. Slaves. They just don't talk about it."

A coldness slides down my spine like a sliver of ice and disgust curls in my gut. Anger boils up in my chest, igniting a smothering heat across my skin, and it takes every ounce of my strength to remain standing in place and not rip Leo's throat out.

"That's what people know, do they?" I reply tightly.

"You don't even deny it," Leo snarls. "I knew it. You're fucking disgusting, Marco. Just because you have an old name and a fancy estate, people are willing to look beyond your crimes but I noticed. All the women and *children* that go missing around you?"

Leo begins to pace, unfazed by the rifles trained on him. "When

Elodie went missing, and her husband turned up dead after you went there for dinner? I was suspicious. There was no way you were killing everyone in that house and she was quite a woman." Leo's mouth snaps shut with a click. "So I started digging. The Netcis, their don was found floating in the river and his two daughters? Gone. The Calderones? His wife went missing and then a month later, his three kids were gone. Then he ends up dead. The Morellis? Same thing. Dead husband, missing wife and kids. The list goes on."

Leo paces back to me and we lock eyes. "I looked into it. All those people had dealings with you, Marco. In the dark, they whisper that you're the devil. You snatch the women and kids to sell, then you off the rest of the family so no one comes looking. You're a fucking curse, Marco."

So, that's Leo's angle. He acts on incomplete information and now he taunts me with my sister for what reason? Revenge? Payback?

"And my sister?" I bite out through tension so strong it's a wonder my jaw even opens.

"No wonder she ran away from a monstrous family like yours. She knew, didn't she? She probably feared she was next the second she stepped out of line."

Leo strides forward and weapons click, ready to fire the moment he acts. He doesn't strike me, though. Instead, he shoves the paper against my chest.

"Well I found her, Marco. And I will keep her safe. And if you want to see her alive ever again, you will do exactly as I demand."

My attention drifts to the paper, which is an enlarged photograph of a woman. My heart seizes painfully in my chest because I expect to see a photo of Emilia, and Leo's words scare me for a split second—how did he get ahold of her?

But it isn't her.

I let Leo leave because I want him to think he has the upper hand, and part of me is still rooted to the spot as a cold realization creeps over me. This woman isn't Emilia, but why does she look so familiar?

I don't know her—but somehow, I feel like I should. Leo is so completely convinced that she is linked to me, and that concerns me far more than Leonardo's threats.

Who the hell is she?

11

GIANNA

"Here, let me—" I rise from my chair and take the small, porcelain milk jug from Emilia's trembling hand.

"Sorry," Emilia murmurs, curling her hands into her blanket-covered lap.

I wave off her apologies and add a drop of milk to her tea, then retake my seat. "It's fine, it's just milk."

"One day it's just milk, the next it's my medication, or my cane in the bathroom, or a fragile glass," Emilia says softly.

"Right. I'm sorry."

"No, I'm sorry." Emilia shakes her head. "No one can know what it's like to live like this, and I don't expect you to understand so quickly. I'm just ..." She briefly closes her eyes. "I'm worried about Marco."

"And Leo?" I ask, wrapping my hands around my own cup for warmth, but not intending to drink. I can't because my own stomach is in knots from this revelation with Leo and the woman I saw at the party. Suddenly, this safe bubble no longer feels safe.

"Yes." Emilia repeatedly smoothes out her flat blanket. "Leo's accusations suggest we have a leak. A mole. Marco was here the other day, interrogating the team I have helping me and now everyone is on edge. And I am as well because I can't help but wonder if one of them lied and is a danger to me or if there is something else going on."

"Marco strikes me as the kind of man that gets answers," I assure her softly, also trying to calm myself. "I don't think anything would get past him."

"Perhaps." Emilia smiles but the warmth doesn't reach her twinkling eyes like usual. She closes them again and remains silent for a long time before she speaks. "He is such an angel. He has given up so much for me, done so much to keep me safe and I'm scared that in doing so, he's losing himself and forgetting to live. I am grateful, I am. But I worry."

"And you think this thing with Leo will just make Marco redouble his efforts to keep you safe?"

"Exactly," Emilia says and her voice cracks. "And goodness." She reaches one hand across and places it atop my own, and I'm shocked by how cold to the touch she is. "Now you are caught up in this mess."

"Don't you worry." Squashing down the acidic warmth that sits at the base of my throat, I give Emilia my strongest smile. "I can help. I'm actually pretty great at running and hiding, so if we have to do that to keep you safe, then we will. And Marco is living. He just wants to keep you safe. One doesn't prevent the other."

I'm not entirely sure if my words soothe Emilia, but her spirits do seem lifted for the rest of our afternoon tea. She tells me about some new saplings she's been cultivating and explains at length how this time of year is crucial in making sure some of her plants survive the winter. She speaks with such passion that I'm almost jealous.

I have no love for a hobby like this. My life has always been fight-or-flight, with no time to stop and enjoy something just because I can. Maybe I would garden if I ever had the opportunity.

Tea lasts until Emilia grows exhausted and I excuse myself as her team takes over to care for her. I head back to my room and immediately dive into my laptop. I can't do anything to help with the Leonardo situation, but my own situation is something I can take charge of.

Having a fake Mafia husband comes with a lot of perks, including a laptop that's already connected to a server that makes getting information easy. I've been focusing on trying to get all the information on the woman I saw at the party.

If she is coming for me, I need to be prepared.

I'm not sure how long I spend bent over the laptop, but when someone knocks at my door and I sit up, the back of my neck is stiff. "Come in!"

Tara pokes her head around the door. "Hey, you didn't come down for dinner so I brought you something. Are you okay?"

"Tara!" A friendly face is exactly what I need to lift my spirits. I pat an empty space on the bed beside me and slide the laptop onto my knees. "Come in."

She enters and places a tray of soup and bread onto my bedside cabinet, then she settles next to me. "What is it?"

"Nothing. I'm okay, I just want some company."

"If you wanted company, you would have come to dinner," Tara points out. "You've been off ever since the party. Did something happen? If someone hurt you, you have to tell Marco!"

"No, no it's nothing like that!" I clutch at her arm and my heart lurches at her concern. "It's nothing, really."

Tara squints at me then glances down at the laptop screen. "Why are you looking at prison records?"

I slap the laptop closed, but the cat is out of the bag and I groan softly. "Do you promise not to judge me?"

Tara smiles and rolls her eyes. "Look where we are. None of us are in a position to judge."

Taking a deep breath, I reopen the laptop and a tremor runs through my shoulders. I've never told anyone this, but Tara is the only friend I have here, and in the event that I do end up dead before Marco can find out, then at least someone can give him clarity.

"I ..." Emotion suddenly clogs my throat and heat prickles behind my eyes. "Sorry."

"Hey." Tara's face crumples with concern. "Gianna, what's wrong? Whatever it is, it can't be that bad?"

The tears flood my eyes and vulnerability makes my chest ache. "I don't know," I sniffle. "It might be." Closing my eyes, I will back the tidal wave of repressed emotion and begin.

"When I was younger, about sixteen, seventeen, I was running with this gang. I didn't know it at first, y'know? I thought we were all friends, and I would see stuff but I was on the streets so I didn't care. I thought I had friends, and they were a reason to get up in the morning, so I was fine with it. They taught me a lot of things, and we would pick pockets and scam men in bars for money or like, a night at a hotel room."

Tara nods along as I speak, and she pulls some tissues from the pocket of her uniform then presses them into my hand.

"I didn't know a lot about them but it was fine. They didn't know me either. There were two women I ran with the most. They called themselves Mango and Cherry. Nicknames, I suppose. Anyway, one night I chose someone at a bar, but he freaked when he figured out I was only seventeen, and he started waving a gun around. I thought I was going to die."

My heart races as if I'm suddenly back in the alley of that seedy bar, staring down the barrel of a gun. Tara reaches for my hand and squeezes tightly.

"Mango and Cherry took over. They disarmed him and then they started harassing him. Accusing him of all sorts of stuff because I was underage. I think they wanted to scare him because he terrified me. They got him to empty his bank accounts and we left with the cash."

"Honey, that's not your fault," Tara says tenderly. "One, you were a kid. And two, he almost killed you. Losing his money? The least of his worries."

"No, it gets worse." My vision blurs and saliva thickens in my mouth. "A few nights later, he got really drunk because we'd basically ruined him. He went driving and ended up killing himself and another person. The cops tracked us down pretty quickly, I guess because of his bank accounts and then the bar. I was so *scared*. Someone died because of us. He might have been a terrible person, or just scared. I don't know. But he died. And he killed someone else. Because of us."

Tara moves closer and places an arm across my shoulders, but I resist her comfort. I don't deserve it.

"I was scared of the cops too," I continue. "So I told the truth. And because I was young, they offered me a deal. I guess they'd been after Mango and Cherry for a really long time and this was what they finally needed. I felt so guilty that I told them everything and Mango and Cherry went to prison. They let me go because I was a small fish I guess."

"Is that why you're looking them up?" Tara asks. "To see if they're still there?"

Dabbing at my eyes, I pull the laptop closer and swallow hard. Each breath scrapes against the rawness in my throat, and my chest throbs.

"Sort of. After that whole thing, I became so much better at choosing marks. And I never forgot them because I knew they would know I put them away." Digging around in my pocket, I pull out a small, worn photograph that's been folded so many times my own face is creased out of existence. I show it to Tara.

"That's Cherry. And that's Mango." I point them out in the group photo and Tara nods slowly. "But I saw Cherry the other night, at the dinner."

"What?" Tara hands the picture back as her head snaps up. "She's free?"

"I think so. It's so early, though, so I've been trying to find out how that's possible because they got sent away for a long time. I half thought it was a trick of my mind but I saw her a few times. Enough to be sure it's her."

"Not a twin?" Tara suggests with a small smile.

I shake my head and fold the picture back up.

"So if she's out, she knows I put her away. And suddenly she's here, so I'm ..." I have no words. I can't imagine what she will do to me if she finds me, and knowing Marco is busy with Leonardo leaves me feeling adrift and alone.

"I can ask around," Tara says suddenly. "I have loads of contacts with the other families, especially with the staff at that dinner. I can poke around and see if anyone knows anything. Maybe we can find out who she was with."

"You would do that?" I gaze up at Tara with wide eyes.

"Of course." Tara squeezes my hand. "You've been so kind to me since you got here. It's what friends are for, right?"

For a moment, I'm speechless. Deep down, I was expecting Tara to be horrified by what I had done, but then again she lives in this Mafia world. Maybe my actions are tame compared to what she has been around.

"Thank you, Tara. Thank you so much."

"Of course," she smiles. "At least then you'll have some facts, and it won't be your mind running with what-ifs."

"Can I ask for something else too?"

"Anything."

"Could you pick me up a pregnancy test?"

Tara's eyes drop to my stomach. "Are you … ?"

"I don't know. I don't think so, but Marco was supposed to bring me the morning-after pill last week, and he hasn't yet. I don't want to take any chances."

"I'll take care of it."

Just as Tara slides from the bed, the door opens and Marco strides in. I shove my old picture under the pillow and adjust myself so Marco doesn't see.

He glances at Tara, and with one look, she bows her head and scurries from the room, but not before flashing me a comforting smile. With her gone, I wipe my eyes.

"Why are you crying?" Marco demands, pausing at the foot of the bed.

"Tara and I were watching videos of animals greeting owners that had been away for a while," I lie smoothly. "It always gets me emotional."

"Oh. Right."

"Are you okay?" I ask, quickly redirecting to him. "Are you still trying to find Leonardo?"

"I found him last night but it ..." Marco shakes his head. "That bastard makes no fucking sense."

"Does he know about Emilia?"

"No. I mean ... he's convinced about my sister but then he gave me this." Marco pulls some paper from his pocket and hands it to me. "He thinks this is my sister and seems pretty set in that knowledge."

I glance down at the paper, and my body freezes like I've been tossed into a frozen river. My chest tightens and I can't breathe; the picture before me dances in and out of focus.

It's a picture of Cherry.

12

MARCO

The next few days are spent trying to find out who that strange woman is, and why Leonardo is so convinced she is my sister. I showed the picture to my father but there was no recognition in his eyes when he looked at her. That ruled out a secret sister running around. Emilia didn't recognize her either, and after a few days of chasing my tail, I decided the only plan was to beat it out of Leonardo.

The problem was, he was in hiding. Either he knew he was sending me on a wild goose chase, or he was smart enough to know I'd rather talk with my fists. Either way, my search for the strange woman turned into a search for Leonardo with my best people on it.

All I had to do was wait. And I'm not a patient man.

Luckily, when I headed to bed that night, there was the perfect distraction two doors down.

I knock once and enter swiftly to find Gianna lounging on her bed with her face buried in her laptop. She's been busy on that thing ever since she got it, and I'm happy she's found something to keep her busy, but I'd much rather it was me.

"What's wrong?" Gianna closes the laptop and slides it out of the way as I approach her.

"Take off your clothes."

She narrows her eyes. "No foreplay?"

"This is the foreplay. Take off your clothes before I rip them off."

Gianna, wearing only a light pajama top and shorts, folds her arms across her chest. "I think I'd rather you ripped them off," she states.

I accept.

I tackle her onto the bed and she squeals, laughing as I shove her down and claim her smiling mouth in a deep kiss. Her hands slide into my hair and pull sharply, so I return the favor. The light fabric of her sleepwear is no match for my strength, and with a strong pull in either direction, her sleek top rips at the seams.

Gianna giggles as the loose fabric falls away, exposing her bare breasts to my wandering hands. I grip both mounds tightly, squeezing her nipples between my knuckles and shoving my tongue into her mouth. She moans loudly, but when I pull back to rip off her shorts, Gianna immediately scrambles away with a squeal.

I catch her by the ankle and drag her back toward me, earning another delighted squeal as she rolls onto her stomach, kicking out at me.

Flipping her back over is too easy, and I grasp the waistband of her shorts, bunching up the fabric and pulling up until the seam between her legs presses firmly up against her pussy. Gianna gasps and yelps but I keep pulling until the fabric is bunched tight between the lips of her gorgeous pussy.

"Where do you think you are going?" I growl, grasping her jaw.

Gianna's eyes sparkle up at me, and she playfully bites at my nose. "Can't make it too easy for you, can I?" she grins.

Fuck. This *woman*.

I jerk hard at her shorts, and as Gianna yelps loudly, the fabric finally rips, and her shorts fall to pieces in my fists, leaving her naked and flushed before me. Her chest heaves as she pants and then spreads her legs wide, exposing her glistening pussy.

I'm a simple man, and I can't resist.

I crawl over her, shedding my clothes as I kiss up her body until

I'm as naked as she is, then I slide up onto my knees, grab her by the hair, and thrust my cock deep into her mouth.

Gianna slots into the role immediately and she clutches at my thighs.

She bobs her head up and down the shaft, choking softly each time she takes me deep into her throat. As she's lying on her side with her head in my lap, I graze my fingers down her waist and settle them between her legs. Thrusting them into her deep, silken heat, Gianna jerks and moans deeply, then chokes once more on my length. Her throat closes around my cock like a glove and I groan deeply.

I can't stand it for long. When my hand is soaked in her juices and my cock throbs in time to my heartbeat, I release her. Gianna is right with me when I reach for the condom and she tears the foil with her teeth, then slides the silicone into her mouth. Dipping down, she uses her tongue and lips to apply the condom, then she flops back onto the bed with a grin.

Her face is flushed, her eyes bright as I enter her swiftly with a loud cry that mingles with her eager moan. Her legs wrap around my waist and I slide my arms around her body, hauling her up into my lap. With my hands up her back to grip her shoulders, I start to fuck her hard, which draws an immediate scream of lust from her throat.

I hold her tight, I fuck her hard, and Gianna comes apart in my arms. She claws at my back with her nails, bites my shoulder with her teeth, and tosses her head back each time the pleasure gets too much. I think of nothing other than driving my cock as deep as I can inside her, fucking all my work frustrations into her with grunts.

She comes within a few thrusts, but I don't stop because I'm not done. Gianna moans openly, whimpering without pause, and in between marking up my back, she pulls hard at my hair and drags my head back so she can kiss me and fight for dominance over my mouth.

I give her that as I pound her pussy until my thighs throb and my back aches.

I come with a deep moan into her mouth and she reaches her second orgasm at the same time. We clutch at each other, trembling and twitching, then we collapse into a sweat-slicked pile on the sheets, panting.

"Holy shit," Gianna gasps. "That was amazing."

I agree with a grunt because when I look in her eyes, my heart soars.

Am I falling for her?

I think I have.

Because the thought of our deal coming to an end and her walking away suddenly leaves my lungs without air and I tighten my grip around her, pressing her naked body against me.

Would it be terrible to turn this fake marriage into a real one?

Could I actually have a real family?

Just as I'm about to ask her, my phone blares from my jeans pocket and Gianna slides away from me.

"I'm going to take a shower," she says. "Wanna join me?"

"Definitely," I reply, watching her shapely ass sway toward the en suite.

I have to check my phone first, and I'm glad I do because a single message flashes on my screen.

We've got him.

They have Leonardo.

The shower clunks on behind me and my cock twitches.

I'll let him stew. Then I'll go to him and beat the truth out of him.

But first?

I need a shower.

13

GIANNA

The sensible choice would have been to stay at the mansion and soak up the wildly intense, growing feelings I have for Marco. They've swept up so quickly that he takes my breath away just by being near me, and the way he fucks me leaves me feeling owned and claimed.

Like I finally have a place to belong.

But after our shower together, I overheard his phone call. He has Leonardo cornered and he's going to kill him.

If Marco succeeds, then I'll have no idea what the connection between him and Cherry is.

Duping Anton and Ben with a fake illness was rather terrifying since they've been on me like bees on honey since the last time I snuck away to see Emilia, but I put on an incredible performance of stomach pains, sickness, and the threat that if they didn't get me help, Marco would surely kill them.

In their absence, I used all my skills to sneak out of the manor, making it into the back of one of the last cars to leave the parking area.

Ideally, this would be the perfect way to escape if that was still my priority, but Cherry's arrival has changed all of my plans. I need to know the truth because if she is here for me, and revenge, Marco may be the only thing standing between me and death.

I tuck myself down on the floor of the backseat, hidden by shadows. It's cold and uncomfortable, but as two guards climb in, grumbling about the time of night, I know I've made the right choice. Thankfully, neither of them checks the back seat, and I remain undiscovered as the car roars to life.

"He's not walking out of this alive," the one driving says, sliding his leather-clad hands around the steering wheel.

My heart punches hard against my ribs as I'm uncertain who exactly they are talking about.

"About time," says the second. "Leo's too much of a playboy. He's a gentle fucker trying to stand tall and fill the boots of his sadistic father."

"You sound like you feel bad for the fucker," replies the first.

"Nah he's just playing the hand he's dealt, y'know? He lacks his father's cruel streak so when he barks, it sounds like yapping. No wonder he resorts to mind games. He just picked the wrong target."

"You think there's truth to it?"

"No chance," scoffs the second man. "You think if Boss's sister was out there, she'd be undiscovered for this long? Boss is a fucking bloodhound. No one gets away from him."

Marco really has done everything in his power to keep Emilia safe, to the point that his own men don't even know she's been living under the same roof. That's incredible—and rules these two out as the leak.

They settle into useless conversation about sport for the rest of the drive and I remain hidden, running through everything I know about Cherry. Never once in our past did she ever mention any of the well-known Mafia names. She was on drugs, but it's the Barrones that control the drug trade around here. Even I know that.

So why is she with Leo?

Nothing makes sense. The deeper I fall into this world, the more confused I become. I almost miss the simplicity of the streets but after a month here, becoming entangled in all these secrets, I'm certain that life is over.

Marco will never let me go, even if we continue to be friendly.

I know about Emilia and that is indeed a death sentence if I try to leave.

By the time the car pulls to a stop, my hands and feet are numb, and a gentle tremor runs through my body from the cold and adrenaline. I remain hidden, listening to a dull hum of voices outside that eventually fades with time.

Then, there's only silence.

I count to sixty and then slowly climb from the car. A bitterly cold wind hits me when I step outside, and the scent of salty sea air floods my lungs with each breath. We're in a parking lot filled with badly parked cars and several flood lights struggling to hold on to full power. At the opposite end of me stands a gigantic warehouse that creaks and snaps every so often, complaining just like an elderly man complains about his old bones.

That must be where they are.

I take a step forward, then the night air is suddenly filled with an explosion of gunshots like the crack of a whip. Instinct forces me to duck down beside the car with a squeak and a storm of gunfire takes over. It's like a fireworks show located entirely inside the warehouse, and my heart pounds so hard that the taste of iron flashes over my tongue.

I made a mistake.

What the hell was I thinking?

"Gianna?" says a voice. I glance up from where I'm cowering by the car to see one of the guards who drove here standing over me with an assault rifle in his hands. "What the fuck are you doing here?"

I have no answer for him, and I don't resist when he grabs me by the upper arm and hauls me toward the raging inferno of shooting inside the warehouse.

By the time he scrapes the door open and shoves me inside, the fighting has stopped and a sickly yellow light spills across the empty warehouse floor.

People are dead. Countless men lie across the floor like discarded rags in all sorts of positions. They share one thing in common—their torsos are mottled with red holes and crimson puddles surround them.

Those that weren't killed are at the mercy of Marco's men, kneeling and facing the wall at the back of the room with weapons aiming at them, ready to fire at the slightest movement.

To my immense relief, Marco is mostly unharmed. Blood streaks his striped shirt and his left cheek looks injured, but he's standing tall and proud with his handgun pointed at the man cowering under his boot.

It's Leonardo, who has both his hands clutching at a spilling gunshot wound on his thigh.

None of them look up when we enter and the guard making me walk abruptly halts.

"The truth," Marco states, oddly calm for someone who just tore through a warehouse. "My patience is wearing fucking thin with you."

"You want her?" Leonardo asks, wheezing from the weight of Marco standing one foot on his chest. "I can—I can get her for you!"

"Stop lying!" Marco barks suddenly and he fires his gun twice, one on either side of Leo's head.

I slap one hand over my mouth in fright, and my ears ring from the sound. This is ... this is insane. This is too real.

Marco leans over his knee, placing more of his weight on Leo's chest and he taps the barrel of his weapon against Leo's cheek. "The truth, Leo. Or I will kill you right here and one of your useless goons over there will tell me what I want to know."

"Alright!" Leonardo wheezes. "Alright, lemme up and I'll—"

"No." Marco's voice is flat, almost bored now as he glances at his watch. "Time is ticking."

"Fine! Fine, I ... it was a hoax, alright? Just some stupid game to try and throw you off so you would make stupid mistakes, and we'd be able to take you out in a way that would look fair to all the other families."

"Since when does a Simone care about *fair*?" Marco spits.

"I care!" Leo gasps. "Before—before my father passed, I heard him talking about you and your sister. The way he spoke, I don't know. I put two and two together and figured it would be the best way to mess your head up. Everyone knows how awful that attack was and there's always been rumors, y'know? Is she dead or missing? So I went with it. I thought that's what my father had planned and so I took it, alright? I made it up. I just wanted to knock you down and sweep in."

"And the woman?"

"No one."

Sharp tingles, like the prick of a thousand needles, skitter down my spine and my stomach twists. She's not no one. Not to me.

"Adios." Marco takes aim with his gun, pressing the barrel right between Leo's eyes.

"Wait!" The word is out of my mouth before I've even thought it through, and suddenly, all attention is on me. Marco's face is open in alarm to see me, then it hardens like a rock and his anger becomes clear.

"The fuck are you doing here?" he barks. "Frederick, get her the hell out of here."

"No, wait—" I jerk my arm free from the guard, and my thoughts scramble for an excuse. If Leo dies, I'll lose the truth about Cherry, but I also have only a minimal understanding of how things work here.

Will this break some unspoken rule?

"Wait?" Marco growls and his hard gaze hits me like a blow to the chest. "You *know* what he did."

"I do," I gasp, stopping a few feet away. "But wouldn't it be better to let him live? And then just take over his business and fuck up his life or something? Sure, he's stupid and he's done a bad thing but killing him ... it will send the message that he got to you. That your head is easy to fuck with."

I'm rambling, scraping together the tail end of unfinished thoughts in a desperate attempt to save this man's life. It doesn't even cross my mind to tell Marco the truth because I don't want him to look at me differently, not until I have no other choice.

There's a deadly silence, and from the uncomfortable look on the faces of some of his men, I get the impression that no one has ever stopped Marco from doing anything.

Marco taps his gun against Leo's forehead, making him whimper in fear.

"Hm." Marco suddenly straightens up, and his men shift their stance like trees reacting to the flow of the window. "You have a point. This snake has a pretty big family and I'm not sure I have the time to wipe them all out. But I hear you have a pretty good hook into the weapons circuit with the Russians." Marco leans down very slowly and Leo audibly wheezes.

"That's my hook now, do you understand?" Marco growls. "And now, every breath in those pathetic lungs of yours are a gift from my wife, so you better kiss the fucking ground she walks on."

"I will," Leo rasps.

"Do it," Marco snaps, finally stepping off of Leo.

A hot, uncomfortable tightness sweeps through my chest and the back of my neck tingles while watching Leo roll over and crawl toward me. He makes it two feet before Marco's boot lands on his back, forcing him back down to the ground.

Then, Leo begins kissing the blood-slicked, oil-stained floor. Over and over, he kisses the ground near me and keeps doing it even when Marco strides away from him.

I feel sick, and yet there's another strange sensation that I can't quite decipher. It's pressure, but fluttering too like butterflies in my gut.

Is it from Marco's show of power, or Leo's obedience?

I have no idea.

"Kill the rest," Marco says to Frederick, then grabs me by the arm. His contact is molten, but it brings me a flood of relief that he is okay.

"Marco," I say, my voice trembling from how frantic my heart dances around my chest.

"Not here," Marco grinds out between clenched teeth as he hauls me with him back out of the warehouse. "You have some fucking explaining to do."

14

MARCO

"What the hell were you thinking? Are you trying to give me a heart attack or something? Were you trying to *scare* me?" I crowd Gianna up against the wall in her bedroom, studying every detail of her flushed face.

I'd been far too angry to speak to her on the drive home but now, in the safety of her bedroom, I can let loose.

"No," Gianna says breathily, panting softly. "It was nothing like that!"

"Then what? Sneaking out of here, giving your guards the slip. Coming to that meeting?" My heart punches against my ribs, skipping a beat every time my mind flashes to the disaster that Gianna could have faced. "You could have been hurt. You could have been shot! What were you *thinking*?!"

"I wasn't though," Gianna says softly and both her hands cup my face, stroking my jaw. "I was concerned because of Emilia. I wanted to be there in case anything bad happened, that's all. And I'm okay, look at me Marco. I'm okay. You're okay."

I should be furious. I *am* furious but something about looking into her deep, sparkling eyes is slowly diffusing that rage. It's not lust that drives me to keep Gianna safe anymore. There's a deeper connection here, and I need to protect it.

If she ends up like the rest of the women in my life, there'll be no coming back from the dark pit that will swallow me whole.

"I need to be able to trust you," I snap. "When I tell you to stay here, I mean it. I told you what happened to Fawn, you saw my sister —" My throat tightens and the words catch in my throat. "I need you safe, you hear me? I need you *here*."

"I need you safe too," Gianna murmurs, and her thumb trails over my chin. "You expect me to wait here like some good little wife when I didn't even know if you would come home. How am I supposed to deal with those feelings?"

"By not putting yourself in danger!" My skin flushes hot, like the first burst of a too-hot shower scalding my shoulders, and the sensation sweeps down my back and across my torso. Gianna's eyes dart between mine, then she leans in and kisses my lips sweetly.

"I'm sorry," she whispers, so close that her lips write the words against my own. "I'm so sorry."

"You will be." I kiss her hard, dragging her away from the wall and spinning us around until I'm facing the bed. Then I shove her down onto it. She bounces once, and as she settles, I crawl over the top of her. I need to feel her. Every inch of her. I need to imprint every single detail into my mind, and I won't stop until the image is pixel perfect.

Our kisses are hard and biting, devouring one another as a scorching heat rises between our bodies. I thrust my tongue into Gianna's mouth and she moans, rolling her hips up to meet mine. I bite her lower lip, and there's a spark of blood as she hisses and jerks her head away, then I bury my face into her neck and sink my teeth into the juncture of her shoulder.

I crave her harder than any drug that's ever crossed my lips. Clothes are tangled and torn in our desperation to free ourselves, and we snatch breathless kisses in between grunts and growls. I pin her to the bed, lavish attention over her throat and down to her gorgeous breasts. She pulls my hair. I nibble her nipples and suck until they peak red and sensitive. I kiss her belly, tracing the curves that flow as she breathes and begs me for more.

When I thrust inside her heat, I maintain eye contact and hold her in my gaze watching every emotion dance across her beautiful face. The pleasure at being filled and stretched, the satisfaction at being held and cared for, and then the impatience when I don't move.

"Please," Gianna gasps.

"Promise me," I growl, nose to nose. "Promise me you will never put yourself in danger ever again."

"I promise," she swears, and I believe her.

I fuck her hard, pouring every ounce of my desire into each thrust. Gianna is shunted up the bed toward the pillows, so I slide one hand around her throat and lightly pin her in place while my other hand slides between us and toys with her clit. Her eyes widen and she moans, draping her legs around my waist as both her hands clutch at my wrist. She doesn't try to pull me away. She just holds on and clenches her pussy around me like a vice each time I pull out.

It's like she doesn't want me to leave as much as I never want to.

The air is filled with heat and the slick sound of flesh impacting flesh. The song of our moans interrupts each time we kiss and soon, there's nothing but the primal, desperate chase of pleasure. Gianna scratches down my arm as she comes with a scream, arching off the bed like the curve of a bow. Her tight muscles milk me, drawing my orgasm out of me with the force of a punch and I bury myself as deep as I can, flooding her insides with me and only me.

Then I kiss her slowly and take her hands in mine. With interlaced fingers, I stretch her hands above her head and pin her there.

"Never again," I whisper against her. "Or I'll never fuck you again."

"No," Gianna whines lazily. "Never again."

I'm about to pull away when my knuckle grazes something sharp under Gianna's pillow. Releasing her hand, I grasp it and pull it free. It's just a photograph and I almost toss it when something—or rather someone—catches my eyes.

My entire world freezes, like a sudden cold snap has swept through the room and encased me in ice. My change must be instant because Gianna is immediately wiggling out from underneath me.

"Marco?"

I sit up slowly and the warmth of my post-orgasm haze vanishes. Staring at the picture, nausea curls through my gut and I swallow so hard it echoes in my ear.

"What is this?" I ask tightly.

Gianna is pale, her cheeks absent the rosy orgasmic glow she had a moment ago.

"Why do you have this?" I repeat. "Why is *she* in this picture?"

"I'm sorry," Gianna gasps and she stands abruptly, shaking her hands as she stumbles about on unsteady legs. "I'm so sorry. I was—fuck—I was going to tell you, I swear, I just couldn't. I was scared you wouldn't look at me the same again."

The picture is old, but clearly cared for with the creases of being folded up for an age.

I can't take my eyes off the picture, and I stare at it as a cavernous hole opens up in my chest. "Explain," I say, strained. "Now!"

"I know Cherry," Gianna blurts out. "Or I did, okay. I used to run with her when I was a teenager and I didn't know any better. She should be in prison because I put her there, but she's out and I don't know why, okay? I've been looking into it, and she got an early release but I have no idea why. I'm sorry, okay? When I ran with her, a man died because of us and I was the witness. I put her away so when I saw her at the party, and then you showed me that other picture, I realized she was connected to Leonardo, and if you killed him, I'd never find out why she was here!"

Gianna is sobbing now, stumbling over her words but she still isn't answering my question.

I stand abruptly and catch her by the wrist, jerking her toward me as I thrust the photograph into her face. "Not her," I bark, having barely noticed Cherry in the picture. "*Her.*"

The taller, older woman in the background of the picture. It's her that I recognize. Her that makes the air around me feel so thin.

Gianna whimpers and looks at where I'm pointing, then she frowns and honest confusion flashes in her tear-filled eyes. "Her? I—I have no idea. She was there a few nights, I think, but she was just on the arm of some guy that Mango met. She was a prostitute, I think?" Gianna looks up at me with eyes like glass. "Why?"

I release her and sink slowly down onto the bed with a long, low groan, the picture clutched in my hand.

"She ..."

Gianna slowly sits beside me, wiping her tears and staring at the picture.

"She looks like *Fawn*."

Gianna tenses up immediately. "Wait ... your ex? The one who was killed by her ex-boyfriend."

I nod stiffly, struggling to process. She was the love of my life when I was eighteen, and while it's been a couple of decades since then, it makes no sense why she's in the background of Gianna's photo. Gianna who is much younger and never would have met her.

"I don't understand," Gianna says softly. "Did Fawn have any sisters, maybe?"

"No," I reply tightly. "She had no family. And at times, I felt the same, so we were perfect, in a way."

As the shock fades, the chill of the room makes itself known, so I grab the end of the blanket and pull it over Gianna's shoulders. This is Fawn. I'd know her face anywhere. The guilt keeps her fresh in my mind.

"You need to tell me everything." I turn to Gianna and clutch at her hand. "I need every detail, everything you remember about everyone in this picture."

Gianna's mouth opens and closes. "Marco, it was so long ago I—"

"Please!" I snap, then I catch myself and lower my voice. "*Please*—"

"Sir!" Anton suddenly crashes into the room while knocking rapidly on the door, and a surge of rage rises through me like vomit. With one look at him, I know the stability I've been clinging to is about to unravel before my very eyes.

"What?!"

"Sir, Tara has been shot."

"Oh my *God*," Gianna chokes and she clutches at my arm.

"And Dante—"

My heart becomes steel. "What about him?"

"He's gone, sir. He's been kidnapped from Mario's where he was having dinner!"

15

GIANNA

I hate hospitals.
    The acidic, chemical smell burns the inside of my nose and clogs my throat, the air is cold and dry, and the machines around Tara's unconscious body beep like a continuous threat.

She looks peaceful, almost. If I ignore the bandages around her arms and shoulder and the bruises and lacerations from the beating she sustained, then I can pretend she's asleep. If I ignore the look on the doctor's face when she told me Tara had been shot in the gut, and was clinging to life, then I can pretend she just has a cold and is getting some rest.

It's a weak lie, one that doesn't hold up against anything, but I try. I try as the hours tick by and nothing changes. My legs grow numb from the hard plastic chair, and I burn through two boxes of tissues sobbing, but still nothing changes. Marco is absent, out searching for whoever has kidnapped his father, and he's left me here with Anton, Ben and a host of others to watch over Tara and wait for her to wake up.

I wait for her to tell me who did this to her, but I think I already know.

The weight of the guilt is crushing, suffocating me with each passing hour. This is my fault. The last time we spoke, I asked Tara to dig into Cherry and now, suddenly, she ends up like this. She's paying the price for my curiosity and there is nothing I can do to help her.

She is my only friend, and I may have just gotten her killed.

A fresh wave of tears warm behind my raw eyes and I close them over, sniffling tiredly.

How do I fix this? Telling Marco the truth hardly made a difference because some fucker has snatched his father and that is an open declaration of war.

While Marco kissed me hard and promised to protect me, I knew he needed to do this. This left me to help Tara, and I have no idea how. I'm not a doctor. Not a surgeon.

I just have to watch her heartbeat dance sluggishly across the monitor, and watch the pump helping her breathe hiss up and down.

"Tara," I weep softly. "I'm so sorry I got you into this. This was my fight and I never should have involved you. I'm sorry, I'm so so sorry." Clutching at her motionless hand, my heart aches to feel a twitch of recognition from her but there's nothing.

She took a beating that was surely meant for me.

"Fuck," I whisper, using up the very last of my tissues. The thought of leaving the room to get more pains me. I don't want to be away from Tara until I have to, so instead I locate Tara's belongings and quickly rummage through her purse in the hopes of finding a hidden packet of tissues.

I do find them, but I also find the pregnancy test I asked her to buy for me. I'd forgotten all about it with everything else that was going on. Another thing Tara was selflessly doing for me.

Glancing around the dark room, Tara remains dead to the world and the door is firmly closed against the guards.

Do I take it?

I should. She risked a lot to get me this so I can't let it go to waste. Leaning over Tara, I gently kiss her warm forehead and then slip into the attached toilet to do my business. In theory it's simple, but it's rather difficult to pee on a stick when you've been crying on a numbing hospital chair for two days straight. I get more on my hands than on the stick, but it glares up at me with a small countdown as I scrub my hands clean.

I don't know what to hope for. Positive? Negative? Will either result magically fix all of my problems?

No.

Will either result bring a distraction? Or just disappointment.

I don't have the answer. A baby was always in the back of my mind since the moment Marco and I met. He made the deal clear. But with Tara in hospital, Dante missing, Cherry in the wind, and Leonardo likely scheming his comeback, this is not a safe world for a baby.

The test beeps and a small animation of a baby appears on the screen.

Pregnant.

"Fuck," I whisper into the eerie silence of the bathroom. "Hey Tara." Moving slowly back into her room, I hold up the test. "I'm pregnant. And you're the first person I'm telling, so you gotta wake up and tell me what the hell I'm going to do with a—a *baby*."

In another time, another place, this might have been a moment of joy, but right now, all I feel is terror.

How can I bring a child into this? Into a life where bullets fly as easily as words, where the people I care about end up in hospital beds or worse? Where revenge and betrayal are the language of survival?

A fresh wave of tears overtakes me, and I sink down to the floor, sobbing into my hands. This should be good news, but under the crushing weight of my guilt and my fear of Cherry, it feels like the end of the world.

I need to tell Marco.

I cry until I can cry no more, then I return to my vigil by Tara's side until a little after midnight when Anton eases himself into the room.

"Gianna?"

"Go away."

"Marco is coming," Anton says. "He wants to take you home to wash and eat. You've been here three days."

"I'm not leaving until she wakes up."

"He's not taking no for an answer."

I stare up at Anton, searching his face for the answer to all my problems but there's nothing other than a soft sadness in his eyes.

"Ben will stay and watch her," Anton continues. "She won't be alone."

"You promise?"

"I promise."

I kiss Tara's head and promise to return the moment I've appeased Marco, then I follow Anton out of the room. Ben flashes me a sympathetic look as he heads inside to take my place, then I numbly follow behind Anton as we head out of the hospital.

Marco has Tara in a secluded wing with an entire private medical team at her disposal, at my request, but it doesn't feel like enough.

My mind spins, weaving between grief, guilt, and the shock at the results of the pregnancy test I left in the trash.

It's too much.

Maybe I do need to sleep.

Out in the parking lot, a light rain drifts down from the sky as Marco's black limo pulls up from the street, flanked by two other cars. His door opens, and the sight of him with the wind in his hair and his silver shirt ruffling around his body causes a squeeze of tension through my chest.

I need him.

I need to sink into his arms and have him comfort me.

Life has a different plan.

Marco takes two steps toward me, and suddenly, several cars around us turn on their headlights, blinding Marco and all the other guards around him. Gunfire erupts through the parking lot, and I can only watch in sickening horror as three explosions of blood erupt from Marco's chest.

He stumbles back with a cry and then disappears from view as

Anton's body slams into me. We crash to the ground and he uses his body to cover me as guns fire, men yell, and tires screech.

No. No no no!

It replays in my head like a loop. The crimson splashes, the twist of pain on Marco's face.

Not Marco.

Not him too.

Anton lunges upward, opening fire over the top of the car we are hiding behind. As he does so, his trouser leg rides up and exposes the gun strapped to his ankle.

I don't think. I just grab it.

Then I'm on my feet and sprinting toward Marco while firing in the direction of anyone I don't recognize. I can't tell who is shooting at who, my only target is Marco.

If I die, then at least we die together.

I can't do this alone.

I reach Marco just as the attackers flee. Those that aren't dead are driven off by Marco's men.

I collapse down onto the ground next to him with small stones digging into my knees. Dropping the gun, I slide my hand over the pooling blood on his shirt.

"Marco! Marco don't you dare! Don't you dare leave me!"

Hot, sticky blood spills over my fingers and soaks into my skin, staining me as Marco remains silent on the ground, dead to the world. Men run around me, people yell and scream. There's a few more gunshots and then suddenly, arms grab at me, pulling me away.

"No!" I scream as my heart races so fast it becomes a blur. "No!" I try to claw my way back to Marco but the guard holds me back, allowing members of the hospital to sweep in and do their job.

"Marco!"

He doesn't answer me. I'm released as Marco is hauled onto a gurney and raced into the hospital, along with those around me who also took a bullet or two.

I can't breathe.

I can't think.

This cannot be happening.

Marco's blood stains my hands, and Tara's stains my soul.

How is this happening? How is my life suddenly crumbling apart as fast as it came together? How are the people *I* love taking the brunt of this?

"Fuck," I whisper, wiping my tears with the back of my wrist. Around me is a sea of carnage; dead bodies, injured men, restless guards, and bullet-riddled vehicles.

My head spins and I turn on my heel as acid rushes up my throat, only it has nowhere to go as I come face-to-face with a woman I haven't seen in years.

A woman with bright green eyes and deep red hair that looks almost black from the rain soaking into the strands. She regards me with a stony look, then delicately wipes the corner of her red lips.

"Cherry?" I gasp, gurgling the word as my body seeks to eject the bile in my gut while shock keeps it at bay.

"You don't have a lot of time," Cherry says, placing one hand in the pocket of her tan coat. "I remember you were always a little slow, so I'll keep this simple."

"What—what are you doing here? *How* are you here?"

"You have one choice, if you can even call it that. Walk away, Gianna."

"What?" I blink furiously as the rain grows heavier, blurring the world around me. This feels like a dream—a terrible, terrible dream.

"Walk. Away." Cherry sighs wistfully. "Do you need me to spell it out for you?" She walks closer, her heels clacking on the ground like the gavel sealing my fate. "If you enter that hospital, I will kill Tara. And Marco will be next."

"What?" Confusion explodes out of me and I spit the words. "What the fuck is wrong with you? What did they ever do to you?"

Cherry smirks like a cat. "Them? No, Gianna. This is on you. All of it."

My stomach falls out of my ass and tension pulls across my forehead. "Wh-what?"

"You know, when I got out of prison on the dime of someone oh so kind, I was excited to get back on my feet. So imagine my disgust when the man I spent a *year* marking, ends up with *you* on his arm. The fucking rat that sent me to prison. I spend a year working contacts to get close to him, and you snatch him up in one fucking afternoon."

"*That's* what this is about?" I gasp. "He was your mark?"

"Don't act so surprised," Cherry snorts delicately. "I know your game, Gianna. I know you were doing the exact same thing."

While true in the beginning, her words cut deeply because they are not true anymore.

The utter agony I felt at seeing him get shot and the sickening coldness at touching his motionless body alerted me to one very true, very real fact.

I love him.

I don't know when it happened, or how. But I love him.

"I'm not—"

"Don't." Cherry holds up one well-manicured hand. "I don't care. He's mine, you understand? I took out Tara as a warning, but I will kill them both if you don't leave right here, right now. This is bigger than you know, and I won't have you fucking me up any longer. You can't protect anyone, Gianna. I remember how fucking toxic your loyalty is."

And then, like a cruel twist of fate, my hand instinctively rests on my stomach, over the child I now know I'm carrying. The child Marco can never know about. Not in this world. Not with Cherry hunting us.

Given the carnage around me, her threats hold weight and fresh, hopeless tears prick my eyes as I wrestle with my decision.

"If I leave," I whisper. "You won't kill them?"

Cherry smirks again, catlike. "Not tonight. No. So do what you do best, Gianna, and abandon the people that took you in. They'll be safer without you around."

What hope do I have? I have nothing. I can't protect Marco and I put Tara in danger.

I blink quickly, trying to clear the tears and half hoping Cherry is just a mirage from my guilt, but she remains there, staring at me and standing between me and the hospital.

If this is what she does to send a warning, I can't fathom what she will do if I don't obey.

So I do.

I leave.

"Fine. I'll go." On trembling legs, I turn from the hospital, from Marco, from everything I thought I could have.

With every step, my heart fractures, but the weight of the life growing inside me demands this sacrifice.

Now I have to do everything in my power to make sure no one finds out about this baby.

16

MARCO

Gianna is gone.

Those three little words are scarred into my mind, surrounding my soul like barbed wire.

I woke up from an operation to have three bullets removed—two flesh and one internal—to find the woman I'd fallen in love with, the woman the world thought was my *wife*—was gone.

Anton found a note left on the windshield of the limo stating that watching me get gunned down so soon after Tara made this world far too real and dangerous for her. It broke her heart, and so she left.

Part of me understands. The fear I felt the moment those bullets impacted my body armor, and my world turned black, was chilling. I was out for two days and woke to a missing wife and a missing father.

Every person I know is on it, searching the entire city for any sign of them because neither of them are safe. Whoever took my father is asking to be sent to the bottom of the ocean in an oil barrel, but Gianna? She flees to be safe, but I know for a fact she isn't. Not after what happened to Tara. This Cherry woman has proven herself dangerous and she's shot to the top of my hit list.

"Anything?" I bark at Ben as he enters my office with a phone in hand. "Have you found her?"

"No," Ben replies quietly and he hands me the phone. "But we found your father."

"Leo?"

"Nah, a smaller family. The Ricci's? They're based on the outskirts and as far as I can tell, they have ties to no one."

"But they kidnapped my father?" I mutter, scrolling rapidly through the information on the screen. "A bold fucking move."

"Yep. But we know where they are keeping him. Frederick is already there, waiting for the go ahead."

"No." I hand the phone back to Ben. Too much has happened without me there to witness it: my father, Tara, and now Gianna. "I want to do this myself."

Carnage isn't a cure for heartbreak, but it's one hell of a distraction. Ben drives me to my father's location, and my men surround the building when we arrive. It's an old abandoned bakery with a sign hanging by just a few threads. The thought of my father, the great Dante Barrone, being held in a place as shoddy as this is almost laughable.

I kick down the door, raise my handgun at the first asshole I see, and open fire. Nothing stops me. Rage pours over me like molten oil, seeping from every vein and flooding from every pore. Too many people are screwing me over, and there's too many things I can't keep in control of.

Do people not see me as a threat anymore? Do they think I am someone that can be messed with like this? This Cherry woman, and now an outskirts family daring to kidnap my *father*?

No one survives.

They fight back and I'm glad they do. I punch faces to pulp, shoot entire clips into the chests of others, and rip and tear my way through every pathetic guard that's stationed between me and my father. They snatched him from a restaurant where he was just eating dinner, and each day he has been missing is a day they could have grown bored and killed him.

I yell his name until it bounces off the walls as my own reply, drive a crowbar through the gut of someone who tries to tackle me down the stairs, and shoot three men with the last of my bullets. Then I kick down the last door and find my father bound to a chair amidst old, moldy sacks of flour.

My heart stops.

His head is down. His chest is motionless.

My heart crumbles further. I take the steps two at a time and charge toward my father, dropping to my knees as soon as I reach him.

"Dad?" There's a wound on his forehead, surrounded by dried blood, and his skin is pale but when I touch his cheek, he lifts his head and the tension snaps in my chest like a rubber band.

"Marco?"

"*Dad*, holy fucking shit, you scared the crap out of me." I pat his cheek, studying his tired eyes. "The fuck happened? When was the last time someone got the jump on you?"

Dad coughs roughly as I move around him and untie the rope keeping him down, then I slide an arm around him and help him to his feet.

"My son," Dante coughs. "They told me you'd been shot. That you were in the hospital, dying."

"I'm fine," I assure him. "I was shot but my armor took two of them, and I'm on so many painkillers I can't find the third."

"My boy." Dante clasps my cheek and wheezes, then he straightens up. "I am so relieved to see you alive."

"Me too." Once he is steady on his feet, I pull my father into a crushing hug that makes both our bones creak.

"Give me a gun." A nearby guard meets Dante's request. "We have to kill the rest of these fuckers. I ain't letting some scumbag, lowlife family think they can snatch a fish as big as me and get away with it."

"You're speaking my language," I reply, seeking out a fresh magazine for my gun.

"What's wrong?" Dad stops in front of me and his pale eyes weave across my face. "Something is wrong."

"Gianna," I say tightly. "She's missing."

"Someone took her?"

"No, she uh …" I almost don't want to tell him. When it was just me, I could tell myself that I would find her before the pain became real. Telling my father brings that pain into my reality, and I don't want to hear his *I told you so*.

"She left."

Dante's eyes narrow. "I told you this would happen, marrying outside of—"

"Don't," I snap, pushing past him. "Are we gonna kill the rest of these fuckers or what?"

"Sir." Ben approaches through the door, his face twisted into an expression I can't quite read. Something between excitement and dread. "We've found her."

My entire body stalls like a snapshot and I wobble, half up one step. "What?"

"Facial recognition flagged her at an airport. Her name wasn't on any of the manifestos, so we checked the private charters, and we found her."

"Take me there," I demand. "Take me there right now!" As I move to sprint back up the steps, my father catches my elbow with a surprisingly strong grip and pulls me back.

"Marco, you can't be serious. What about the Ricci's?"

"She's more important," I snarl, jerking my arm free. "I have to get to her. I have to talk to her, explain—"

"Explain what?" My father's face darkens. "She's an outsider, Marco. You knew this. She's not worth *shit*. Look at the mess she brought with her, huh? A street rat bringing her messy life into ours like it means nothing. Your maid got shot, *you* got shot. This here is a real problem, I was kidnapped for fuck's sake!"

"We don't know who shot me yet," I grind out.

"That's beside the point. Why do you think the Ricci's were bold enough to attack me, hm? Because we've slipped. Because you disrespected everyone with that rat—"

His words end when my fist slams hard into his face, sending him reeling backward into Ben. "Don't talk about my *wife* like that," I snarl, then my furious gaze moves to Ben. "Take me to the fucking airport."

Ben doesn't need to be told twice, and he leads me down to the car and then tosses his phone into my lap as he drives.

The picture of Gianna on the screen makes the rest of the noise in my head fall silent. She looks sad, pale and strained. I don't blame her for running. I don't blame her for being scared, but I need to talk to her, to show her I'm okay and that I can protect her.

I stare at her narrow eyes, the slope of her nose, and the slant of her chin. She's dressed much like she was when she first met, and I can only assume she found an old contact to help her get on this flight.

Each beat of my heart is like dragging myself through razor blades. Each breath scrapes my throat and she is my only focus.

I need to tell her I love her. That I will do everything in my power to protect her.

We reach the airport two minutes before her flight is due to depart and Ben doesn't need to be asked to drive straight through one barrier and onto the tarmac itself. He seems to know where he's going, and in any other situation, I would applaud his preparation, but right now, Gianna is my focus.

We race down the smooth tarmac, gliding toward our target and narrowly avoiding several public planes. Ben races us through another fence and we skid onto the tarmac of the private planes where a single, solitary plane sits.

No, not sits. It's moving.

"Drive!" I yell at Ben, unsure what the hell we can do but as Ben slams his foot down on the accelerator, the plane lifts off the tarmac and glides into the sky like a white dove. Ben slams on the brakes and I stumble out of the car before it's even fully stopped, tripping over myself as the love of my life is carried far away.

"Gianna!" I scream, as if my voice could somehow reach the plane that takes her further and further away from me with every passing second.

The ground rises quickly and I crash to my knees as the remaining shards of my heart crumble into dust.

I lost her.

What have I done?

17

GIANNA

I'll never grow used to the chemical scent that exists in a hospital. It's so sharp that my nose burns as I crack open my eyes and take a slow look around the room.

Pale light creeps in through the half-shut blinds, trembling due to the force of the rain pouring down outside. An endless gray sky stretches out like a turbulent ocean, and I gaze at it from where I lie, working through a drug-addled, sluggish mind.

It's been eight months since I left Marco. Eight months of running and hiding, using every trick in the book to survive. Those tricks grew fewer and fewer as my belly swelled with new life, and soon, there was nothing left for me to do but scrape together my last few dollars and try to make it back to familiar territory.

I failed.

Stress, exhaustion, and malnutrition tossed me into early labor in the middle of a supermarket in a small town well off the beaten path. My last memory is of a terrified store clerk yelling into her headset about an ambulance. Everything after that is a blur: doctors and nurses asking me questions I couldn't answer, demanding insurance information, and then a mask over my face as they tell me my baby is coming.

My daughter came into the world via C-section at 4:32 in the morning.

I slowly adjust myself on the bed and wince as a dull pain—kept at bay by the painkillers in my blood—throbs across my lower abdomen. It's jarring to see a much smaller bump under the covers. I press my hands over the area as my mind races through the fog, struggling to organize my thoughts.

Just as I'm gathering myself, the door to my room swings open and in walks a smiley nurse with tightly curled blonde hair. She pushes something on wheels in front of her and it's not until she stops beside my bed that I realize what it is.

A makeshift cot.

"Oh look! Mamma's awake!" The nurse says cheerily, cooing down at the baby. "How are you feeling, Mom?"

I blink hazily up at her, and when I speak, my tongue rests heavily in my mouth. "Tired," I say. "I'm sorry, I—I don't remember ... how did I get here?" My eyes drop to the baby bundled up tightly in a pink blanket. "Is she okay?"

"You're a little under the weather so the doctor had to sedate you, but don't you worry, everything went perfectly. You're both happy and healthy!"

She's far too happy for my liking and I fight the urge to roll my eyes. "I can't afford to be here," I murmur, bracing my hands down on the bed and easing myself painfully into a sitting position. "How long until they kick me out?"

"Listen mamma, don't you worry about that right now," the nurse grins, and she bustles about my bed for a minute or two, then she pauses next to me. "Do you want to hold your baby?"

Your baby.

I feel so strangely detached from those words and my heart begins to race.

What if something is wrong? What if I hold her and she cries? What if I feel nothing? What if she can tell that I'm not built to be a mother?

Those thoughts and more swarm my mind as the nurse holds my

gaze, and after a few seconds, I nod. I can't think of anything else to say.

The nurse beams at me, and with practiced ease, she scoops the baby up from the crib and gently eases her into my arms, giving a few quiet instructions to support her head and keep her close.

In an instant, the baby becomes *my* baby.

My daughter.

The room fades to nothing, and the nurse's words grow muted as I stare down at this absolutely gorgeous, perfect little face. My daughter scrunches her nose, and she gurgles faintly despite her closed eyes.

She's perfect.

A painful warmth suddenly blooms out from my chest, and I can't *breathe* because of how intense the rush of love is. Tears warm behind my eyes, and all my stresses and fears are momentarily forgotten.

"See?" the nurse speaks softly. "Holding her makes everything else unimportant."

She's right. From the first touch, all I care about is keeping her safe. The surge of love is unlike anything I've ever experienced before, and with it comes a stab of sadness in my heart.

Did my mother ever feel like this? And if she did, how could she give me the terrible life I lead?

"Is there anyone I can call for you?" the nurse asks.

I shake my head. "No," I whisper, lightly touching my daughter's forehead. "There's no one."

"Have you thought of a name?"

Staring down at her adorable, scrunchy face, I nod just once as the tears come. "I'm going to call her Freya."

∽

THE SECOND TIME I wake up, my attention is immediately on the crib by my bed. The nurse had been kind enough to talk me through breastfeeding, though a deep sense of failure sat heavy in my chest when I failed to provide any milk for Freya. According to the nurse, it's very common and we were to try again later after more rest.

My room is dark now, and the only light comes from the machines around my bed monitoring me and my baby. My body aches, and my heart is full, yet weighed down at the same time, and I can't take my eyes off her as she sleeps soundly next to me.

How did I do this? How did I keep myself hidden *and* grow another human inside of me? This miracle is almost beyond my understanding because someone like me should not be capable of creating something as small and perfect as her.

"Cute kid," says a husky voice from the darkness.

My heart lurches and I jerk upward on my bed, scanning the shadows for where that strange voice came from. I see nothing at all, yet just as I fear it was my imagination, there's a scuffle of fabric.

My hand shoots out to the alarm button near my bed, and as I repeatedly press the button, husky laughter flows from the shadows.

"I already cut the line," says the voice. "But go to town."

The voice is right. Lifting my hand, the alarm button is attached only to two inches of cable. The rest is cut and out of sight. My heart pounds against my ribs so hard it's a wonder the bones don't break, and a wave of dizziness washes over me.

"Who are you?" I demand hoarsely, scanning the darkness and straining my eyes. "Show yourself!"

"Careful," says the voice. There's a click and the small lamp beside the couch turns on, revealing the owner of the voice. "You'll wake the baby."

A beautiful woman clad in leather pants, a white T-shirt, and a leather jacket sits on the couch, watching me with dark-lined eyes. Her ruby-red lips purse into a small O as she toys with the sleek, sharp knife in her right hand.

Our eyes meet, and there's a familiarity about her that I can't quite place through the haze in my mind. All I can think about is the knife and that this stranger is in the same room as my baby.

Stitches be damned, I will protect her.

"Are you here to kill me?" I ask. My voice wavers from the force of my heart racing, and I swallow around the dryness parching my mouth. "Here, in a hospital?"

"No," the woman says. She stands slowly and her heeled biker boots clack softly against the floor. "I'm not here to kill you, Gianna."

"You know my name." I can't remember what name I gave to the doctors when I arrived here, but I'm certain medical staff don't dress like her. She looks like an assassin right out of some kind of action movie, and I can't take my eyes off her.

"Of course I know your name," the woman says as she wanders slowly toward the end of my bed. "You don't recognize me?"

I squint through the low light, mapping out the slopes of her angular jaw, small nose, and the flow of jet-black hair. Should I recognize her?

"I'm hurt," the woman says, sounding not very hurt at all. "I would have thought you'd recognize me instantly."

"I just had a baby," I mutter, tensing as she walks closer and closer to where Freya lies sleeping next to me. "I barely remember my own name."

"Think," the woman says. The knife glints dangerously in the light as she stops next to the crib, and my heart leaps into my throat as a pulse of sickly fear washes over me.

I stare at her, then at Freya, wracking my brain for any inkling of recognition.

And then, as the woman leans over the crib to stare down at my daughter, it clicks like the snap of a lock in my mind.

"Amanda?"

She straightens up suddenly, and smiles coldly. "Of course. I forgot I went by a different name when we met. But you know my real name too, don't you?"

I nod slowly, thinking back to Marco's reaction when he found that picture of my past. To me, that woman was Amanda. To Marco?

"Fawn," I say softly. "You're ... you're really not dead?" Part of me had hoped Marco was just mistaken but here she is, standing in front of me and very much alive. "I don't understand."

"Of course you don't." Fawn rests one hand on the edge of the crib and I can't take my eyes off it.

I'm terrified she's about to do something to my daughter and I'm useless, with only a few staples holding my insides where they're supposed to be.

"You look ... good," I say, searching for the right thing to say.

Fawn eyes me through narrow lids. "Leaving behind a life of sex work does wonders," she says. "But you, my little dove. Imagine my surprise when *we* crossed paths again. From the look in your eyes, you really are as clueless as I suspected."

I have no answer for her, unable to breathe until she removes her hand from Freya's crib.

"Maybe you can enlighten me," I say weakly, watching as she walks slowly back to the end of my bed. "These drugs aren't kind on the mind."

"Killer painkillers though, right?"

I nod. "Sure."

"Well, Gianna. It's been a long time since we saw one another so I'll be straight with you. We have history beyond what you could ever imagine. My name is Fawn Deleware but my real name?" She spins the knife in her hand. "Fawn Simone."

"*Simone?*" I choke on the word as Leonardo bursts into my mind, "Leo is your brother?"

"Yes. But he thinks I am dead too, and I plan on keeping it that way. You see, I was training to be an assassin under my father's instruction when I was just a teenager. I was pretty good at it, and still am."

From how effortlessly that knife dances around her fingers, I have no cause to doubt her.

"And I was given a task. A simple task that I had done a hundred times before. Kill Marco Barrone."

My heart skips a beat.

"But instead, I fell for that bastard's sickening charm and chose love over death. How fucking foolish."

As Fawn talks, I subtly pull on the chord and draw the crib closer and closer to me. I need Freya as close to me as she can get. "Marco told me you both fell in love. He called you the love of his life, but you were there to kill him?"

"Of course he did," Fawn scoffs darkly. "That man is a fucking puppy."

"I don't understand. You were there to kill him, and you ... didn't?" Marco never mentioned any of this. If anything, it sounds too far-fetched to be real, and I get the impression she is toying with me.

"Is it really that hard to believe?" she says. "You know the little crooked V-shaped scar Marco has on his hip?"

I frown at the thought, distantly aware of the scar. As much as we fucked, I never spent much time exploring his body.

"That was from an attempt. He thought I was into knife play, so I let him think what he wanted. And then he seduced me." She speaks as if recounting something affectionate, and then her voice hardens to steel. "I thought we were going to be together forever until he sold me into the sex slave trade, and my life turned to hell."

"What?!" I balk at the accusation and a sickening coldness seeps through my gut. "You lie!"

"Do I?" Fawn snarls slightly. "Do you think I *chose* a life of prostitution? I was sold into it by Marco Barrone as punishment for being sent to kill him. Any decent man worth their salt would have challenged me in a duel, but not that fucking scum bag. And I knew! I knew about the rumors surrounding his family and the whispers in the dark, but I was fooled by his dreamy eyes and that fucking smirk."

"No," I whisper, and the sting of bile crawls slowly up my throat. "This can't be—no, he would never!"

In all our talks and everything I overheard while at the mansion, I never once got any hint that Marco had anything to do with human trafficking.

"I don't believe you," I spit at her. "You could say anything and then stand there, expecting me to believe the word of a stranger?"

Fawn is over me in an instant—she moves so fast I scarcely even see her. She grips my throat with unexpected strength and shoves me back down against the pillows.

"Don't you *dare* call me a liar," she hisses in my face. "Are you really so blind? Did you wander that estate with your eyes and ears closed? Everyone knows the reputation of the Barrone family. Their reputation and his presence are tied to the disappearance of countless women and children, with their men slaughtered so no one goes looking. The Barrones are balls deep in the skin trade, Gianna, and your ignorance doesn't change that. Even his own *sister* wasn't safe from their twisted ways!"

I almost blurt out the truth about Emilia in an attempt to save myself from Fawn's claws, but I stop myself just in time. Despite everything, I can't betray her like that.

"No," I gasp, gripping Fawn's rigid wrist as hard as I can. "You must be mistaken."

"Stop being so foolish!" Fawn snarls and she rips herself away from me, leaving me gasping for air as the phantom pressure of her palm clings to my throat.

I gasp for air, massaging my neck as I slowly sit back up. "When we met," I say raggedly. "Were you in the sex trade then? Four years ago?"

Fawn scoffs. "If I say yes? You can't pick and choose what you believe to be the truth, Gianna. I tell you yes, and you believe me, but you refuse to see what's right in front of you about Marco. He's dangerous. No one touches the skin trade but the lowest of low scumbags, and Marco Barrone is one of them."

My heart races so loudly that my blood roars in my ears. Marco. The man I fell for, who was so painfully gentle with his sister? It doesn't fit. I can't believe it.

And yet, Fawn is real. She is right there and it's clear she has been through hell.

"You know." Fawn begins to pace. "It was you that spurred me to grasp for freedom. I saw what you did to Cherry and Mango, turning on them like that?" She lets out a low whistle. "It was the wake-up call I needed. I killed my captors, freed myself, and spent the past four years hunting down and killing all the powerful men that purchased me. All of it has been practice. A way to hone my skills."

"For what?" I ask, still massaging my throat.

"To come back and kill Marco. The fucker that started it all. But imagine my surprise when I saw you hanging off his arm all of a sudden. You know, it was me that got Cherry out of prison. She might be a bitch but she's fucking skilled and exactly the type of woman that could get close to Marco. And instead ..."

Fawn's eyes glint at me through the low light and finally, she slides the knife into a sheath on her thigh.

"It was you. Pretty little Gianna. Innocent little Gianna."

My head spins, warring with what I feel to be true, and all this new information Fawn provides.

"And I saw myself." Fawn's voice is suddenly soft. "I saw his next victim and I knew I had to get you out of there."

"No," I whimper as tears flood my eyes, fueled by conflicting hormones and confused thoughts. "Marco was nice to me. He was always nice, and I was on the streets, Fawn. I know the Barrone's only deal in drugs!"

"Of course that's the word they put out on the street," Fawn snorts. "Do you think anyone would buy from them if they knew the truth? I can give you names. Countless names of missing women and children he sold on the black market. I could show you pictures that would make you sick."

She sighs deeply and her tongue clicks behind her teeth.

"Instead, I got you out. Shame about Tara, though."

Cold prickles down my arms and through my tears, I glare at Fawn as the pieces slowly click together. "Tara?" I say tightly. "You did that? You hurt her?!"

Fawn nods. "A necessary incident."

"What the fuck did she do to deserve that?" I yell suddenly, and Freya snuffles in her crib. "You nearly killed her!"

"She was feistier than I expected," Fawn admits. "But I needed to make you see the danger you were in, Gianna."

"So far, the only danger here is *you*," I mutter.

"Your little Tara was digging a little too close to home about Cherry, and I could see how you looked at Marco with fucking doe eyes. As soon as you learned that Cherry was up to something, I knew it was only a matter of time before you told Marco. And then he would sell you, like he sells everyone else. So I did what I had to do to get you away from him."

Thinking of Tara in that hospital bed makes me weep and I ache to know what happened to her. "You couldn't have picked up the phone?" I ask through my tears, sobbing softly as my chest cracks with grief.

Is Marco really a monster? Has he been selling women and children on the black market? Was his story to me about needing a wife all part of some elaborate ruse?

"You wouldn't believe me," Fawn says. "Because you don't believe me now after everything you've seen. But I would rather you don't believe me while being miles and *miles* away from those monsters. So I don't really care."

"Then why are you here?" I snap, raising my head to her. "I'm out! I left him. I've been running. So why even come here and tell me all of this?"

"I check in on you from time to time," Fawn says, and her voice is softer. "Cherry found the pregnancy test in the bathroom not long after you left, and I realized there was a danger you would go back to him. Pregnant and alone? He would look like Fort Knox. So when I heard you went into early labor, I came to make sure that never happens."

"You just expect me to believe you, huh?"

"No," Fawn says. "But look into your heart, Gianna. Think about what you know, or even how little you know. You have a daughter to protect—"

"I swear to God," I spit, rising slightly on the bed. "If you harm her, I will kill you, do you hear me?!"

Fawn laughs lightly. "You wouldn't stand a chance against me, darling. But I'm not here for that. I am not the monster here. I'm here to offer you safety."

"*Safety*?" I spit, wiping furiously at my tears. "You harm my friend to force me away from the man I love, then you tell me all of these horrific things in order to keep me away from him. Where is the safety in *any* of that?"

"I'm not the only one on your tail," Fawn says. "I'm just the one that got here first. You have to understand, Gianna, that while Marco is a monster, his child is like liquid gold to his enemies. The both of you are."

Hopelessness washes over me in a suffocating wave. "So what?" I whisper. "What the hell do you expect me to do?"

"You mustn't tell anyone about me, but Leonardo can help you."

"Leo?" I gasp, thinking back to the last time I saw him in that warehouse. "He's Marco's enemy."

"For good reason," Fawn mutters. "But he is a good man and he can keep you safe. You can't run anymore, Gianna, not with a newborn. You need protection."

Fawn has clearly endured hell, but her hatred for Marco might be clouding her judgment. Still, the offer of safety for my daughter, for a life away from the violence, is tempting.

If only to give me a few months to bond and rest with my child. Leonardo, to his credit, has always been kind to me. That doesn't change how I feel deep down, though. My love for Marco is boundless, and yet it sours in my mind with the new information.

She was right. As soon as I held Freya in my arms, I was overwhelmed with the urge to return to Marco.

But what if Fawn is right? What if staying with Marco means endangering Freya's life?

My chest tightens like a rubber band as I weigh my options, my mind clouded with hormones, fear, and doubt. "I need time to think," I whisper, shaking my head.

Fawn's laugh cuts through me like an icicle. "Did you listen to a word I just said? There's no time, Gianna. You have no idea who else is watching you. You don't have forever to decide. I'm here, offering you one single chance."

My aching heart pounds as Fawn's words sink in. Fawn found me, so who knows who will be next to walk through that door?

I'm running out of time, and my decision now won't just determine my fate—it will decide my daughter's future.

As Fawn's cold eyes bore into mine, I grow sick under the weight of the horrifying truth:

No matter what choice I make, someone will pay the price.

I have to do what is best for Freya.

18

GIANNA

Twelve months ago, I turned up on Leonardo Simone's doorstep drenched from the storm and begging for his help.

With my emotions in constant fluctuation from giving birth, it was painfully easy to fall into the role of *damsel in distress* just to get safety and security for Freya and I.

I told myself I didn't believe a word Fawn said about Marco, and yet I couldn't risk possibly endangering my daughter. So, Leo was my only hope as the wolves closed in around me.

He took me in without question and was very clearly *eager* to save someone from Marco Barrone. I cried in his arms for days and he never left my side. To his credit, in the first few months he was very attentive, and Freya and I were taken care of to the highest degree.

It was only supposed to be a few months—just until I was able to feed Freya properly and get her all her vaccines and required injections. Then, it was until I could get her to sleep through the night and get both of us back up to a healthy weight. The days turned into weeks, and the weeks bled into months. Before I knew it, six months had passed, and I was no closer to understanding anything Fawn had told me.

It was difficult to dwell on that when my baby daughter now consumed my entire life.

And she was thriving. Thanks to the intense security Leonardo had at his home estate, she was happy, healthy, and safe. To my knowledge, no threat ever reached my door, and it became almost too easy to keep up the pretense of needing saving.

Leonardo would ask me often how I escaped from Marco, and I would tell him a vague tale of escaping from the hospital after sending Marco away for the nurse. Leo would always get the same sad look of understanding on his face whenever I told that story, then he would promise me constantly that I was safe and no one would harm me and my daughter.

I came to enjoy that security because, unlike Marco, Leonardo was rather absent. He would always call ahead to let me know when he was coming, and we would spend a lot of time together when he helped me with Freya, but all in all, I was given my privacy.

And then Leonardo proposed.

It came as a huge shock when he got down on one knee and declared that he had fallen in love with me. He wanted to ensure the safety and security of me and my daughter for the rest of our lives and I was completely lost for words.

I warmed to him, but I didn't love him.

And yet, I got the distinct impression that I couldn't say no. If he decided to toss me out on the streets, I would be right back at square one with no idea who was a threat, or how to keep my daughter safe. It was one thing to pick pockets and scam men for money; it was quite another to support myself and a seven-month-old baby.

So I said yes.

Protecting Freya became my priority from the second she was born and keeping Leonardo on my side was the best way to do that.

With the engagement came a new freedom as Leo left me to plan every detail. In his words, he wanted me to have a dream wedding so everything would be under my control.

During the day, I would do just that. But as the nights drew in and my mommy brain no longer became the main ruler in my mind, I started to dig.

I dug into Marco and his father, Dante. My time spent looking into Cherry had made me rather deft at connecting dots and finding out things that were meant to be hidden, so within a few weeks I was knee-deep in hell. It wasn't that hard to find information on the families that did dealings with the Barrone's. I remembered most of them from that dinner where Marco and Leo were at each other's throats.

From there, I followed thread after thread and a semblance of the truth began to become clear to me.

Fawn was right, to a degree.

Many families involved with Marco ended up culled, one way or another. The men would end up dead through accidents that I knew to be code for murder, and the families of women and children would vanish. There would be no trace of them anywhere, and from those disappearances came the rumors.

Rumors now backed up by Fawn's story and the obvious pain of her past.

Every piece of evidence I scrape together after hours of digging, points at Marco's direct involvement, but my heart refuses to accept it. On one hand, he's a dangerous man leading an even more dangerous Mafia. He's callous and brutish, and I witnessed firsthand how eager he is to kill when he had Leo cornered. That version of him might be capable of Fawn's accusations.

But each time my mind reaches that conclusion, my heart twists in a different direction and I think of the man who would do anything for his sister. The man who has given up his life to protect her and keep her safe, who even sacrificed his own happiness to prevent her from being married off.

It's like I'm dealing with two different versions of the same man.

And he is the father of my child. The idea that he could be capable of such a betrayal is more than I can bear, and my researching nights always end the same; sickened as I war with myself over what is the truth.

Fawn truly believes her truth, and it's not completely baseless given what I've found. But I struggle to accept the idea that he sold her into slavery.

And that I could have been next.

That kind of research fills the next few months and then, in a blink, I've been with Leo for a year. Freya's first birthday is a grand affair in the estate, and Leo puts on such a show that I entertain the idea of staying here for good.

I'm safe. Freya would have a good life, a safe life.

That is what I should want.

And yet Marco never leaves my thoughts. The truth is mucky and I'm being pulled in two directions, each as unforgiving as the next.

Without confronting Marco, the truth remains muddied like garden puddles after a downpour, and each time I look into Freya's eyes, all I see is him.

Did I really fall for a monster? Did I wander like a lamb right into the jaws of the lion?

I'm no closer to the truth when yet another day of research ends at the same conclusion; no one knows. There's nothing concrete, but there is enough belief and suspicion that the Barrones are deep in the skin trade and no woman is safe.

"What are you looking at?" comes Leo's voice as he wanders close, rocking Freya in his arms. She gurgles up at him and he smiles widely, then he tries to peer over my shoulder.

I slam the laptop closed and grasp his collar, distracting him with a light kiss on his cheek. "Wedding surprise," I say, throwing him off the track.

"You can't give me a hint?" When he moves in for a real kiss, I slip away and ease Freya from his arms, then shake my head.

"The wedding is next week, you can't wait that long?"

Leo rolls his eyes and fixes me with a steady stare. "I'd wait forever for you."

It's painfully romantic and so misplaced that my heart breaks for him, but I force a smile regardless, trying to ignore the strange, cold look in his eyes.

It hits me at that moment that Leonardo isn't just my protector anymore—he is my captor. And he's beginning to sense that my heart isn't in this engagement.

I have to stay strong and see this through to the end. Once I'm married to Leo and Freya's safety is secured, I can plan my next steps.

Until then? I am the perfect fiancée.

19

MARCO

Today is the day Leonardo Simone marries the love of my life. It doesn't feel real, like some kind of cruel joke is being played on me and I'm waiting to wake up.

It's been almost two years since I last laid eyes on Gianna, and not once has she left my thoughts. She lingers like a ghost, haunting my every step. Even after her scent faded from her pillows and her voice became nothing but a distant jingle in my mind, I kept loving her.

They say absence makes the heart grow fonder. But that doesn't include finding out the woman you love is staying with your mortal enemy. For a few long months, I thought he had kidnapped her, so I did everything in my power to rescue her.

Then I heard the engagement announcement.

My world crumbled that day, and her memory turned to ash in my mind. Leonardo and I have been warring over territory for over a year with no end in sight. As far as I'm concerned, that engagement signed his death certificate.

Deep down, buried under all the hurt and the anger, my love for Gianna still lives on. There's something about her going to him that I can't settle with. It doesn't feel like something she would do, and there's a part of the puzzle I'm missing.

I'm sure of it.

"Marco?" Dante snaps me out of my turbulent thoughts and I lift my head from my desk to eye my father where he stands by the door.

"What?"

"We lost fourteen more men today," he says, sighing deeply. The war has been tough on everyone, but it seems to affect my father especially. He tells me it's because he's watching men he nurtured die for something pointless, and then we usually argue. I want to kill Leo. I want to crush his family name into dust. In my father's opinion, I'm draining the family because I can't let go of a woman who doesn't care for me.

Part of me knows this is the truth. The rest of me won't believe it until I hear it from Gianna herself.

"Send flowers," I say, then I return to the plans on my desk. While Leonardo gets married, I plan on burning down every warehouse with even a remote connection to the Simone family.

"Half of them don't have family to send flowers to," Dante says. He walks forward, scanning the plans on the desk. Then he snatches up a photograph of Gianna from near my elbow. The picture is of her in front of a window at Simone estate, and if that place wasn't some kind of fortress, then I would have taken her back already.

"How many more," my father says with a bite of disgust as he tosses the picture back down. "How many more will die before you concede to Leonardo's demands and bring an end to this war?"

"You would have me give up?" I glare up at him. "And spit on all the respect holding up our family name?"

"If you keep going this way, there will be no family name left," Dante says. "Marco, please. You have to pull us back from this path before it's too late. No one is worth this much carnage."

"Do you think fucking Leonardo has people telling him to bow to *my* demands?" I snarl, standing so abruptly that the chair tips back against the wall. "No. He has men who burn down the schools our children attend, flood the market with contaminated drugs, and pay the cops enough that half our men end up locked up on bogus charges. He doesn't back down, so why should I?"

"You are both fighting different battles," Dante mutters. "Why can't you see that?"

"You know what I see?" I prod him firmly in the chest. "I see a *coward* who wants to turn tail and give up everything we have ever worked for."

"Am I a coward?" His bushy brows knit together. "Your path is destroying my legacy."

His *legacy*? "I am your legacy."

I push past him, unable to stomach another round-robin argument, and leave the room. I stride through the mansion, intent on seeking out my sister but on the way there, I run into Tara.

She is the only other person who has a chance to understand my turmoil over Gianna.

"Sir." She greets me with a tight smile and holds out a small piece of card. It's no bigger than a business card. "This arrived for you."

I take it and eye the gold swirls across the surface, then I glance at Tara. "You know what day it is?"

She meets my eyes and nods. "Yes, sir."

"Have you … heard from her?"

Tara shakes her head, then speaks softly, "I would tell you if I had."

We part, and I resume striding through the estate. I don't stop until I find myself in my sister's greenhouse.

She greets me with a paper-thin cough and a wide smile. "Marco," she says, taking one of my hands between both of hers. "I have been waiting for you."

"Tell me Emilia, tell me I'm not throwing this entire family into the fire." I drop into the seat across from her and place my other hand over the tops of hers. "Tell me I'm doing the right thing."

Emilia tilts her head. "I can't tell you that because I don't know what the right thing is."

"Father thinks I'm blinded by rage, that I'm obsessed with only killing Leonardo."

"Are you?" she asks, running her pale eyes over my face.

"Maybe."

"But for Gianna, you will do anything."

"Yes. She left because she was scared. And I understand that. This world—my world, it's intense. She's a flower and I'm the frost."

Emilia snorts and turns her attention to her tea. "You are a terrible poet."

"You know what I mean." I sigh deeply and fish the card Tara gave me from my pocket. "She wanted out of this and he dragged her back. And I don't know what game he's playing with this wedding, but I know I need to save her."

"Brother, have you considered that she doesn't want saving?" Emilia asks softly. "A lot can change in eighteen months."

Her words spear to my core, but she is the only one who can say them without facing my anger. With no answer to give, I open the card and my blood runs cold.

I lean forward and my mouth falls open in shock. "It's from her."

"What?" Emilia's cup clatters back into her saucer. "Gianna?"

I tilt the card so Emilia can read it alongside me.

Marco,

I know you know what's happening with Leo and I. But I need to know the truth. Come and meet me, but only if you are prepared to tell me everything.

Gianna

Below her signature is the best kept secret in the world—the address of where Leo and Gianna are getting married.

"The truth," Emilia repeats, taking the card from me. "What does she mean by that?"

"I have no idea," I reply hoarsely, and my heart skips a beat in my chest. As my stomach twists into anxious knots, my mind races. Is this a trick? Or is it really from her? Do I go alone and end up facing death, or do I turn up with an army only to find her?

"Emilia," I say tightly, forcing the words through the lump in my throat. "What do I do?"

"Marco." She clutches at my wrist. "One way or another, this war has to end. You know where she is, so you go to her and you listen to her. And whatever she tells you? You use that to bring this bloodshed to an end so I can have my brother back."

Her encouragement chases back the chill creeping through my veins and I nod. I can't force Gianna to come back to me, and I would never hurt her. But this might be my one chance to hear the truth from her own lips.

The reason she left. The reason she chose Leo.

I have to go.

∽

I TURN up to the church alone, parking across the street and observing the people who pour through the doors. Every single person wears a pin with the Simone crest, and most are armed. Some are obvious as they guard the perimeter, and others are more subtle, with bulges in their suits and handbags just large enough to hold a powerful handgun.

But the address is correct. Which means Gianna is there and she wants to talk, or I've been lured to watch the love of my life marry my enemy right in front of me.

Both are painful concepts.

Suddenly, cars screech around the corner and flood the street, pulling up at all angles on either side of the road. Leonardo's men leap into action, but they don't stand a chance against the men who climb out of the new cars brandishing assault rifles.

A handful are gunned down within a matter of seconds, and it's so fast that I barely have time to register what's happening.

I'm out of my car in seconds, gun in hand and I'm sprinting toward the church until I spot someone I recognize, and my feet stumble on the sidewalk.

"Dad?! The fuck are you doing here?" I crash into my father a second later, and he grabs me by the collar of my shirt.

"Me?" he yells. "You are the fool that came here alone!"

"I can do this!" I yell back as gunfire erupts inside the church. "You didn't have to turn this into carnage!"

"I may not agree," Dante snarls. "But I won't let my son walk into enemy territory armed only with a fucking pistol. Count yourself lucky I had you followed!"

As the cacophony of bullets floods the air, my heart punches up into my throat at the thought of any of those stray bullets hitting the wrong person.

Namely, Gianna.

"This wasn't supposed to be a fight!" I yell, wrenching myself free of my father.

I charge into the church and I'm immediately met with carnage. Those people who were there purely as guests lay strewn across the pews and the aisles, nothing more than bodies in the way. My men tear through the sea of Leonardo's men, using the element of surprise to their advantage, but it's not long until Leo's men begin fighting back.

I have no idea where Gianna could be, so my target is the back of the church where she might be hiding in one of these rooms. The church floods with men, and soon, there are far too many to decipher who is who. Guns are abandoned as the fight turns to close quarters and gunshots are replaced by the slick, wet sounds of knives and blades cutting into flesh.

Men drown in their own blood, dropping like flies, and I fight through the sea of them fueled by rage and panic. All it takes is one bullet and my life is over.

Without Gianna, I am nothing.

I punch, bite, and claw my way through anyone who tries to stop me, losing my father in the crowd. I am a man obsessed and no one stands a chance.

By the time I stumble through into the back rooms, my shirt is torn and blood soaks into me as if I've just swam through a pool of the stuff. My knuckles ache, my jaw throbs, and several lacerations litter my body but I made it.

The first door I stumble through is empty, but the second is like a breath of fresh air.

I charge into the room and a squeal rises from the woman there.

Gianna.

She stands before me in a pristine, floor-length white wedding dress, with her long hair scooped up into curls on top of her head. She has one hand over her mouth as she stares at me with wide eyes lined with black and glitter. Ruby-red lips peek out from between her fingers and for a moment, she looks terrified.

"Marco?" she says, and her voice punches through me harder than any of those earlier blows ever could.

It's been so long since I've seen her, or heard her, that I almost fall to my knees.

"Gianna," I murmur her name like a prayer and a sensation like static rises behind my eyes. It's her, it's really her.

And she looks *stunning*.

"What—what's happening?" she gasps. "What have you done?!"

"Me?" I wipe away blood that flows from a deep cut in my lower lip. "I didn't do this."

"People weren't supposed to get hurt," she whispers, and tears well in her big doe eyes. "I thought you would come round the back and we would talk!"

"This was my father. He thought I was in danger and he—" I wave one hand. I don't know how long we have, and I don't want to waste it talking about him. "Gianna, what did you mean in your note?"

"What did I mean?" she asks, pressing her other hand to the jeweled bodice of her dress. "I wanted to talk. I thought that was clear," she whispers.

"About what? About why you left me?" I straighten up and hurt swells like a gigantic balloon in my aching chest. "Why you abandoned me? Why you broke my heart, and why the fuck you are marrying *Leo*?"

"I can explain!" Gianna steps forward, but her explanation has to wait as the door behind me crashes open and she flinches back with a cry. I spin around, expecting to see Leo but instead, it's my father who stumbles through the door, gasping. Blood soaks his shirt and his skin is pale.

"Dad!" I fly forward, catching him before he can hit the floor and I drag him toward the nearest chair.

"It's chaos," Dante gasps. "I'm sorry, Marco."

"It's okay, *fuck*. Gianna." I look up at her and she remains frozen in place. "Can you watch him? I have to end this. I will be back, I promise."

Gianna nods hurriedly and as much as it tears my soul in two to do so, I leave Gianna with my father and sprint back to the fight.

The carnage is never-ending, but we gain the upper hand through sheer numbers. My father brought an entire army.

I fight alongside my men until Leo's numbers start to trickle down. Once I am sure victory is secured, I trudge to the back room with a doctor in tow for my father.

Only when I open the door, my heart crumbles to ash.

The room is empty.

Gianna and my father are gone.

20

GIANNA

We are meant to stay and wait for Marco to return, but no sooner has he left than Freya begins crying loudly from all of the noise. As soon as the shooting happened, I tucked her into her bassinet and hid her in the closet in the hopes of saving her life.

My eyes lock with Dante as the wails of a baby fill the air, and I find myself hoping that he will bleed out so my baby will remain a secret for a little while longer. As it turns out, his wound is only superficial. He stands strong and I have no choice but to show him Freya.

He takes one look at her, and then suddenly he's carrying her and dragging me out of the church through the back door. He tells me over and over that it's not safe and we need to get away from here because no one in that church will pale at harming a baby.

When I try to fight him, he grabs my arm and tells me to listen to him, as a father speaking to a mother. He can't protect his own son, so he will help me protect my daughter. I try to lie and tell him that the baby isn't mine, but he doesn't fall for it. "Your eyes," he tells me. "I can tell by your eyes that you would die for this child."

A few hours later, Dante is true to his word. Freya ends up with

Tara and Dante at a safe house in the city, and reuniting with Tara is more overwhelming than I can put into words. Tara brings me a change of clothes and I dress in jeans and a T-shirt while warning Dante that Leo suspected I would leave him. This whole thing looks like an elaborate plan from the outside and he will come for me.

Dante assures me it won't come to that, and to prove to me that he's trying to end the war and keep everyone alive, he then takes me to a safe house on the outskirts of the city to face Marco. With Freya safe with Tara, the only person I trust without a doubt, I tell myself that no matter how this goes, it will be worth it to finally get answers.

Which is why, five hours after the carnage of my supposed wedding, I stand in the lounge of a run-down building eyeing Marco as he walks through from the kitchen.

He stops dead in his tracks when he sees me, and the glass of water in his hand slips from his grasp. It crashes to the floor and shatters, sending glass and water over his bare feet but he doesn't even flinch. His naked torso is wrapped in a multitude of bandages and part of his face is swollen from too many punches.

And just like in the church, my heart throbs like a bruise at the sight of him. Love and doubt war with each other inside my chest and I almost can't breathe when he locks eyes with me.

"Gianna," he says, and I nearly melt for him right there and then.

"Marco," I reply.

There's a moment when time freezes, and we both stare at one another, waiting for the other to move or speak first. The air is thick with tension and the sharp scent of antiseptic.

Then Marco rushes toward me, scoops me up into his arms and kisses me so hungrily that I momentarily forget my own name. Nothing exists but the firm press of his body and his hot lips crashing into mine over and over. He kisses me like he's trying to consume me, and I give in to it for a few desperate minutes.

My hunger and love for this man haven't faded one bit.

Then I push him away, and we stumble apart as reality crashes back into my mind. No matter how I feel, no matter how I yearn for him, it's not worth it if he is the monster in the dark.

"I missed you," Marco croaks, dragging one hand through his hair. "I can't believe you are here."

"I told you," I say shakily, fighting to remain confident. "I need answers."

"Anything," he says, and his voice is soft. "I will tell you anything."

"I learned some ... horrifying things about you, Marco." My voice trembles. "I need to know if they are true."

"Is that why you left?" he asks, taking a step forward.

I take a step back. "One thing at a time."

He nods. "Okay. Ask me."

I spent twenty minutes telling him everything about Fawn. His shock is visible on his face as I explain how she came to me in the hospital after an accident and how she presented me with an ultimatum to protect myself. I tell him everything she told me, and Marco's face is a flip book of horror, pain, and sadness.

"How could you?" I ask as tears threaten behind my eyes. "How could you do that to someone you love? To *anyone*? People aren't a commodity, Marco. You can't just sell them off because the money is good!"

Marco doesn't speak. His dark brows knit together as he appears to be processing everything I've said, and it's almost infuriating. My heart races, and sickness takes hold. Where is his immediate denial? Why is he just sitting there?

After a long period of silence, Marco stands. "Follow me."

"What?" I step back as he passes me, then I follow him down a hallway to a small office at the end. The air is thick with dust and I cough slightly as Marco approaches a small wall safe. He enters the combination, then opens it and pulls out a thick tan file. Then he hands it to me.

"What is this?" I ask, moving to sit in a leather chair near the desk.

"Open it," he says in a strained voice.

I do as he asks. What's inside makes my stomach cramp with nausea. There are pictures. Hundreds and hundreds of pictures of women and children. Their photos spill across the page, taped next to paragraphs of information and large sums of money scribbled in red.

"What is this?" I whisper as my hands tremble while flipping the page. "A trophy book?" So many of the pictures are familiar from my own investigations and Fawn's story roars in my mind.

She was telling the truth.

As I study the pictures, Marco pours us a drink from a bottle of scotch and sets my drink in front of me.

"Yes, I am responsible for those people disappearing," Marco says, and he leans against the desk in front of me. "It's because I saved them. After what happened to my mother and sister, the sheer audacity that some of these families think they are owed a daughter just because they're in charge sickens me. I meant it when I said I keep people safe. I learn of wives and daughters being abused, sold off, and hurt, so I save them. Rescue them. Give them new identities and new lives, and then kill their abusers."

Marco's next breath trembles audibly, and he drains his glass in one gulp. "The money at the bottom? That's how much I set them up with in their new lives. It's a secret of course, so if people think I'm in human trafficking, then it's the perfect cover. But all of them are alive and safe in new lives. I could call any one of those people and they would answer. In fact, if you need to …"

Marco digs his mobile out of his pocket and hands it to me.

"Call them all if you must."

I am stunned.

My head spins and the pictures blur together as I stare down at them. Could it be that Fawn was wrong? That she believed the lie that Marco let exist in the world just so he could keep all of these people safe?

My heart pounds against my ribs like a rock and I swallow down the acidic taste of churning gut.

"And Fawn?" Marco remarks, puffing out his cheeks. "Fawn being alive makes sense, and if she's mad at me then it explains why several of my lieutenants have been assassinated over the past year, but it wasn't me that hurt her. I swear to you, Gianna. I had no idea she was trying to kill me and I certainly never sold her. All these years, I thought she was dead. Genuinely. Someone else is the bad guy here. I have no clue who but it's not me."

I slowly close the folder, knowing how dangerous it would be for this file to fall into the wrong hands. If anyone learned the truth, all these people living new, safe lives would instantly be at risk.

I look up at Marco through tear-filled eyes, and it's like I'm seeing him for the first time. That tender man I would watch with Emilia wasn't some trick. That was Marco in his true form. The aggressive, war-torn bully is the disguise.

How could I have doubted him?

"I'm so sorry," I whisper through my tears. "Everything was fitting, you know? And after Tara, I was so scared that I—"

An explosion of gunfire suddenly erupts in the distance and I lurch upward as Marco pushes off from the desk.

He looks past me, then he cups my face and looks deep into my eyes.

"You being safe and alive is all I care about, do you understand? Nothing is more important to me than that. Here." He digs around in his pocket once more, then pulls out his wallet. A second later, he presses the American Express Centurion Card into my palm.

"What? What is this, what are you doing?"

"Use this," he says. "It's your turn to take care of yourself, Gianna, because Leonardo won't stop. To him, I've ripped apart his family and now destroyed his wedding. Only one of us will walk away alive."

"No!" I clutch at his chest. "I don't want to lose you again! We've just learned the truth and I want to stay—"

"No." Marco kisses me deeply, pressing himself against me as if he's trying to imprint his presence. "The war won't stop until it consumes us, but not you, okay? You go. You hide, and you live, and then when it is safe, I will know how to find you." He glances at the card. "I won't risk your life. I will end Leonardo. I will find Fawn. I will make things right with her, and then you will be safe."

I want to stay, but Freya needs me. I open my mouth to tell him the truth, to tell him that he needs to survive so he can come and be a father to his daughter, but all I do is squeal as the distant sound of a door splintering reaches my ears.

"Quick!" Marco takes my hand and we run into the hall but skid to a stop as Fawn, dressed in her assassin outfit, stands in our way. But I know it's her, I'd recognize those cold eyes anywhere.

"You," she snarls when she locks eyes with me. "I warned you, Gianna. I fucking warned you!"

She flies down the hall toward me, but Marco throws me against the wall and intercepts. As they grapple, Marco yells at me to run so that's what I do.

With the card clutched in my hand, I sprint through the house and stumble outside to find an overturned motorcycle and Dante panting heavily with two dead bodyguards at his feet.

"Dante!" I yell, running toward him. "You have to get help! Marco, he—"

The house behind me suddenly explodes in a gigantic ball of flame, and the force of the explosion sends me crashing forward into Dante's open arms with a scream. We both hit the muddy ground as flames engulf the house; pieces of wood and brick begin to rain down around us as I roll over, completely winded.

The house is ablaze, crumbling in on itself and with it, my heart shatters into a thousand pieces in my chest.

"Marco! No!"

21

GIANNA

"Mommy! Mommy!" With a sweet cheer, my darling six-year-old daughter flies into my room and throws herself up onto my bed, exploding into a burst of giggles.

In the five years we've been in hiding, Freya has grown into the most adorable child ever. She has Marco's ice-blue eyes and my auburn curls, making her the perfect creation from the both of us.

And she is blissfully unaware of the turbulent life she has been born into. She kicks her legs in the air, sending the frills of her skirt flying toward her hips, then she rolls over and stares at me as I push myself up onto my elbows.

"Well, good morning Freya."

"Morning!"

"You have a lot of energy for eight o'clock."

"No school!" Freya slides from my bed and then runs out of my room, cackling.

I laugh softly, sliding from the bed with a yawn. Ever since Dante brought me here five years ago, I've never stepped foot outside because it's far too dangerous. Which means my only option for Freya was home-schooling. It's been a challenge and sometimes I feel like we're both learning something new, but I enjoy watching her grow and flourish.

It's the only thing I have any control over.

Dressing quickly, I follow the sound of her giggles and find her in the bathroom attempting to brush her teeth. Together, we make a game of it and then it's breakfast time.

The secluded penthouse Dante brought me to after my life exploded into smithereens has more luxury than I could ever dream of. With a full wall of floor-to-ceiling windows, I'm spoiled with a gorgeous view of a city torn apart by war.

A war that makes it impossible for me or my daughter to leave. Not until she's older.

So, for the past five years, I've lived here raising Freya by myself with scarce visits from Dante who often only brings bad news. News of death and rioting, of murder and more.

The world went to shit after Marco died.

At least, the world *thinks* he's dead.

Sometimes, I'm not so sure.

After a breakfast of fruit and yogurt, I carry Freya to her playroom and set her down in front of a hand-crafted doll house. She immediately sets about entertaining herself, and I sit nearby and bury myself in my laptop, keeping one eye on her at all times.

In the beginning, grief swamped me, and I didn't do much of anything. The weeks after the explosion, I felt like I was adrift in an ocean surrounded by sharks. Leonardo was on the warpath because he thought our engagement and the wedding were an elaborate plan to kill him. Someone else took over leading the Barrone family and they certainly wouldn't look at me kindly since, as Dante put it, to others it looked like I led the assassin right to Marco.

I hadn't even considered that Fawn would still be shadowing me, and my heart breaks every time I think of her standing in that hallway with murder in her eyes.

So, I had no choice but to lay low and try to piece some semblance of a life back together. Focusing on raising Freya made the months fly by and before I knew it, the world was moving on and I was mostly forgotten.

In the streets of the city below, an exhausting war still rages between Barrone and Simone. It's bloody and consuming the entire city by this point, but it's been going on for so long that no one really remembers why it even started. For the Barrones, I suspect they were seeking revenge for Marco's death, and Leonardo was responding in kind, but after five years, there's just a lot of anger and death.

When Freya turned three, I started to notice a few things that stuck out to me. Dante would visit and constantly tell me I was safe here, and that it wasn't safe to leave. I believed him, until one day I was climbing the walls and decided a walk would be the best way to clear my head. That was when I discovered I couldn't leave.

The single elevator was fingerprint activated, and my prints were not in the system. When I asked Dante about it on his next visit, he told me how important these security precautions were and claimed he was only keeping me safe out of respect for Marco. Otherwise, he would toss me to the two families eager to slaughter me, and then who would protect Freya?

I realized that day that I wasn't being kept safe. I was being kept prisoner.

Then Dante stopped visiting.

The lights stayed on, and food was still delivered each month, but other than that, I had no interaction with anyone. Dante never picked up his phone when I called, and despite spending so long shadowing me, I never heard from Fawn either. Without any idea what happened to Tara or Emilia, I slowly realized that the life I thought I had ended the moment Marco died.

But that didn't keep me down for long.

Now, I'm researching.

I've become pretty deft at it by now, but reclaiming details from memory is complicated. In my last conversation with Marco, he showed me a folder containing the names of women and children he had helped escape this life. It was his proof that the Barrone family never touched the skin trade.

All that proof burned up with Marco, so I've been compiling it myself to the best of my ability. Going off of the phone numbers and names I remembered, I've been able to contact quite a few women that Marco helped, and all of them have been safe in new lives and speak so highly of him. I didn't have the heart to tell any of them that he blew up and instead congratulated them on their new lives.

Unfortunately, none of them remember much about the people Marco used to get them a new life. Part of me was hoping that whoever rescued those women could help me out of this predicament, but Marco covered all his bases.

There's no trail for me to follow.

For each five women that I find alive and safe, there's one I can't contact. The missing women could have simply moved on and continued to live in secret, but each time I find a woman who remains missing, I can't help but wonder.

Marco mentioned that someone else was the bad guy, and swore he wasn't responsible for what happened to Fawn. Was that person involved in his rescue operations, or was it just a coincidence?

My days are spent chasing shadows of the past and raising my daughter. As she gets older, my determination grows to give her the same free life that Marco gave these women, but I'm severely lacking resources.

I still have his card, but I haven't needed to use it since Dante placed me here. I have no idea if those kinds of cards have an expiration date, or if it will even work since his death but I keep it all the same.

Because sometimes, in the dark of night when I'm buried in exploring news articles and reports on the Mafia war tearing apart the city, there will be something that catches my attention. A shadow in the crowd of the news report or a story of a heroic act with no picture and a bare-bones description; things like that catch my eye.

And I begin to wonder if Marco is alive.

Wishful thinking.

I spent the day researching a woman named Maria. Once I track down her new name, Hayley, and give her a call, I quiz her about the people who came to her house the night of her disappearance. Just like the others, she remembers faces but no names and never saw any of them again. She asks why I'm calling after eight years, and when I tell her I'm looking for those people to help someone, she wishes me luck.

It's sweet but ultimately useless.

Freya and I eat dinner together and then I abandon the laptop and spend the rest of the evening playing cafe with her. She's an amusing tyrant in the workplace and each time she cackles like a maniac, I'm reminded of the sharp edge to Marco's laugh.

I miss him. I'm trapped with no way out and the longer I'm here, the more I contemplate smashing the windows and trying to climb down the outside of the building.

It works in movies, right?

By the time Freya has served me my eighth cup of cherry tea, she's yawning her little head off, so I scoop her up and we begin our nightly routine.

A shower, a story, and then she's tucked up in bed claiming she's not tired right up until she falls asleep against me. I kiss her head and tuck her in, then slip from her room and begin *my* nightly routine.

I pour a glass of wine and wander from the open plan kitchen to the lounge with my phone in hand, intent on calling Dante until I get pissed off.

Only, instead of hitting the dial on his number, my wine glass slips from my fingers and smashes on the hardwood floor as a dark figure melts out of the shadows in my lounge. I'm a split second away from screaming in fright when the figure lowers their hood and I meet the familiar, cold eyes of Fawn Simone.

Her black hair is long gone, replaced by a platinum blonde.

"So," Fawn says, looking me up and down. "You're actually alive. Here we all thought you were dead."

22

MARCO

From the safety of my apartment, I stare out over the balcony at the gigantic blaze tearing through the streets of New York. The fire started small in the kitchen of one of Leonardo's clubs, but it quickly consumed the entire building and is now spreading like falling dominoes to each neighboring building.

From this high up, the fire looks like orange lava slowly seeping through the streets. I watch grimly, draining my glass of vodka and then pouring myself another.

"You drink that shit like water," comments my father who stands next to me, watching the inferno.

"Your point?"

"It's not good for you."

"Nothing in this fucking life is good for me," I snap, drinking deeply. "If I die from vodka, wouldn't that be a good death?"

Drinking myself to death isn't an active plan in my mind, but I don't care. I haven't cared about my life ever since I woke up in hospital from an eight-month coma after something triggered the emergency explosives in my safe house five years ago.

I don't remember much. I remember Gianna and her giant doe eyes staring up at me in fear, then the assassin in the hallway and the strength with which she attacked me. We tumbled down into the cellar and then all the charges blew, consuming us under a mountain of rubble.

I woke up eight months later to the news that I was the only one pulled out of the carnage, and that Gianna was dead.

Dead, my father told me, at the hands of the assassin after his escape convoy was attacked and ran off the road.

No one knew how she survived the explosion or how she tracked down Gianna, but the one thing we did know was that she was working with Leonardo.

I spiraled into a deep, dark grief that kept me secluded from everyone as I slowly pieced my physical self back together and learned to walk again after being unconscious for so long. Dante thought my determination was to return to the head of the family, where he had situated a temporary decoy as a leader, but as soon as I left the hospital, he learned my true goal.

Killing Leonardo and Fawn.

Nothing else mattered to me. They both had a hand in taking the woman I loved from me, and they would pay. Nothing else mattered to me then and it's the only thing that matters to me now.

I got close once. It was a sheer stroke of luck that Leonardo managed to escape my grasp and he's been in hiding ever since. So, I have decided to burn him out. The fire raging in the streets below is the seventh club of his that I've reduced to ashes, and I will keep going until there is nothing left.

Until that bastard has nowhere left to hide, and then I will kill him slowly, making him feel a fraction of the pain that's consumed me ever since Gianna was ripped from me.

So, dying by vodka would be a luxury.

"Marco." Dante grabs my wrist as I reach for the bottle once more, and a pulse of rage flashes through my heart. I'm about to snap at him, to tell him to get fucked when the achingly familiar click of a cane on the wood floor reaches my ears.

Turning, I see Emilia.

Her health has been rapidly deteriorating this past year and she stands at the entrance to the balcony looking more like a ghost than anything else.

My heart softens immediately. I abandon my empty glass and move to her side, taking her arm in mine. "Emilia, what are you doing? You should be in bed, resting."

"I wanted to see the stars," she says weakly, yet her smile is as strong as ever. The oxygen tube around her nose shifts as she speaks, and she slides it back into place with a trembling hand.

"I'm pretty sure round-the-clock bed rest means exactly that," I say, but I can't resist the yearning in her eyes when she looks at me, so instead of guiding her back inside, I lead her out onto the balcony.

"Are you cold?" I ask.

She shakes her head. "I don't feel the cold anymore."

Dante watches her for a moment, then he excuses himself and vanishes into the apartment. He's been acting strange around Emilia ever since we brought her from the estate to here, but I suppose she serves as a reminder of mother and what he lost.

"So, the stars." I look up at them, fighting through the low haze of alcohol to pick out their sparkles above, but when I glance back at Emilia, her gaze is down on the fire below.

"Was that you?"

My jaw tenses. "No."

"I don't believe you."

"Then why ask me?"

"Marco." She turns to me, placing a weak hand on my cheek. "You know she wouldn't want this."

"I have no fucking clue what she would want because she's not here, is she."

"I know she wouldn't want you to lose yourself to anger, to this terrible war. You know as well as I do that she would be horrified to learn how many people we've lost to this."

"I care about none of them," I say tightly, and the burn of alcohol in my throat thankfully keeps my emotions at bay. "Mom. You. Fawn. I couldn't take another. I couldn't. And now she's gone, and I don't have any more pieces to slot back into myself. So this is it. This is my final hurrah."

"You talk like you are the one dying," she says and her eyes sparkle with unshed tears. "I hate to see you in pain."

"It doesn't hurt anymore," I lie. "I'm at peace with this choice."

"You have never known peace." Emilia shakes her head, and when she closes her eyes, tears leak down her cheeks.

She is all I have left. The only softness that survives this terrible life. I'm at the edge, my sanity teetering over an abyss as grief consumes me daily. And when Emilia takes her last breath, I know I will be right there with her.

Deep down, I'm tired.

I'm tired of losing the people I care about. Even Fawn—as much as I hate her guts now, her *death* was very real to me as a teenager. I'm tired of fighting for survival. I'm tired of not being able to save my heart.

"Come on," I say softly, wrapping one arm around Emilia's frail shoulders. "Back to bed. I don't want you catching a chill."

"I told you," Emilia sniffles. "I don't feel the cold."

"I'm pretty sure that's a bad thing." With her tucked under my arm, I slowly guide her back to her bedroom. Each step is slow, and with it my drunken thoughts stumble over one another. I drink so that I don't drown over the countless *what-ifs* that swarm me each night, and so I don't have to feel the pain each time my broken heart yearns for a woman who was ripped away from me.

Five years is a long time, and yet no time at all in my world.

Easing Emilia back into bed, I kiss her forehead and tuck her up as tightly as I can. "Do you need anything?"

"Just my brother back," she says sadly, patting my cheek.

"When I have Leonardo and Fawn's heads on a platter, I will be back."

It's not the most satisfying answer but it is the truth. Distantly, I hear a knock at the door and tension immediately tightens across my shoulders. Only a scarce few people know that we are here, so a visitor is never a good sign.

"Sleep," I soothe Emilia. "You need to gather your strength."

She rolls her eyes, but they close a moment later and she falls fast asleep within seconds. Such a short walk to the balcony really exhausted her. I kiss her forehead, then slip from the room and close the door quietly behind me just as my father passes me in the hall.

"Who was at the door?" I ask, noting that no one has joined us and he has nothing in his hands.

"What? Nothing. No one." My father vanishes into the lounge, leaving me alone in the hallway and a spark of suspicion ignites in my mind. There's no way it was no one. This building is thought to be abandoned so it wouldn't have been a salesman or a neighbor. There's only one reason we would get visitors, so why would my father act like it was nothing?

Is he trying to hide something about Leonardo from me?

Grumbling to myself, I storm into my own room and seek out my tablet. In a few taps, I pull up the security system and it only takes a few seconds for me to pull up the cameras on the exterior of the building.

My heart jumps into my throat as a familiar figure I haven't seen in years flashes across the screen, hurrying across the street and into the night.

Tara.

What the hell was she doing here?

23

GIANNA

"Dead?" The word is ash in my mouth as a hurricane of thoughts swarm me in three seconds.

Fawn is here.

Somehow, she is in my penthouse, and I have no idea how she got here. The last time I saw her, she was grappling with Marco intent on killing him, and she was successful. With Freya asleep in the other room, I have to do everything I can to keep Fawn focused on me.

"I'm not dead."

"Yeah, I can see that," Fawn mutters. "All this time ..." She trails off, pinching the bridge of her nose and then she begins to pace in front of my unlit fireplace.

"I'm sorry. Why on earth would you think that *I* am dead?" It's the only thought I can latch on to amidst the rush of confusion. I've been in hiding, certainly, but Fawn is a woman of many talents, and I had been led to believe she would be hunting me down to kill me. Yet she stands in my lounge looking very nonlethal.

"What?" Fawn looks up at me, then her shoulders slump. "You have no idea, do you?"

"Look, if you're here to kill me then ..." I glance around, looking for anything I can use to protect myself. "Just so you know, I know how to look after myself now and I won't make it easy!"

Fawn sees straight through my lie and laughs dryly. "Kill you? The last time I tried that, I got this." Fawn lifts up the hem of her red tank top to reveal a large, twisted burn scar across her abdomen. It's long healed but the sight of it still makes my gut twist uncomfortably.

"That?"

"Yes, that." Fawn lowers her shirt. "Please tell me you remember the explosion and I'm not dealing with some insane memory loss here."

"The explosion? When you killed Marco?"

Fawn stares at me blankly, then she snorts. "Wow. Okay, let's get something straight. I didn't kill Marco, okay? Believe me, I wanted to. I watched and waited for him at the wedding but had no idea that he would bring an entire blood bath with him. I knew he wouldn't be able to resist you and yes, I followed you because I was going to kill him."

As she speaks, I continue to scan the room for anything I can use as a weapon, but as far as decorations go, my only options are a tasseled lamp and a metal dolphin statue.

"I failed," Fawn mutters. "It turns out Marco fights like an animal when he's trying to protect the woman he loves. I'd admire it if I wasn't so disgusted by him." She sneers slightly. "Anyway, after the building came down on top of us, I barely made it out with Cherry's help. The next thing I know, I'm hearing that Dante and his convoy gets attacked and you were killed in the firefight."

My heart skips a beat and a static sensation fizzes just beneath my ribs. Fawn's words almost don't make sense, like she's trying to tell me some kind of story that I know in my bones not to be true.

"What?" I whisper. "That ... that's not true."

"Well obviously," Fawn mutters. "You wouldn't be standing here right now if it were true. But the story is out there. Everyone died except Dante. He barely escaped with his life, not that it mattered because Marco was in a coma for so long that he didn't know until it was too late."

"Wait—" Without thinking, I surge closer to Fawn. "What do you mean he was in a coma?!"

Fawn's sharply lined brows lift. "Exactly that. The building came down and he took the brunt of it. Eight months he was dead to the world. I would have finished the job but ..." She indicates to the scars of her old wounds and purses her lips.

"So he ... I'm sorry, are you telling me that Marco is alive?"

Fawn meets my eyes, and for the first time I see something other than coldness in there. A flicker of warmth mingling with confusion. "Marco is alive, of course he is. The guy's harder to kill than a fucking cockroach."

"Oh my God ..." The room spins and the air grows thin as I struggle to breathe, pressing one hand against my chest. Fawn is there with me, and while her lips move, I can't hear anything she's saying.

Marco is alive.

All this time, he's been alive.

And they think I am dead.

What the fuck is going on?!

It takes Fawn twenty minutes to calm me down, in between assuring me that she isn't here to kill me. She reveals that she has been looking for Marco to finish the deed and after countless dead ends, stumbled upon the old deed for this building. According to city records, this place was demolished thirty years ago but it still stands, so Fawn started digging.

A fingerprint-controlled lift is no match for her.

We move to the kitchen and I begin to make tea until Fawn demands something stronger.

Vodka it is.

"So," I say after getting my breath back. "Everyone thinks I'm dead?"

Fawn rises up from where she was cleaning up the broken glass from my wine, and nods. "Everyone. Why do you think the war between Barrone and Simone has been raging for so long? They both think each other killed you. Of course, Marco is in hiding because he's fucking smart. He can cause a lot more carnage from the shadows."

"But why?" I say, passing Fawn her drink as she sits beside me. "Dante knows I'm alive. He's the one that brought me here with my daughter. He told me there were guards downstairs and he visits every few months."

Fawn frowns over the lips of her glass as she drinks, a look of disgust in her eyes. "Gianna. There are no guards downstairs. This building is empty. It's just you and your kid."

"But ..." I lift my hands and massage my temples. "He still visits. I mean, I haven't seen him in maybe six months, but the food still arrives and the power is still on. Why would he do all of that if not for Marco?"

Fawn drains her glass then she sets it down, rocking it back and forth. "I'd say to protect you from his sex trafficking son, obviously, but he's just as fucking twisted as Marco."

It hits me then that Fawn doesn't know the truth, and I clutch at her arm without thinking about how dangerous she is.

"No, Fawn. You're wrong! I confronted Marco about everything you told me and he denied it."

"Of course he did," Fawn mutters, snatching her arm free.

"No, listen. He showed me proof and he told me everything. All of those women and children, the ones you were so convinced he sold into the black market? He wasn't selling them, he was *saving* them. From abusive husbands, and arranged marriages, and cruel families. Each time he caught wind of someone suffering, he took action and saved them. Often killed the abusive pricks they were scared of so that no one would come looking. He'd set them up with new lives, new identities, and allowed them to live in peace."

"Cute story," Fawn growls. "I ain't buying it."

"You must! He has all this documentation that was destroyed in the explosion, but this past year or two, I've been digging too. Everything I could remember about what he showed me. I tracked them down, I spoke to some of the women, and they are all safe and happy. All the ones I could reach at least. Marco told me he was happy to let the rumor build that he was in the skin trade because it was a good cover."

"He lied to you," Fawn says tightly.

"No!" I clutch at her hand. "I'm telling you, I spoke to them. He's not the sex-trafficking monster you think he is. And when I told him you were alive, he was genuinely stunned. Please, Fawn. You have to trust me on this. He's telling the truth."

"No." Fawn jerks her hand away. "I know it's bullshit."

"How?" I press forward, my heart racing. Is it stubbornness or pain that prevents her from accepting the truth? "He saved those people, Fawn."

"No he didn't," she spits. "That's impossible because not long after I was kidnapped and sold, I was bought and used by *Dante*. So tell me, Gianna. Tell me how he saved those people!"

My blood runs cold. The pain bleeding into Fawn's voice is the most emotion I've ever heard from her, and it brings me no reason to doubt her.

My stomach churns and I feel sick.

She was bought by Dante? I can't fathom such a thing.

How can this be? How can the man who is protecting me and my daughter be the same man who subjected Fawn to such cruelty?

Something is still missing.

My heart breaks for Fawn as she drums her fingers on the counters.

"Fawn I ... I am so sorry, I can't imagine—"

"No, you can't," she snaps. "You need to stop, Gianna. Stop trying to justify the twisted acts of that fucking family!"

Suddenly, she pulls her phone from her pocket as it jingles to life, and all emotion vanishes from her face. The cool, collected assassin is back.

"We need to get you out of here. Now."

24

MARCO

"*No one.*"

My father's lie weaves an unruly path through my mind as I stand on the balcony, observing the sunrise over a smoldering city. He lied right to my face and told me no one had been at the door last night. He even seemed irritated at being questioned.

But I saw her on the security cameras.

Tara.

I haven't seen her in years. She was gone by the time I came out of my coma, and when I queried the whereabouts of the people who ran with us at the estate, my father put it simply: dead and gone. Just like Gianna.

But Tara is clearly very much alive.

As horns blare far below and sirens rise up through the morning smog, I study the printed screenshot I took from the security footage. There's no mistaking her slender build, but how did she find us? And why was she here?

Why would my father lie?

A quick search through the system revealed that Tara did appear to fall off the map shortly after the explosion at my safe house.

Leonardo's men raided my home not long after he sent his assassin after me so she must be working for Leonardo.

No one else hates me as much as he does.

And I him.

I'm convinced he also had something to do with the explosion at my safe house, but that mystery refuses to unravel itself. If I get my hands on him again, I'll beat it out of him right before I kill him.

"Tara," I murmur, staring at the picture. "How do you fit into all of this?"

Just as I'm considering asking my father one more time, my phone buzzes to life in my pocket, and the strained voice of one of my remaining lieutenants scrambles across the line.

"Boss! Boss, we have him! I see him right now?"

"Who?"

"Leonardo!"

Tara's picture ends up crumpled in my pocket and the call becomes a shared video. Through the shaky hands of my lieutenant, sure enough Leonardo Simone is deep in conversation with someone outside one of his last remaining clubs. It seems my fires have finally brought the cockroach up for air.

"You watch him," I order, racing through the apartment and grabbing my car keys. "You watch him and if you lose him, I will rip out your eyeballs and shove them so far down your throat you'll end up with four fucking testicles, do you understand me? Watch him!"

∼

"He's still there, boss," my lieutenant gasps in fright after I hit my knuckles sharply against the rolled-up window of his car. "He hasn't left, I swear."

"He better be," I snap down at him. "Because if I go in there and he's slipped out the back, losing your eyes will be the least of your worries."

"He's there, I swear. See, even his car is still there." The man points across the street to the black sedan I saw earlier, so I nod and unholster my gun.

"Boss, don't you want to wait for backup? Anton is five minutes out!"

"I've waited long enough."

Leonardo has been in hiding for almost eighteen months and I won't let that snake slip through my fingers again. This is it. This is where I will kill him.

And finally avenge Gianna.

Leaving my lieutenant to wrestle out of his seat belt in a vain attempt to come and help me, I race across the street and hop up onto the sidewalk. Then I gently test the handle on the door to the club.

It opens easily.

It seems the threat of arson leaves Leo light on the locks.

Inside, the lights are low despite it being early morning, and low music rumbles through the building. I walk red-lined floors, passing glittering curtains and sparkling decor that depict a starry night sky—something that would be pretty if I wasn't so focused on murder.

"Leonardo!" I bellow as I charge out of the entryway and into the club's main floor. Four spotlights above drift listlessly back and forth as Leonardo Simone, my target, jolts up abruptly from the table he was leaning over. He has four guards with him, all of whom reach for their guns the moment they see me.

I'm one step ahead and firing off bullets as soon as I spot Leo. The first man to his left takes one between the eyes and collapses like a sack of bricks onto the neon floor. The second man on his right takes three in the chest and he crashes back over the pink leather couch, vanishing through a dark curtain.

As Leo's men open fire, I continue to sprint forward, blinded by Leo. I don't feel the bullet that grazes my ribs and tears open my shirt or the spray of glass raining around me when one poorly aimed bullet ricochets and kills one of the spotlights above me.

"You son of a bitch!" Leonardo yells and dives to safety behind the DJ booth, firing widely. I shoot his third guard in the knee, bringing him down, and then when I'm close enough, I kick him hard across the face. Blood and teeth spray through the air, and then the man collapses down next to his dead colleague. The last guy tries to tackle me and as we grapple, Leo rises over the DJ booth and fires directly at me.

I use his bodyguard as a shield and three bullets impact the back of the man I'm fighting.

He coughs and sprays blood in my face, then crumples forward onto me and I'm forced back a few steps under his weight. With a grunt, I'm able to shove him aside and dive behind one of the leather sofas to avoid the next few bullets coming my way.

"Burning down my shit!" Leonardo yells. "You crazy motherfucker! You should be dead, why the fuck aren't you dead?!"

"You can't kill me!" I yell back, seething with such fury that saliva sprays between my teeth. "I'm alive just to kill you, you fucking asshole!"

We take pot shots at each other, trying to find an opening to get closer or, in Leonardo's case, escape out the back door.

"Do you have any idea how many people died in that blaze last night? You fucking psychopath!"

"They would have survived if you hadn't been hiding like the little weasel you are!" I peek up my head and then immediately duck, narrowly avoiding two bullets. Lifting my hand, I fire a few toward the booth and pray to hear a noise of pain, but none of the bullets hit their target.

I don't know how many I have left.

I need to get closer.

Panting, I slide across the floor to the edge of the booth and peer around. Leonardo is doing the same thing, and we momentarily lock eyes. Then all hell breaks loose as we each fire widely while diving back behind cover.

"Give it up!" I yell. "Your time is over, Leo. I'm here now and I'm not letting you out of my sight, you hear me? I'm going to kill you so fucking slowly, you have no idea and I'm going to enjoy every *fucking* second of it. Because you have made me suffer ever since you killed Gianna. So I'm going to peel the flesh from your face, I'm going to make you watch as I pump you full of drugs and keep you awake so you can see as I cut up your flesh inch by inch!"

"Me?!" Leonardo yells back. "Nah, I'll be doing that to you, you twisted fucker because we both know you're the one who killed Gianna!"

What? Is he so caught up in his rat ways that he can't even remember killing her? Was she that unimportant to him? Just another notch on his belt?

"Oh, you don't even remember, huh? Killed so many defenseless women that one more doesn't even make it into your mind, is that it?" I spit on the ground as my blood boils hot with rage, and every fiber of my being screams out to get my hands around that bastard's scrawny neck. "Her name was Gianna and you killed her! I'll etch her name into your fucking bones you cunt, so you'll never forget!"

"Killed her?" Leonardo sounds like he's choking on himself. "I tried to save her! From you! You and your fucking curse. She died in that explosion, the explosion that should have killed you, but by some fucking *joke*, you're still here to terrorize all of us!"

"Bullshit!" I lurch upward and fire at the DJ booth. "You and your fucking assassin killed her!"

"My assassin?!" Leo leans around the booth and fires back, forcing me back into cover. "You can't pull that shit with me, I see your assassin following me like a fucking shadow, like a threat. And I knew as soon as I poked my head up, they would tell you and lo and behold, here you fucking are!"

"Do you even hear yourself?! I'm here to kill you with my own bare hands, I don't need a fucking assassin and I sure as hell don't have one! Your assassin came for me, or did you think the coma would wipe my memory?! And after blowing me up, she blew up the convoy Gianna was in. I don't know how you two even met but I know she works for you!"

There's a sudden moment of silence when Leo doesn't reply, and when I peek around the sofa, I see that he's standing upright with a strange look on his face.

I take aim immediately and fire, but Leo doesn't finch and my gun stalls.

I'm out of bullets.

"The assassin, clad in black?" Leonardo says, his voice calmer. "Tall? Lanky? Killer curves?"

"Like you need to describe that piece of shit to me," I snarl. I don't even want to know how Fawn and Leonardo ended up working together, but my thoughts about her have warped over the years. In that safe house with Gianna, I was willing to track her down and make amends with her. It was a promise I made. Then I woke up and Gianna was gone.

No one has been safe from me since then.

"She doesn't work for me," Leo snaps, waving his gun. "I thought she worked for you!"

"Bullshit," I snarl, throwing my empty gun aside. "You're trying to stall until she gets here so you have back up, aren't you? Can't fight me like a fucking man because you're not a man, you're a fucking coward!"

My muscles are coiled so tight that walking toward Leonardo is painful. All my joints protest the overflowing tension in my body, but I can't focus on anything else.

"She doesn't work for you?" Leo says and he takes a step back, raising one hand. "I'm telling you man, she doesn't work for me either."

Something about his tone finally reaches me through the fog of fury blinding me, and I hesitate.

Isn't Fawn working with Leonardo? All this time I had viewed them as a package deal since killing me is a goal they share, but learning that she's been flitting around Leonardo like a reaper changes things.

I lower my fists, and Leo lowers his gun.

"Then," I say tightly. "Who the fuck does she work for?"

A sudden blast of heat rushes across my back, followed by a deafening explosion, the force of which sends me forward and over the DJ booth. I crash into Leonardo who yells in shock. The heat becomes unbearable in an instant, and then darkness follows as an explosion rips right through the heart of the club.

25

GIANNA

"Mamma," Freya whines, yawning widely as tears cling to her lashes. "I don't wanna!"

"I know sweetie, I know. I'm sorry, but we have to, okay? So choose which stuffie you want to take with you or I will." I do my best to soothe her but being woken up this late has her in an understandably cranky mood, and my heart aches to see her so distressed.

Fawn stands nearby, busy on her phone as I wrestle Freya into some clothes and then set her down. "Do you want the pig? The hen? How about Mr. Hippo?"

Freya sobs softly and stretches out her hands for the hippo, then she clutches it to her chest. Having her a little calmer gives me the peace of mind I need to tear through the drawers and deposit as many clothes as I can into the suitcases. I don't care about my own clothes, only Freya's.

"This makes no sense," I mutter as I drag clothes from their neatly folded home. "Why would Dante keep me here for so long if he wasn't keeping me safe? If he was as cruel and as twisted as to …" I trail off and glance at Fawn who regards me cooly.

I'm still shocked to my core at her revelation, and it throws everything into doubt. Everything I thought I knew about Marco and his family, everything he did to convince me that he was helping those women and not hurting them. The truth, it seems, is to remain clouded and out of reach.

I pack clothing, underwear, and everything else I can think of into the small suitcase, and by the time I close it, Fawn has moved to play with Freya. An unexpected warmth blooms across her narrow features as she does so.

"Marco thinks I'm dead. And all this time, I thought he was dead. I don't understand." Dragging one hand through my hair, I pull at the roots and try to ground myself with the flare of pain. "That's why he's tearing up the city, isn't it?"

Fawn nods. "He's clever. Has people doing his dirty work for him. I thought if I shadowed Leonardo for a while, Marco would appear and I could kill him but no such luck yet."

"Fawn," I warn. "I may be completely lost in all of this but I'm still like 80 percent sure you would be killing an innocent man. Or at least, innocent of what you think he did to you."

The warmth on Fawn's face vanishes and she stands abruptly. "You really want to have that discussion now?"

"No, I—I just mean that there's more to this than we both realize. I think." My hands take another path through my hair. "Fuck, how did I get caught up in this insanity just from picking a pocket?"

"That's not important. Are you packed? We have to leave *now*." Just as she finishes, a soft ding rings through the apartment and we both freeze.

I stare at Fawn with wide eyes. "The elevator."

She presses a long finger against her lips, pulls a long blade from her pants and slips from the room. I run to Freya and scoop her up into my arms, along with the pillow, then retreat to the farthest corner of the room.

I don't know what the fuck is going on but someone else turning up this late at night can't be good. I'm defenseless, but I will protect Freya with everything I have.

Silence fills the air and it's almost suffocating. My heart pounds painfully against my ribs and it's all I can hear other than Freya's sniffles. Then the sounds of grunts and something heavy falling in the hallway drifts through the door.

Then, more silence.

I kiss the top of Freya's head, smoothing her hair down repeatedly while I stare at the door, terrified of who might walk through. What if it's not Fawn?

What if it's Dante?

The hinge creaks as the door slides open and my heart punches against my throat, then Fawn's head pokes through. "Come on," she demands as I breathe a gigantic sigh of relief. "We've lingered too long already."

I'm on my feet instantly and I hurry after her, cradling Freya while Fawn takes my suitcase. Out in the hall, the moment I glimpse blood I hide Freya's face against my chest.

"Don't look," I whisper, stepping over the two bodies in the hallway. "Don't look, sweetie. That's it."

She remains innocent all the way to the elevator, and I refuse to let her look until the doors have closed. The control panel on the inside is hanging off the wall by a few wires and I glance at Fawn.

"Your handiwork, I take it?"

She shrugs. "Fingerprint scanners are too easy."

As the elevator rushes down, my stomach twists into knots. I have been here for so long that stepping outside feels alien. Like I'm doing something wrong or spitting on Dante's kindness.

His kindness has grown sour with Fawn's revelation.

"Come on." The doors open and Fawn steps out, then she holds out a hand for me to follow. "You have to trust me, Gianna. If I wanted to hurt you, don't you think I would have done that upstairs?"

Stepping out of the elevator into the crisp night air. The very edges of the skyline begin to turn pink, teasing the early sunrise as emergency sirens screech through the air.

I haven't been outside in so long.

The city stinks, and I wrinkle my nose.

"You're right," I reply, adjusting Freya against my hip. "You're right."

Fawn nods, then she leads me to a silver car that's parked nearby. My heart continues to race as I constantly have to evaluate how safe each of these decisions is for my daughter, but all of that screeches to a halt when I spot Cherry in the driver's seat.

I haven't seen her since that fateful night at the hospital and my eyes widen.

"Trust me," is all Fawn says as she opens the rear door for me. "Please?"

Once again, I find myself with no real choice to make. Going back isn't an option because I have to assume Dante sent those guards. And sending them tonight, on the same night that Fawn appears? That's one hell of a coincidence.

"Just so you know," I mutter, sliding into the car and having to keep Freya in my lap since there is no car seat. "I will never forgive you, Cherry, for what you did to Tara."

"Six years is a long time to hold a grudge," Cherry replies, popping some gum as Fawn slides into the car. "You'll change your tune real soon pumpkin."

The sliver of time before late night becomes early morning is an odd time to be awake. The streets are quiet except for emergency vehicles and a few people driving home, and Cherry takes multiple back streets and alleys on our way to our destination.

Which turns out to be an old, run-down building on the outskirts of the city. As I climb out of the car with a sleeping Freya in my arms, I glance behind me to the hill that arches down to the city below. It looks so beautiful this high up. It's difficult to believe so much of my pain has existed in there.

Fawn leads me inside and shows me a room to put Freya to bed. She's so tired that she doesn't even wake up as she changes from my arms to bed, and I kiss her forehead repeatedly. Then, I follow Fawn to a rundown kitchen.

Despite the peeling paint, faded tiles, chipped countertops, and windows stained with age, there are warm signs of life here. Dishes in the sink, magnets on the fridge, a pot bubbling on the stove and the scent of coffee in the air.

"I'd offer coffee," Fawn says. "But you're going to need something stronger."

"Why?" I ask as Fawn unscrews a bottle of vodka and fills a glass she takes from the drying rack. She slides it toward me and then tilts her head, indicating behind me.

I turn around.

"Tara?!"

Tara, looking every bit like the girl I remember and yet somehow more beautiful, stands in the doorway with a bright smile on her face. "Hey, Gianna. It's so good to see you."

I throw my arms around her and drag her into a tight hug, and then the wall breaks. The last thread of my sanity that's been focused on keeping Freya safe, snaps at the sight of a true friend, and I sob on her shoulder as I clutch at her.

"I can't believe it," I wail. "I can't believe you're here, I can't believe you're really here!"

Tara hugs me back just as tightly and guides me back toward the chair Fawn pulls out for me. We sit, and Tara laughs softly.

"I'm here," she says. "I'm more amazed that you are."

"I'm not dead!" I say as we part, and tissues appear in my hands. "I'm not dead."

"No," Tara says warmly. "You're not."

"Are you okay? I saw that bitch, Cherry, and I was so mad that I —" It's then I realize where the tissues came from. Cherry stands in the doorway and snorts.

"You did nothing," Cherry says.

I glare at her through tear-soaked lashes. "Yeah, but I've planned it."

"Hey." Tara takes my hand, drawing my attention back to her. "Cherry and I are good."

"What? How can you say that after what she did to you? Seeing you in that hospital because of *me* broke my heart."

"I know," Tara soothes. "But we've had a long time to work out our differences." She glances at Cherry with a warm smile.

"Five years," Cherry says.

"Five years," I repeat. Turning to face the table, I take the vodka that Fawn prepared for me and down it in one gulp, wincing as the burn tears down my throat. Screwing up my eyes, I focus on the pain as Cherry excuses herself and Tara squeezes my thigh.

"Okay," I say hoarsely as the burn fades. Opening my eyes, I look at Fawn. "You have to tell me what's really going on. I'm tired of being in the dark."

Fawn sighs. "Okay." She pours me another drink, and then begins to explain.

"After your death, the Mafia world fell apart. Both families thought the other was responsible for your death, so they've been tearing the city apart trying to kill each other."

"For five years?" I croak. "They haven't stopped?"

"You've seen the news," Tara snorts. "They're both like cockroaches."

"Anyway," Fawn continues. "After I got out of hospital, Dante was keeping Marco on a short leash. I couldn't get near him to kill him, and it was pissing me off. That, and I never trusted Dante because he raped me, so I've been keeping an eye on him for years. Partly for revenge and partly because I wanted to stop other women from getting sucked up like I did. Like you almost did."

She briefly closes her eyes, and I try to dry my tears but they just keep coming.

"About six months ago, I noticed he started sneaking away to meetings with members of a third family, the Ricci's. They were the small family who were actually behind Dante's kidnapping that forced Marco to rescue him. Only it wasn't a kidnapping, it was a meeting. Back then, I suspect they were hoping to kill Marco, but he was so hell-bent on finding you that he was just too good." Fawn rolls her eyes. "So, while Leo and Marco rip each other apart, they're destroying the two largest families, leaving space for a smaller one to sweep in and pick up the pieces. To me, it looks like Dante has a plan. He's letting Marco and Leo kill each other so that the Ricci's can come out on top, then Dante will join them likely by marrying their heir, Tianna, and becoming top dog once again."

"Holy shit," I breathe out. After a few seconds, I take the next glass and drink a few mouthfuls. "Why doesn't he just kill Marco then if he wants power back so badly?"

"Killing one and leaving the other wouldn't give the Ricci's the smooth entrance to power that they clearly want. They're banking on Marco and Leo draining themselves and killing each other," Tara explains.

I clutch at her hand, giving her a watery smile. "Look at you," I whisper. "You've grown so much."

"So have you," Tara murmurs. "I saw Freya, she's beautiful."

"Thank you."

Fawn clears her throat sharply. "One thing I do know is that we don't want the Ricci's to fill any kind of hole left by the other two, because they *are* involved in sex trafficking. Their previous don was someone I killed several years ago because of that, and clearly, they haven't learned from their crimes."

"But Marco," I say softly and my heart clenches at the thought of him. "You have to believe me, he really did help those women. The people I called were all real, and I don't know if there was something else going on or if he was oblivious to something, but I looked into his eyes. I truly believe he thinks he helped those people. And he was *stunned* to learn you were alive. So ..."

Maybe my heart is blinding me to the truth, but of all the awful things Marco has been accused of, I can't believe he's a sex trafficker. Not my Marco.

Even now, the flames of love haven't died down. Mourning him did nothing to quell those feelings and now learning that he's alive has ignited them like a bonfire.

Fawn drums her fingers on the table. "Given ... what you have told me," she says tightly. "I'm inclined to believe there is something I am missing."

"I need to talk to him." I press both hands flat against the table. "If you can get me to him then maybe I can—"

"Fawn!" Cherry bursts through the door, cutting me off with a yelp. "The girl we had on Leo just called. Marco raided him at that club, the Newt, downtown and when they were both inside, it exploded!"

Fawn is on her feet as fast as my heart jumps painfully in my chest.

"They're on their way to hospital," Cherry finishes.

"It's the Ricci's," Fawn mutters. "It's gotta be. They'll never make it. We need to hijack those ambulances!"

26

MARCO

I can't breathe.

    I can't move.

    My limbs are heavy. My lungs clog with brick dust and ash. Pain throbs through me, pulsing in time to my sluggish heartbeat, but the sensations are oddly distant, more like a memory than anything else.

How has it come to this? Another explosion just when I was close to getting Leonardo.

Leo, who claims to know nothing about the assassin and now I have to believe him because there is no way he would blow himself up.

I need to get up.

I need to find him and talk to him and get to the bottom of this once and for all, but I don't have the energy. I can barely even open my hands.

Hands grab me, pulling in all directions and I don't have the strength to resist. I'm shunted back and forth like a piece of meat and while a distant voice in my mind screams at me to do something about it, I can't.

I just ... can't.

"Boss?" Anton's familiar voice drifts toward me, and I finally crack open my eyes, glimpsing a light blue sky and then Anton's sweaty, dirt-streaked face. I want to thank him for always being by my side. For taking care of me and never doubting me. For giving me such unwavering loyalty.

My lips don't move.

"You're gonna be okay, boss!" Anton says distantly. "We'll get you to a hospital!"

The blue sky vanishes and a white ceiling takes its place as I'm loaded onto something. Anton is gone, and the crash of doors closing is muffled to me.

I'm tired.

I close my eyes.

Is this it?

Is it finally going to be over?

I yearn for peace. Deep down, it's been my only goal ever since I lost Gianna. I crave to be with her, and yet loyalty kept me alive and eager for a decent death.

An explosion isn't a bad way to go. I survived one. I'm pretty sure that's all the luck you get.

My mind drifts, keeping the pain at bay as things touch my face and something sharp pricks my arm.

In my mind, I dream.

The sharpness is suddenly Gianna as she wakes up beside me in bed and stretches out like a long cat enjoying the warmth of a sunbeam. Sleep calls to me, but the duties I face today force me to sit up with a groan. She grips my arm and her nails pierce into my flesh, drawing a gasp from my lips. Giana laughs and it's a warm sound that makes my soul cry out for her.

I face her and she nestles into the pillows with her hair framing her head like a halo.

"Hi," she grins.

"Hi."

"Stay in bed," she pouts softly. "It's too early to get up."

"I'm sorry. I have to. I have stuff to do."

"What kind of stuff?" She walks her fingers slowly up the back of my arm.

"Stuff that you don't need to worry about."

"But I'll get lonely." Gianna pouts once more so I lean down and capture her perfect lips in a sweet morning kiss.

"I'll treat you to lunch. That will cure your loneliness."

She rolls her eyes and loops her hands around my neck, toying with my hair. "Okay. I'll hold you to that."

The dream lurches suddenly and melts away from me, like sugar dissolving in water. My chest hurts so much, and I open my mouth to cry out, but no sound comes.

I want to go back.

I want to stay in bed with her.

But the dream is gone. Gianna is gone.

And I am still here.

Something jolts me, and I would roll to the side if not for the straps holding me in place. There's distant gunfire, a squeal of brakes and yelling, but it's all too far away for me to care. I just want to return to the dream with Gianna and spend the rest of my time there.

Warmth envelops my left hand, moving in slow circles. Then it moves up my forearm and something about that touch makes my heart break. It's familiar in a way that makes my chest crack open and I beg for death in the darkness of my mind.

Opening my eyes, everything is bright and white. Am I still in the ambulance? I think so. The ceiling looks the same. The world is so blurry and the bottom half of my vision is obstructed by a mask over my face. I blink, wincing at how heavy my eyes feel, and then suddenly, like a ghost, Gianna is here.

Her face floats right above me with eyes filled with tears, and the brightness grows glaring.

"Heaven?" I whisper weakly. "What did I do to deserve heaven?"

Darkness consumes me not long after, and I sink into its cold embrace, safe in the knowledge that Gianna came to greet me at the pearly gates.

THIS IS NOT HEAVEN.

When I first open my eyes several days later, the first sight I'm struck with is a pale yellow lace curtain clinging to the frame of a gnarly old window. The curtain and the window clearly haven't seen any love in years, and the sight of it immediately puts all thoughts of heaven to rest.

This is definitely still the real world.

Nothing else smells so musty and old than the mortal plane, and I groan softly then close my eyes.

Maybe I'll be lucky and the next time I open them, I will be dead.

No such luck.

Grunting, I gaze around the room. There's a worn wardrobe in the corner near the window and several shelves on my right-hand side piled high with books mostly covered in dust. A few show obvious signs of interaction, meaning someone has been in here since the last layover of dust. The bedside table holds several bottles of water and orange pill bottles.

Right. The explosion.

I lift the covers and glance down my body to see several stitches and patches of gauze littering my torso and left leg. Seeing my ribs alerts me suddenly to the throbbing ache that rises each time I breathe in, and doing that alerts me to the burning need to piss.

"Fuck," I grunt, bringing one hand to rub at my eyes. Soft bandages greet my fingertips around my head, and when I sit up fully, I glimpse my reflection in the mirror next to the door.

I look rough.

Tired.

My hair is sticking up at all angles and the bandage around my forehead is the cleanest thing in this room.

Wait a second ... why the fuck am I not in a hospital?

That thought spurs me upward and I heave my aching body out of bed. Clad only in black boxers, I shuffle toward the door and my sluggish mind slowly plans some kind of escape. Maybe I can open the door and rush whoever is outside.

They'll either kill me or I'll get away.

Assuming I can do anything with a body that throbs like a skinned knee. Grasping the handle, I wrench open the door and freeze.

On the other side stands a woman holding some blue linen and her hand is poised toward the handle as if she was about to enter.

Her eyes widen and her lips part as we stare at each other, and for the first time in five years, the breath I take seems to fully reach my lungs.

"Gianna?"

I can barely get her name out. It feels forbidden to say, and even more forbidden to taste but it's true. Gianna stands in front of me and the world screeches to a halt.

My heart breaks.

She looks exactly like I remember. Sure, there are a few more laughter lines around her eyes, and she looks worried and stressed, but it's her. It's definitely her.

I don't understand.

"Marco," she says, and hearing my name in her voice kills me. I break down as a sudden, overpowering wave of emotion crashes over me. Tears fall, my chest cracks like my heart is fighting to break free, and I sag forward with a wet gasp.

"How?" I croak as I take her in my arms. "How is this possible? How are you *here*?" I've never sobbed in my life, but in this moment it's all I can do.

She cups my face, letting my tears run over her thumbs and then she very gently kisses my lips.

"It's okay," she says softly. "I'm right here, Marco. I'm alive."

27

GIANNA

I know we should talk.
    But seeing him again after so long is surreal. I feel like I've stepped into a dream seeing his face, awake and alert for the first time in four days. Fawn wasn't kidding when she said she was going to hijack the ambulances and she took me along, convinced that only my presence would prevent Marco from going insane and killing her.

    It turned out he was far too injured to care about that for the moment, and all I had to do was soothe him in the ambulance until he and Leo were brought here and tended to by some of the other women Fawn had gathered over the years.

    Watching them all work together reminded me of years ago when Cherry, Mango, and I were against the world.

    Things change a lot, and yet not that much.

    Marco breaks down in my arms, and his sobs rip my heart wide open. I have nothing but my presence to soothe him through his pain, knowing I share a similar ache in my own heart.

    The ache of loss and grief and the shock of barely daring to believe what you see in front of you—that person you love and have loved dearly is back with you. After so long, I didn't expect the surge of love to be so intense, with so many years in the ocean between us.

But it's there, pulling me in with the tide like we were always fated to be together. No matter what, it's him and I.

I help him to the bathroom, giving him the time he needs to clean himself up and then he's back with me in the hallway.

Suddenly, Marco sweeps me back into his room and slams the door shut, then he presses me up against it and kisses me deeply.

I should tell him about his injuries, warn him to be careful, tell him to take it slow, and tell him there will be plenty of time for that later.

I don't tell him any of that.

Because I want this.

And I want him.

He kisses me deeply, like he's trying to imprint himself against my lips and I drink up the sensation. Marco smells exactly like I remember, with the added antiseptic cream on his wounds. Wrapping my arms around his neck, I pull him closer and arch my body into his.

If he feels any pain, he doesn't announce it.

Marco's hands cradle my face with his thumbs stroking the shells of my ears. He kisses me repeatedly, with a soft gasp each time he needs air, and we switch angles with practiced ease. It's like we were never apart.

Then his tongue trails across the seam of my lips and I open my mouth to him. As his tongue tangles and dances with mine, he slides one hand down my torso and grasps my breast through my T-shirt while shoving one thick thigh between my legs. He's much taller than me so when he cocks his knee, I'm forced onto my tiptoes with my weight against his thigh.

A hot thrill shoots through me, sending a cascade of shivers across my arms and legs. My fingers thread into his hair and—mindful of the bandages—I tug just hard enough that he gasps into my mouth.

"Fuck," Marco growls, rolling his hips eagerly against mine. "Fuck —I can't think. I can't *breathe, you're* so intoxicating."

"Oh, I'm the problem?" I laugh breathlessly and my head falls back against the door. Marco lays multiple open-mouthed kisses over my throat, and his second hand falls to my breasts, kneading and massaging while he kisses and licks down to my collarbone.

He kisses until his lips find fabric and then it's a whole other game. Marco tears at my clothes as if they suddenly personally offend him, and I'm right there with him. I want to feel his skin on my skin, feel the heat of his body, and touch all those familiar marks and scars. My T-shirt lands on the floor and my bra follows. My jeans are more of a struggle, but once they're off, Marco is on his knees, kissing his way up my legs.

I'm so wrapped up in everything *him* that no other thought breaks through the lust fog that descends.

We need to be together.

We need to feel each other.

Dampness warms my thighs and Marco kisses higher and higher, and my core clenches powerfully as he gets closer and closer to my pussy. It's been so long that I can barely remember what he feels like, only that I want him.

Marco snags my underwear in his teeth and drags them back down my legs. Then he encourages me to step out of them. With them gone, he shoves his face between my thighs and slides his tongue through my soaked folds in one swift stroke.

That touch alone is nearly enough to make me come. I'm so achingly turned on that the edges of my vision fuzz slightly, and when he pulls away from my pussy, I use my grip on his shoulders to pull him back up to face me.

"Fuck me," I demand breathlessly in between kissing him repeatedly. "Please, I need to feel you. I need to."

His cock is rock hard against my bare thigh. He's just as turned on as I am, and as he kisses me deeply, he clutches at my waist with both hands and growls.

One second I'm in the air, the next I'm flat on my back on the bed and he's between my spread thighs. No words are spoken as he thrusts inside me and suddenly, my life is complete.

Marco fits inside me like he belongs there, and while the sudden stretch to accommodate his girth makes all my core muscles complain and clench, it's nothing compared to the sheer delight of having him buried inside me. He reaches deeper than I swear he ever did before, and tears well at the corner of my eyes.

"You're here," I whisper, cupping his face. "You're really here."

"So are you."

When my eyes flutter closed, he gently kisses my lids.

"Open them. I want to look into your eyes while I fuck you."

I obey, opening my eyes and staring up into those achingly familiar ice-blue eyes. As soon as we make contact, his hips start to move, and he pounds me hard and fast. Marco acts with such ferociousness that you would think his very life is on the line with this act, and maybe in some ways, it is.

Because this feels like the only way to prove to one another that we are really here.

His hips pound into mine, his cock spearing as deep as he can reach and his balls slapping against my ass with each rapid thrust. I jolt up the bed with each thrust but his grip on my waist keeps us aligned and not once does he break eye contact.

Neither do I. I can't look away from those gorgeous blue eyes, and the harder he fucks me, the more I'm certain I can see his soul.

There's something about how intensely he looks at me that I'm certain he's baring all to me. And I to him, to the best I can. I stroke his cheek and kiss his jaw as he pounds harder and harder into me. Pleasure swells like a bubble in my core and there's nothing stopping it.

I want to be consumed by it, so I focus on the thrusting of his cock and the stroking of my G-spot, along with how damn good it feels to be in his arms again.

Then, with a soft cry from me and a grunt from Marco, we come together. His thrusts don't stall. In fact, I swear he fucks me harder, and each breath is punched out of me with a little sound as my entire body rattles to his power.

My core clenches rhythmically and pleasure ripples through me, right to my fingertips. With it comes a deep sense of peace.

I am back where I belong, with the person I belong with.

Nothing else matters.

Marco doesn't stop there. His cock remains hard post-orgasm, so he flips me onto my hands and knees and fucks me from behind just as aggressively.

With each powerful slam, he lavishes attention over my back and kisses down my spine while panting against my skin. His hands wander over my tummy and clutch at my breasts, pulling on my nipples and sending shocks of pleasure through my core. I clench each time, and suddenly Marco is focusing intently on my nipples, playing me like a fiddle.

I clutch at the bedspread and moan openly, rocking back against him as hard as I can, and far too quickly, we come together again.

There's a moment of respite when we lay together on the bed, tangled up in each other's arms. Marco watches me intently, touching my face and body like he's expecting me to crumble away to dust right before his very eyes. I mirror that feeling and kiss him softly on his lips and forehead just below the bandage.

Light fades outside and shadows dance across our skin as Marco pulls me into his lap and I ride him for all I'm worth. Every bounce of my hips is me trying to get Marco so deep inside me that he can never leave me ever again. I drag my nails down his chest, careful to avoid any skin that looks tender, then cup his face and kiss him slowly.

Mouth to mouth, I moan into his and whisper his name over and over like a prayer. Marco holds me close and strokes my back, kissing my breasts and sucking on my nipples each time my bouncing allows him to do so.

It's amazing and yet not enough at the same time.

I need more. I crave more.

I come first this time, yelling out my desire without a care about who hears me. Marco comes some minutes later, after he's thoroughly fucked my orgasm right out of me and I'm teetering on the edge of oversensitivity.

"I love you," I gasp against him, cradling his head to my chest as I slow my bouncing and come to rest with his cock softening inside me.

"I love you too, Gianna. So *fucking* much."

28

MARCO

It's a lot. It's enough.

And at the same time, it's not enough. Gianna sags in my arms, panting heavily against her chest as the last tendrils slowly leave her. The heat between us is incredible, and her presence keeps the pain at bay.

Maybe I'll regret it later, but right now this is the most magical moment of my life.

Even if I'm dead, I'll still take it.

I can't take my eyes off of her. I need every detail of her burned into my mind so I never forget a single thing about her. From every strand of hair to every eyelash, I need to see it all.

Rolling to one side, I ease my cock out of Gianna and lay her down against the pillows. She pants, licking her lips and smiling up at me with such adoration that my heart clenches repeatedly.

I love her.

More than anything else in the entire world.

"Good?" Gianna asks softly, caressing my cheek.

"Better than good."

I kiss her lips and slowly move to her jaw. With every touch, I'm painting a portrait of her in my mind. It won't hold a candle to the masterpiece she is in real life, but it will be worth it to have her there just in case. I can't go through losing her again.

From her jaw to the soft lobe of her ear, I kiss down her neck and nuzzle into the junction of her shoulder. She sighs softly, lazily threading her fingers through my hair. I kiss across her collarbone and dip my tongue into the small hollow at her throat, then down her chest to where her heart beats rapidly beneath her breast. Pressing my lips to her skin, I can feel the slight vibration from the intense beat, and my own heart matches it like we are one and the same.

Over her breasts, I lavish attention on her sensitive nipples and she moans tiredly, continuing to stroke my hair and the back of my neck. I worship the curve of her stomach, the swell of her abdomen, and right down to her navel, where a scar slices across her body. It's one I don't recognize but it's clearly a few years old. I have questions but I store them for later, and Gianna doesn't offer up an explanation either.

I kiss down to her hips, nibbling along the bone and then to her thigh. Each thigh is worshipped and kissed until I know every line of muscle, every silver stretch mark, and every fine brush of hair. I kiss with every ounce of love I have.

Then I settle between her legs and kiss her hot pussy. Gianna, having lost her anchor in my hair, moans softly and tosses her head back into the pillows.

"Marco ..."

Is she begging me to stop? Or to keep going?

Her legs fall open wider, giving me my permission, so I press my face firmly against her pussy and begin eating her out. I start with long, slow strokes of my tongue over her inner lips while delicately kissing her outer lips. She moans long and slow, coaxing me like a musical note. I slide my hands up her thighs and gently part them wider, then press her into the bed so I can hold her open for my devouring.

My slow strokes run up to her clit, swollen from all the previous activities and when I seal my lips around the nub and suckle, Gianna whines sharply. I remain as gentle as I can, loving each inch of her spread before me until she's whimpering and rocking back and forth on the bed. My tired cock stirs but I have nothing left to give her.

Except this.

Once her moans reach a tell-tale pitch from my tongue, I begin to dip my tongue inside her. She whimpers and gasps, grinding her hips down onto my face and I drink her down eagerly. Every scent and taste is like a golden touch from my memories and I crave her. I never want to stop.

Gianna eventually comes from my mouth, moaning hoarsely as her final orgasm is pulled from her and she is left tired and spent on the bed. Wiping my face, I crawl over her and flop to the side pulling her into my arms. She goes willingly at first, until she touches bandages, and then she's less eager to cuddle against me.

I insist with a kiss, and she becomes a comforting, grounding weight at my side.

"I still can't believe it," I say softly, not taking my eyes off her face. "All these years. All this time and you …"

I can barely say it. Gianna, tucked under my arm, cups my face and gently strokes my jaw. "I know," she whispers. "For so long, I was so sure. Anything else I thought was just wishful thinking, but I never knew that you were … I mean that explosion and everything since. I dreamed and *dreamed* of you, but it was all just fantasy in my mind."

I kiss her again, mildly confused by her words but explanations will come later. I don't want to *stop* kissing her. It's the only thing that brings my turbulent mind any peace.

Now that adrenaline has faded and we're no longer fucking like animals, pain makes a return. My body aches like one gigantic bruise and there's a throb in my skull that flares up each time I move. I was blind to these before, but now that we are calm, they creep back in.

But I will take it all because it means I am alive.

And that Gianna really is here.

Kissing her bare shoulder, I draw the covers up around us, and then her hand finds mine. In the dying light, she laces our fingers together and waves them back and forth, just touching.

I soak it up. Every second with her, every detail of her, will be my focus from here on out.

And then the words come with no warning.

"Marry me."

Gianna freezes, and our joined hands remain aloft. She looks at me with her huge eyes and studies my face. "What?"

"I mean it. For real." I shift slightly so I can look at her better. "This entire time without you, Gianna, I was a wreck. I constantly drowned under *what-ifs* and regretted the things I should have done or didn't have the confidence to do. There is so much that I want to experience with you, and I know in my heart that we are meant to be together."

She blinks and her eyes turn to diamonds.

"I love you so much it hurts. I was eager to die because I thought then I would be with you, and now I am eager to live because I need to be with you. For the rest of my life. Until I'm old and gray or however that may be."

So, tangled together naked in the low light bleeding into this rundown room, I repeat the most important question I have ever asked.

"Gianna, will you marry me?"

29

GIANNA

"*Will you marry me?*"

I should pinch myself to make sure I'm not dreaming. Tangled in Marco's arms as he weaves such sweet words in my ear, how can I resist? Maybe I should say no until everything is sorted and calmed down—but I know in my heart of hearts that he isn't guilty for what happened to Fawn—and if I've learned anything over the years it's that nothing ever settles down.

There's always something more, something worse. Nothing is ever calm, and there's never been a return to normal, so if I wait, I'll be waiting forever. Maybe there's more to think about, but in this moment, I just want something nice—just one thing to go right.

"Yes," I say after a few seconds of staring into the depths of his eyes that hold warmth only for me. "Yes, I would love to marry you!" After five years, I love him as dearly now as I did when it broke my heart to run away all those years ago.

I cradle his jaw and nod as happy tears flood my eyes. "Yes, yes!"

Marco kisses me deeply and rolls us over until he's above me, kissing me repeatedly. "We'll be married for real," he whispers against my lips. "A real wedding with just us and no one in the way. No guns, no shooting. And a better dress."

He kisses me again as we laugh and blissfulness warms my tired body. It will be the best wedding in history.

Sleep comes pretty quickly after that, especially once Marco takes some of the painkillers Fawn acquired for him. I don't tell him that part yet, instead I let him fall asleep next to me while I slip into unsettling dreams. They're a mix of bliss with Marco and fear from the ambulance and seeing the club explosion on the news.

Even asleep, I'm distantly aware of how a third party has been playing all of us for fools.

The next morning, we wake to the scent of coffee and toast, and I show Marco where he can get some fresh clothes. They're not his usual luxury brand but they will do. Then I take his hand and lead him through the house, following the scents. A soft murmur of conversation rises from the kitchen, and when we enter, I spot Tara and Cherry near the stove as they nurse coffee mugs and talk.

Leonardo sits at the table and my heart lurches. I'd momentarily forgotten about him. He woke up a day earlier than Marco and our reunion had been tense. He'd mostly been stunned that I was alive, then more stunned that we had saved him. He'd been subdued by the promise that answers were coming, but I'd become distracted by Marco and we'd delayed that accidentally.

"Gianna!" Tara smiles widely; then, her smile falters when she spots Marco behind me. There is a single second of peace before Marco and Leonardo spot one another, then they lunge at each other like wild animals.

"You fucker!" Marco yells. "Trying to bury me for a second time huh?!"

"Me?!" Leonardo yells back. "You're the one fucking destroying all my property!"

Just as they clash with one another, Cherry and Tara are there to haul them apart and it's alarming to see just how desperately each man claws the air to try and reach the other. Tara slams Leonardo back against the fridge, dislodging a few magnets in the process, while Cherry shoves Marco into the next room.

"Marco!" I run after him, placing my hands on his heaving chest as he seethes with rage. "Please, you have to listen to me okay? Leonardo's not the bad guy you think he is. I mean, he *is*, but in this context, he's really not."

"What?" Marco turns those flaming angry eyes on me and I pull my hands back slightly.

"Trust me," I plead. "I can explain everything."

It takes Marco a few minutes to calm down, but eventually, he sits on the sofa and allows Leonardo into the room. While they sit as far away from each other as they can, they both accept cups of coffee. I sit next to Marco, keeping some space, as what I'm about to say will be hard for him to hear.

"For the past five years, I've lived thinking that you were dead, Marco. I was told and believed that the explosion that night at the safe house killed you and that Leonardo was responsible."

"I didn't—" Leo surges forward but he's silenced by a dangerous look from Cherry.

"And so, for these past years I've been alive living in a safe house. I was put there by someone I thought was keeping me safe and I was … busy." Bringing up Freya is a whole other can of worms I can't get into right now. "And time passed so quickly. And then I began to think that the person keeping me safe wasn't actually doing that. I was really a prisoner."

"Who?" Marco demands, gripping my hand. He sends evil glances toward Leonardo. "I'll kill them. I swear I will."

"Dante," I say softly.

Marco freezes and confusion washes over his face. His lips part and no sound appears. Even Leonardo seems surprised as he shifts in his seat but doesn't speak.

"I don't understand," Marco says tightly as his brows knit together. "Dante—my father—has kept you hidden all these years?"

"Yes. He told me you were dead, and that the remaining family was after me as revenge. He told me Leonardo was also hunting me down because I'd embarrassed him with the wedding fiasco and he also thought that the whole thing had been a ruse."

Leonardo had already been informed about Cherry and Tara, and why I was forced to run so he was soothed in knowing there was no grand plan there from Marco.

"What the fuck," Marco breathes. He's difficult to read as a blanket of anger descends, and he's silent as he stares off into the distance. "All this time, I don't fucking understand. He would tell me over and over that you were dead but that your death wasn't worth prolonging the war. I don't ..."

As he falls silent, Tara begins to detail Dante's involvement with the Ricci family. She explains their low-level status, so low, in fact that no one looks at them twice. As she details how Dante's kidnapping was merely a ruse, and that they've followed Dante several times to meetings with the head of the Ricci family. She's halfway through when Leonardo suddenly lurches up from his seat.

He stares at the doorway, white as a ghost, and we follow his eye line to Fawn. She stands in the doorway, and as soon as Marco sees her, he's on his feet as well. He stands between me and her, so I rise and clasp his hand.

"It's okay," I soothe him. "She's on our side I promise. She won't kill you."

"I'm tempted," Fawn says stiffly. "After our last encounter, I was pretty pissed you got away."

"Didn't have the balls to kill me while I was in a coma?" Marco snaps.

Fawn laughs. "I didn't exactly walk away from that explosion intact. I had to take care of myself. In fact—"

"*Fawn?*" Leo's voice trembles and he steps forward shakily. "I-I'm sorry, you just ... you look so much like someone I used to know ..."

"You're not wrong," Fawn says softly, eyeing Leonardo.

"Wait," Marco butts in. "You two know each other? I fucking knew you were behind it Leo!"

"Marco, no." I squeeze his hand to keep a hold of him. "It's really not what you think."

Leo sniffles, wiping quickly at his eyes. "It can't be," he says. "You *died*. You were killed, I know you were."

"Lots of people come back from the dead," Fawn replies, then she looks at Marco. "Leonardo is my brother."

"What?" Marco explodes. "You're a Simone?!" His hand curls into a fist against my palm. "You better start talking before I put you through that fucking wall!"

"You lay one hand on my sister and I will kill you!" Leo yells, despite the tears in his eyes.

An argument breaks out once again and it's only calmed after Tara and Cherry step in to keep the two raging men on opposite sides of the room. Despite my protests, coffee is replaced with vodka, and after twenty minutes of cursing and threats, we finally have everyone seated once more.

"How are you alive?" Leo asks weakly after downing his glass of vodka in one gulp.

"I was never dead," Fawn replies. She stands in the middle of the room between the two of them and sighs. "When I was eighteen, my father assigned me my first big case. Everything before that was small targets. People were causing issues that he wanted to get rid of. He wanted me to kill Marco."

Marco stiffens against me but doesn't speak.

"So I started scoping him out, one thing led to another, and we fell in love. I thought my father was being generous in giving me a lot of time to kill Marco, but looking back, I suppose he was just hoping my romance with him was a way to get close and kill his entire family. I failed, in his eyes. I couldn't kill a big target so all my training as an assassin was suddenly useless."

"And then you died," Leonardo says tightly. "Dad would tell me all the time as a warning. You *died*."

"I thought the same," Marco murmurs.

"I didn't die. I was sold into slavery. One minute I was asleep in bed; the next, I was in a van being taken somewhere, and I was sure Marco had worked out who I was and what I was trying to do. For *years* it fit. I was sold by Marco because everyone knows the human trafficking rumors around the Barrone family."

"I didn't," Marco says, his voice strained. "I would *never*."

Fawn sighs. "Thanks to Gianna, I think I believe you this time."

"You were ..." Leo shakes his head. "No, Dad told me he saw your body. We had a funeral and everything, I don't understand."

Fawn grits her teeth. "That I can't explain. But I was definitely not dead. In fact, one of the things that convinced me that it was you, Marco, was Dante."

"My father?" Marco shakes slightly as we sit, shoulder to shoulder. "What do you mean?"

"Not long after I was taken, maybe six months or so, I was sold for a night to a group of men having some party. They could sell me for high prices back then because I was fresh." Her words roll with disgust. "Dante bought me that night. Your father raped me, and he definitely knew I wasn't dead."

There's a sudden strong gagging sound from Marco as he clutches at my leg and sweat breaks out across his forehead. "What?" he hisses through clenched teeth.

"The world thought me dead. Your *father* knew otherwise. So from that point on, I was convinced you had learned who I truly was and shipped me off."

"I wouldn't," Marco says. "But I don't understand why—"

"It was him, wasn't it?" Leonardo speaks up, looking rather unwell himself. "Dante. It has to be. Why else would he leave her there, huh? He had to have known she was already there, or had a hand in putting her there, right? And now he's in bed with the Ricci's, letting us tear ourselves apart."

He has a point. All this time, all the good Marco has been working to do; none of it holds up against Dante's cruelty. Why he sold Fawn is still unclear, and why he kept me captive and hidden for so long remains a mystery.

So many questions and only one man can answer them.

"Do you know where my father is?" Marco asks and his voice is eerily calm, like the lull in the ocean before a storm.

"We had eyes on him," Tara speaks up. "But since the club explosion, he's gone to ground."

Marco looks up. "Why did you come to the safe house? How did you know where we were?"

"Fawn's followed Dante back there countless times, but she wanted to investigate another building where she found Gianna. I was to make sure Dante was at home so Fawn knew exactly how long she would have."

Marco nods stiffly, and his hand moves to grip my thigh.

"If he's gone to ground, I'll find the fucker," Leo snaps.

"No," Marco cuts in. "Emilia, my sister, she's still with him."

"Your sister is alive?!" Leo chokes on the words. "What the fuck?!"

"Dante wanted to sell her, marry her off for power and I refused. After what happened to my mother, I couldn't let that happen and I—" Marco pauses. "I don't have to explain myself to you. Either way, we can't go against him until I know Emilia will be safe."

Fawn glances at Cherry who nods once and slips from the room.

"We'll find your sister," Fawn says. "We're already aware of her condition. Moving to that new safe house made it more obvious you had someone else with you."

Marco gazes up at Fawn. "Why are you helping me? By rights you should still want to kill me for what my father did."

"I do a little bit," Fawn replies. "But you could say I've learned a new perspective." She glances at me with the smallest of hidden smiles.

Suddenly, there's a thump and through the door comes Freya who, upon seeing strangers, immediately begins to wail. During all the discussions, she had slipped my mind, but now she runs straight toward me, sobbing.

I scoop her up and feel everyone's eyes burning into me.

It was supposed to go better than this. I have no idea how I would have told Marco the truth, but given the dark topic of conversation, it feels right to mention something nice.

Especially as Leo and Fawn hug each other after decades apart.

"So," I say softly as Marco stares up at me, his eyes locked on to Freya. "Would finding out you're a father be too much for you right now?"

30

MARCO

"What?"

The world falls away, and the people in the room all fade away to nothing. Nothing exists except Gianna standing before me, and the sniffling child in her arms.

A father? I have a daughter?

All my anger at Dante and my conflicted feelings over Leonardo and Fawn suddenly don't matter as I stare into the eyes of a child whose ice blue matches mine.

"I'm a father?" I repeat as Gianna adjusts the crying girl on her hip, and nods.

"This is Freya. Your daughter."

She's grown. Gianna holds an actual small person in her arms, not a baby. A real child who fusses at the strangers in the room and repeatedly hides her face in her mother's neck.

A daughter.

My daughter.

I don't know what to say. My mind is blank. Thankfully, Gianna seems to know what to do because a second later, she's taking my hand and leading me from the room. I follow, unable to take my eyes off the child.

Gianna leads me through to a different bedroom that's filled with toys and stuffed animals. It's definitely Freya's room. She sits herself on the bed and settles Freya in her lap.

"It's okay," Gianna soothes softly, rocking Freya back and forth in her arms. "You're okay. I'm right here sweetie. It's okay. Don't cry, it's okay."

Freya wails loudly for a few long minutes, then she begins to calm when Gianna presses a stuffed hippo into her small arms.

I can't fathom how this is possible. We've been apart for so long, but this child is mine? I try to calculate back, estimating what age she could be based on when we last slept together but my memories from around the explosion are fuzzy because of the coma.

Does this mean poor Gianna had to go through pregnancy all by herself? She had to give birth by herself? Suddenly, the new scar I found on her abdomen becomes crystal clear in my mind and I bite back a soft noise of pain. She had a caesarean and she was all by herself?

That pain bleeds into the anger that beats in my heart. Dante had Gianna hidden for five years which meant he knew there was a child. Maybe he suspected the child belonged to Leo but given how my father seems to operate, I doubt that's the case.

"Freya," Gianna says with a warm smile. "I want you to meet someone, okay?"

Freya nods, clutching at her hippo.

"This man is your Daddy, Freya. This is your Daddy and he's so excited to meet you!"

"Daddy?" she says, and my heart *melts* the second I hear her voice. "Like—like in my story books?"

"Yes," Gianna nods. "Exactly like the book we were reading last night! You would be Baby Bear." Gianna pokes Freya's tummy. "I would be Mommy Bear and this is Daddy Bear. Do you want to say hi?"

I sit beside them on the bed and suddenly my palms break out in a nervous sweat as they rest against my leg. My heart races as I watch

Freya peek through Gianna's hair and stare at me with eyes almost as big as her mother's.

This is a lot to take in so quickly and I try to arrange my face to be as pleasant as possible for a child. It's difficult since I have exactly zero experience with children outside of hugs from the ones I've sent off to a new life. I have no idea how to talk to a child, how to care for one, or how to make sure I don't scare them. Being a father was always a distant thought for the future, and now reality is here with a fully formed child.

"He's not scary," Gianna assures Freya. "He's just big because he does a lot of work, like Santa!"

The comparison seems to work for Freya because her eyes widen and she leans forward to get a better look at me. "Daddy?"

That single word is like a punch straight to the heart and my lower lip quivers even as I smile. "That's right," I say hoarsely. "And you're my ... my Freya."

Freya watches me for a few seconds, then she nods and begins to wiggle so much that she slides from Gianna's lap to the floor. Then she moves off to one of the play mats set up on the floor and dives right in.

My heart pounds and I curl my hands into fists. Was that a good reaction? Did I do something wrong?

I look at Gianna, and she's watching me with a slightly nervous smile on her lips.

"Did I do something wrong?"

"No," Gianna says softly. "She's little. The concept of another parent will be difficult for her for a while, but she didn't cry like she did when she met Cherry for the first time so you're doing good."

I laugh softly, rubbing my palms along my thighs. "Okay. Okay."

"Play with her." Gianna tilts her head down to where Freya is playing.

"I don't know how."

"There's no rule book," she says, reaching for my hand. The warmth of her contact blooms across my knuckles. "Just do what she's doing."

It's more nerve-wracking than charging into a room full of armed men all wanting to kill me. This impossible small human is mine, somehow, and as I settle on the floor next to her, I can't take my eyes off her. She has the cutest button nose with hair like her mother's.

"Can I play?" I ask softly.

Freya shoves a plastic spoon into my hand and orders me to cook, and from then on I become the head chef at the cafe/restaurant she's running. It's terrifying at first. My mind races with the fear that I'm doing the wrong thing or saying the wrong thing, but Gianna never corrects me and Freya doesn't seem to mind anything I do.

After some time, she ends up shuffling around with her toys and resting against my leg. The contact burns, but I'd rather chop my own leg off than move and risk disturbing her. During play, we have to deal with an unruly customer who refuses to pay and Freya punishes them with too much salt in their food.

Then she begins to yawn and rests heavier against me.

"Tired?" Gianna asks. "It's been a long day."

I glance at the clock. A whole chunk of time has just vanished, either because of the earlier meeting or because of play with Freya. Either way, she isn't the only one that could benefit from a nap.

As Gianna stands, Freya suddenly turns against me and raises her arms. I glance at Gianna for permission—who nods quickly—and then as carefully as I can, I scoop my daughter into my arms. She barely weighs anything and immediately settles into my hold like she's been there a thousand times already. Through Gianna's direction, I tuck her up into bed, and then together, we read her the hungry bear story until tiredness pulls her into an afternoon nap.

Gianna then takes me back to the bedroom and remains silent until she prepares my medication. "I'm sure you have questions."

I ease down onto the bed with a grunt as all my aches pull and squeeze. "A few."

"You can ask me anything."

"What age is she?"

"Six, nearly six and a half."

"Six?" I count back and had expected the child to be from when my memory was hazy but instead, I have to go back further.

"When Tara was attacked," Gianna begins, sitting next to me. "That was when I found out I was pregnant. I was going to tell you once you had gotten your father back but then Cherry appeared and threatened me. Of course, she was working for Fawn, and they were convinced you were a sex trafficker, so they were scaring me to stay away."

I nod slowly.

"All I knew was that I had to keep the baby safe from everyone so I just ... I left. And I stayed hidden until she was born and Fawn tracked me down. She also wanted to keep Freya safe and it was her idea for me to go to Leo. She told me the truth of who she was, and I would have told you when we met at the safe house but there wasn't enough time." Gianna sighs deeply. "Anyway, that's why I went to him because I didn't know the truth. I didn't know anything and all I wanted to do was keep her safe. So that's what I've been doing. Even in that apartment Dante put us in ..."

She shakes her head and tears sparkle in her eyes.

"I'm sorry I never told you. All the time I was pregnant, maybe if I'd reached out, then things would have been different—"

"Hey, hey." I stop her immediately and cup her face, caressing her cheek. "Don't talk like that. You've been through this constant hell, with a child to protect all through that. I'm the one that's sorry. If I hadn't been so blinded by grief and hate all of the time, then maybe I would've seen clearly sooner. I've been blind to so much, my father included. You did what you had to do."

Looking deep into her eyes, a small grateful smile flashes across her lips.

"You did all of that alone, and I can't imagine the strength that took. So don't you dare apologize, okay? Don't you *dare*."

Moving in, I kiss her deeply and pour every ounce of my love into the action. Gianna murmurs softly, then her hands slide around my neck and she pulls me closer.

31

GIANNA

His kiss is sweet and soft, unlike any other kiss he's given me before. So much has come out today that I'm just relieved he didn't accuse me of cheating or get mad at me for hiding his child from him.

If anything, his warmth and understanding is almost unexpected. If he'd taken the pills I'd laid out for him then I'd suspect he was just high on pain relief, but they still sit on the bedside table, abandoned in favor of me.

I cradle the back of his neck and run my fingers through the finer hairs just below his hairline. When he angles into me, I align myself just right and sink into his arms.

Part of me wants to cry. Everything that happened in the lounge is still so raw and sharp at the forefront of my mind. Revealing all those secrets and not being met with pushback was a shock, but part of me suspects Marco had his own suspicions that something else was going on. Maybe being blown up together with Leo was a bit of an eye-opener.

I wouldn't be surprised if Dante were behind that too.

Marco and I slowly move deeper onto the bed, barely allowing a second for our lips to be parted. There's no heat this time; at least not the heat that existed last night when we fucked like animals and clawed our way to orgasm like it was the last thing we could do on this earth.

No, this heat is different.

It's deeper and sets my heart fluttering in my chest when Marco reaches under my shirt. My stomach twists into knots and I'm as giddy as I was during our first kiss which feels so long ago now.

"I want to take your clothes off," Marco murmurs against my lips.

"Then take them off."

He does exactly that, with such care that I feel like I'm on the verge of affectionate tears. Marco kisses every inch of my bare skin and chases the hem of my T-shirt with his lips. As each inch by slow inch is exposed to him, he kisses and nibbles promises into my skin, and it doesn't stop there.

Every article of clothing is removed in the same way, like he's worshipping every single bare inch of my body. He kisses softly, murmurs sweet praises against little bites he leaves around my ribs, kisses slowly near the softer skin of my upper arms, and then he's down at my abdomen with his attention on my scar.

I've never been ashamed of the scar. Without it, I wouldn't have Freya. But there's something nerve-wracking about having him down there mapping out the silver line with his eyes. Before I can speak, he kisses one edge of the scar and then very slowly runs his lips along the twisted flesh right to the other end. Then he playfully nibbles and kisses softly.

"Beautiful," Marco breathes against my skin, and my heart swells. Both hands fly up to my face and I have to fight not to cry. I didn't need his approval or reassurance but it's painfully nice to have.

With my eyes closed, I rely on touch to track Marco over my body and not an inch is left untouched. From my scar, he lowers to my pelvis and worships my thighs, my knees, and down my calves to my ankles. He kisses down one leg and then slowly up the other. By the time he's back up near my face, my entire body is pulsing hot and my core is damp with need.

He kisses the back of my hands and gently pulls them away from my face. "Why are you hiding?"

"Because I'm almost scared to look at you," I whisper. "Because sometimes this doesn't feel real. Like I hit my head and I'm still back in that place, and this is a dream."

"It's not a dream," he assures me in the same soft whisper, kissing my lips softly. "This is our reality."

When he enters me, he's slow. While part of me craves the animalistic nature of our fucking, there's something incredibly erotic about feeling his hard cock slide inside me inch by slow inch. It's like I can suddenly feel every single detail of his length as he locks us together and holds me in his arms. We lie on our sides, arms around one another and legs tangled, staring into each other's eyes.

When Marco's hips move, he uses his grip on me for leverage and I do the same for him. We rock together like an erotic dance, using one another to help us thrust and rock. Occasionally, we roll over and whoever ends up on top takes control for a little while, but we eventually roll back onto our sides.

I never look away. I watch as pleasure blooms in his eyes, and he bites his lower lip as his cock twitches inside me. I swallow down his moans as we kiss slowly and he tastes the pleasure of mine.

Time becomes forgotten. Nothing else matters but our entwined bodies and the rhythm we can only find with each other.

We come together with noiseless gasps and pants, eyes locked as if we're in the same cycle of pleasure. His cum floods inside me, a familiar warmth that I crave more each time I experience the sensation, and he gunts each time my pussy clamps down around his cock.

We remain like that, woven together like we are one and then tears spring into my eyes. I'm not sad. It's an emotional moment and the most connected I have ever felt to another person. I can't look away, scared that if I do, he will vanish.

So we stay together, lazily watching each other as our bodies pulse and twitch until blinks become lazy and slow, and tiredness sweeps us both into the land of sleep.

The next morning, I wake up all wrapped in the duvet and tucked up sleeping. Marco is missing from beside me which sends my heart fluttering painfully in my chest. Dressing quickly, I hurry through the building to Freya's room. She's still sound asleep and as I kiss her forehead, I realize just how early in the morning it is.

The sun isn't even up yet. Marco probably just went to the bathroom. Feeling foolish, I trudge back to the bedroom, but low tones coming from the kitchen catch my attention. Curious, I walk over and peek inside to see Marco and Leonardo on opposite sides of the kitchen. They seem amicable at least, which is a surprise. Not wanting to intrude, I step away but not before Marco spots me.

"Gianna?"

"Sorry," I say, flashing them both a quick smile. "I wasn't trying to be nosy, I was just checking on Freya and passing."

"It's fine." Leo shrugs one shoulder. "We weren't discussing anything secret."

"Leo was telling me about what he dug up on the Ricci's. They really are a family from the dirt. Never been on anyone's radar and we have no idea how they got on my father's. Other than that, they're exactly the scummy type of rats he would find if he wanted to sell someone."

"Someone like Fawn?" I ask.

"Exactly," Leo spits.

"So what are we going to do about him?" I step further into the kitchen.

"Nothing," Marco sighs deeply. "Not until Emilia is safe."

"And then what?"

"Then," says Leo. "We scrape together what we have left from this stupid fucking war."

"No clubs, that's for sure," Marco snorts, and his eyes hint of amusement.

"Agreed," says Leo.

"Alone, we don't stand a chance," Marco continues as he moves closer to me and touches my arm. "But together? Maybe there's a chance we can turn this whole wretched thing around."

32

MARCO

The cold wind billows around me, carrying with it the scent of oil, old waste, and salt from the water. Below me, the city stretches out with each building lit up like an urban Christmas tree.

For the past month, Leo and I have been digging while hiding behind our war. On the surface, it looks like we're both still at each other's throats and targeting what territory we have left, but in secret we have been using that distraction to freely investigate the Ricci family. It was clear early on that they were deep in the human trafficking trade, and there were several other smaller families that worked alongside them. The key connection was indeed Dante who, upon my return from the "hospital," was all too eager to listen to my pre-planned rant about how Leo trying to kill me in the club was the last straw.

Keeping Dante busy gave Fawn the opportunity to delve a little deeper into the Barrone financial records. She discovered a link between Dante's personal account and the Russian Mafia. It's been a long time since the Russians were safe on this side of the ocean, and when they retreated, we took that as a victory.

A misplaced victory if Dante has been feeding their skin market all these years.

It was a step forward but a painful one for Fawn and myself. Knowing my father, the man I trusted above all, had a hand in harming the woman I had loved so dearly was crushing. I feel sick every time I try to guess what he had planned for Gianna.

Over the past month, I've watched him closely since Gianna's disappearance surely reached him when those guards he sent never returned, but not once did he give the impression that anything was wrong. In fact, his performance was so good that sometimes I doubted he really was the mastermind behind this hell.

It was proof of how good he really was at hiding the twisted shit.

While I was busy with Dante and Fawn was digging into the money, Leo took the Ricci's. Over time, he accumulated the names and addresses of every single Ricci business and establishment. There were more than a small family of their size should ever have, and most were on Barrone territory. This was another gift from my father, no doubt.

The man placed at the head of my family to throw Leo off the scent was eventually brought in on the plan because without him, controlling what men I had left would have been difficult. I didn't tell him the names of the targets, or even anything about Leo. I simply informed him that soon I would have a list of Leo's places that we would attack simultaneously and bring this war to an end.

If this man betrayed me and told Dante, Dante would think I was targeting Leo, and I kept a fake list of Leo's remaining properties on hand.

In reality, when the time comes, I will send the real list, and every single Ricci establishment will crumble under the combined might of my men and Leonardo's.

"Marco?" Gianna approaches me slowly, picking her away across the rooftop and reaching for me when she was close enough.

The hardest part of this entire thing has been being away from her while pretending to be back on Dante's side, and seeing her again lifts my heart immensely. I'm utterly infatuated with her. She consumes all of my thoughts and even now, with her hand in mind, it's not enough.

It will never be enough.

"Are you sure you want to be here?" I ask, kissing her cheek. "You can stay with Freya."

"No, I have to be here," she says with a firm nod. "Freya is safe with Tara for now and this ... everything has been building to this." She squeezes my hand. "I want to be here."

"Do you think Fawn will pull it off?" This entire night rides on Fawn's ability to break into my safe house and rescue Emilia, who Dante has barely stepped away from the entire month I was back. My own plans to rescue her had to be put to the side, and now Fawn is my only hope of saving my sister.

"I think if anyone can, it's her," Gianna nods. "She's strong. Capable. And she's fighting for a lot more than herself."

"You're right."

"The places you hit tonight, are you going to kill everyone?" She looks up at me with her large doe eyes and I nod slowly.

"Yes. Because every finger in the Ricci family has been in the slave trade pie and no one gets out. The only people seeing a hospital tonight will be the victims we rescue."

Gianna nods as the wind catches in her hair, so she tilts her head to keep her face clear. "So why here? Why this roof?"

I shrug one shoulder and then point down toward the river. "From here, we can see the river and the docks. Any victims we find are likely going to be there, and from here we'll be able to see the ambulances helping them. And then over there." I point to the other side of the city. "Leo's rigged several Ricci warehouses to blow. We'll get to see that too."

"You've really thought it through, huh?"

I study her face as the city lights reflect in her eyes. "I lost you. For five years, I lost you because of this. Because of all of this. Leo lost his sister. I lost Fawn. I missed my daughter growing up. There's no room for mistakes, y'know? Tonight?" I lift her closed hand to my lips. "Tonight, we take back our home and make Dante pay."

Suddenly, my phone blares to life and Fawn's voice fills the air when I hit speaker.

"I've got her," Fawn says. "Your sister's made of stern stuff."

"Marco?" Emilia croaks softly in the background. Cherry's voice drifts through as she soothes my sister.

"Thank you, Fawn. Truly."

"Don't mention it," she says. "Good luck."

The call ends, and I remain silent as I type out a text to the acting head of my family and attach the real location list. Given how long it will take people to head to the right areas, I calculate we have about twenty minutes before it all kicks off.

"Is that it?" Gianna glances at my phone. "Now we wait?"

I nod. "Now we wait."

"IT WAS SUPPOSED TO BE A RUMOR," Gianna says twenty minutes later as explosions rock the city and men and ambulances pour across the docks. "How did it end up being real?"

"Maybe it was too good a cover," I reply softly with my arm around her shoulders. "If I had looked closer at the rumors instead of using them for cover ... if I had even looked closer into Fawn's death then maybe ..." Puffing out my cheeks, I sigh. We could do this dance forever and reach no conclusion.

"Do you understand his goal?" she asks, looking up at me.

I shake my head. "Power? I guess I was too powerful, held too much loyalty otherwise he could have just killed me and taken it. Instead, he does this."

"Maybe the Barrone line is just twisted," scoffs Leo's voice as he melts from the shadows and joins us on the roof.

"A month ago, I would have killed you for saying that," I reply.

"And now?" Leo tilts his head, his hands in his pockets as he stares down at the city.

"Now I'll just contemplate shoving you off the roof."

"I can live with that." Leo breathes deeply. "My men are almost done. There's going to be nothing left."

"Same," I say, eyeing the docks. "You know what happens next."

"What happens next?" Gianna asks, clutching at my shirt.

"We declare open war on the Ricci's and my father will know he is caught. If he doesn't know already. Then it will be a race to stop him before he goes into hiding," I explain.

"And after?" Gianna straightens up, stepping away from me. "What about after? Or is it foolish of me to think that far ahead?"

"I actually have an idea," Leo says, catching both our attention. "Look ... there's a lot of bad blood but without it, I wouldn't have my sister back. And that's all that matters to me. We destroyed each other out there, Marco. We're both ripe for the picking. But together?" He waggles his eyebrows and his suggestion becomes clear.

We could join up.

Gianna laughs. "No Mafia family has enough room for both your egos."

We laugh because she's right, but as I watch her, it suddenly all becomes crystal clear to me. What I want is Gianna, and Leo may just be giving me the means to make sure I can safely have what I want.

"That's not a bad idea," I say. "For a Simone."

Leo shoves me lightly.

"But ego won't be a problem because I will step down."

"What?" they both cry, and Leo's jaw falls open.

I focus on Gianna. "I've lost enough time with my family already. Five years. If we survive this then Leo, you can have all the power. I already have what is precious to me."

"Dude," Leo gasps.

Gianna smiles shyly, her cheeks flushing crimson as I take her hand, and she steps closer. "Are you serious?"

"Deadly. I want to be with you. I want to marry you and spend the rest of my days with you and our daughter, away from everything else."

Her arms drape around my shoulders and she kisses me sweetly as her eyes sparkle. "I love you."

"I love you too."

"Holy shit," Leo repeats.

I glance at him. "I get it. You didn't expect power so easily."

"No, no, not that." He glances up from his phone. "It's Fawn. She caught Dante."

"What?!"

33

GIANNA

"This wasn't part of the plan!" Marco hisses at Fawn, grabbing her arm the second she greets us outside the old bakery she brought Dante to.

The building is smack-dab in the middle of the city and in Fawn's words, it's the perfect place to hold him. No one will be looking right in the heart of disaster, and I have to agree with her.

"No, it wasn't part of *your* plan," Fawn snaps back, jerking her arm out of his grip. "I saw an opportunity and I took it, okay?"

"What opportunity?" I ask before Marco can let out another frustration that might have Fawn turning us away.

She glares at Marco, then turns to me with a small sigh. "When I was in that apartment for Emilia, I took a look at Dante's computer. There wasn't much to go on, but I noticed he had Find My Device turned on, so I secured access and pinged his phone. Easy peasy."

"Dangerous," Marco mutters.

"Amazing," pipes up Leo, but he's quickly silenced by a glare from Marco and Fawn.

"Do you want to spend all night out here arguing about it or do you want to confront the fucker?" Fawn crosses her arms over her chest. "Because at this point, I'm good with either."

Marco grumbles to himself and indicates for Fawn to lead the way inside. On our drive over, he kept telling me that it was a bad idea for me to come and that I should return to Freya, but I refused. I need to know why he locked me up for all those years, for my sake and my daughter's.

Inside, Fawn leads us through the dusty, unused bakery and through a small corridor down to where the old kitchen is. Nothing in here has seen light for years, and the only scent, other than dust, is a faint, acrid stink of rye. Fawn has Dante tied to a chair near the old furnace and it's no surprise that somehow she's managed to stoke the fire and bring the flames to life. The light dances over Dante's bruised face where he's taken one or two punches.

"Oh there she is," Dante spits. "The fucking whore. And who did she bring with her, huh?"

As Marco steps forward, Leo catches my arm and holds me back with him in the darkness. As much as I want answers, Dante is Marco's father and he likely has a great deal to say to him, almost as much as Fawn, no doubt. My heart goes out to Marco as I watch his shoulders bunch up while he steps into the flickering light. Dante flips like a switch.

"Oh my son! You came! Thank God, thank God! Please, you have to help me. This woman, this crazy woman attacked me and killed my guards, then dragged me here. I don't know what the hell is going on, but thank God you're here!"

Marco doesn't reply. He stops a foot away from his restrained father and folds his large arms over his larger chest.

"Don't just stand there!" Dante pulls against his restraints and rocks his chair back and forth. "Kill her!"

"Why did you sell her?" Marco asks, and confusion flashes over Dante's face.

"Sell her? What are you talking about? I don't even know her!"

"You really don't recognize her?" Marco speaks tightly, his voice small. "Take a good, long look."

"Marco, my boy. Whatever she has told you is bullshit, okay? You can't just stand there and let some fucking cunt tie up your own fat

—" His words end in a spray of blood as Fawn punches him hard across the face. He coughs and splutters as she steps back, shaking her hand free of the pain.

Then Leo moves past me and steps into the light.

I watch the pieces slot together in Dante's mind as he looks from Marco to Leo, and then to Fawn who regards him with cold disgust. The moment Dante realizes he's been caught, *really* caught, his whole demeanor changes. He relaxes back into the chair like he's at a bar, and a strange smile creeps across his blood-stained lips.

"I suppose I won't be seeing the Ricci family for some time," he says with a soft grunt. "Figures."

"There's so much I want to ask you," Marco grinds out through clenched teeth. "But I don't know how long I'll be able to hold back my anger listening to the bullshit that spews from your lips so you better start talking, and fucking quickly."

"So this is it?" Dante snorts. "My own son goes behind my back and teams up with the fucking Simones of all people."

"I know, I'm just as surprised," Leo comments. "Isn't it fucked up what brings people together?"

"You were tearing each other apart just last week," Dante scowls.

"Actually, Leo and I haven't been fighting one another for longer than that," Marco says, and he rocks back onto his heels.

My chest aches like a large pressure has settled just above my breastbone, and the air in the room feels thin when I breathe. I want to touch Marco. I want to feel his warmth in my hand to reassure myself that everything is alright, because I'm scared. Scared that Dante may reveal something so awful that this shaky alliance will crumble. Scared that no matter what happens here, the death will never end.

I wrap my arms around myself and bite my lower lip, watching as Fawn punches Dante once again. This time she grabs him by the collar and hauls him upright, then grabs a fistful of his hair and jerks his head back.

"They have more patience than I do," she growls. "So, start talking."

"Fine," Dante spits, spraying bloodied saliva up at Fawn. "What do you wanna know, huh?"

"Everything," Marco says, and there's a touch of pain in his voice. "Why did you sell Fawn? Why the fuck did you get into bed with the Ricci's and the Russians? What the hell were you thinking?"

"Me?" Dante cackles suddenly. "What about you, son? Every step into power, you spat on the old ways and disrespected our traditions. The ways that have kept our family on top for decades were suddenly not good enough for you, and ironically it was all my fault. If your mother hadn't died, you'd have grown up as bloodthirsty as me."

A chill coils down my spine as Marco speaks. "Mom? How the fuck is that your fault?"

"Because *you*," Dante yells, nodding at Leonardo, "were supposed to marry Emilia. Our families were supposed to merge with that marriage, and we would have become so powerful I wouldn't have had to deal with the Russians. Instead, my wife had a few things to say about that and then she never stopped. She was so against it because she was stupid and couldn't bear to be parted from her darling daughter."

A union between Leonardo and Emilia? It's hard for me to picture such an agreement since the two families have been fighting for as long as I've known them. It must have been very different back then.

"But your father, Luca Simone, it was the only deal he would accept. Those were his terms and he was a hard man. So I did what I had to do."

Marco grunts like he's been wounded. "Luca sent those assassins, didn't he? The ones that broke into the estate that day? The ones that killed Mother and maimed Emilia and nearly killed me?"

"They didn't break into the estate," Dante says coldly. "I let them in. And then they were off their leash, and once they were finished with Emilia, there was barely any deal to be had. There was nothing left of her."

Marco's fist flies out as quick as a flash and strikes his father across the head with a solid sound of impact. The force knocks the chair off-balance and Dante crashes backward, landing on his bound arms with a cry of pain.

"Beating up an old man?" he rasps from the floor. "Maybe you're more bloodthirsty than I thought."

"How could you?!" Marco rages, grabbing Dante by the collar and dragging him back up. "How could you let that happen to your wife? Your own *daughter*?!"

"Things got a little out of hand, I admit," Dante chokes. "I realized that your devotion to your sister made you easy to control, but Luca still saw you as being in the way. So he sent *her*." He looks at Fawn like she's the most hideous thing he's ever seen. "Did she tell you she was sent to kill you?"

"Yes," Marco growls, releasing his grip with a snarl of disgust. "She told me everything."

My heart hammers painfully as Dante's face twists. He seems to know that it's completely over for him and now he's just trying to sow discourse and leave behind pain as a final act of revenge.

"Stupid bitch fell in love, and Luca couldn't bear to stomach the disappointment. It was *him* who sold her, not me. You understand?" He glares at Fawn. "It was your own father. I just took the pleasure of fucking that smirk right off your face."

When Fawn launches forward with a scream, no one moves to stop her. She attacks Dante in a fury of punches, clawing and yelling as he mocks her assault. Marco lets her while Leo suddenly doubles over as if he's winded.

"Dad?" he says weakly. "He wouldn't, there's no way because he ..." He pauses and straightens up suddenly, then turns to Dante.

"That's what he meant."

"Huh?" Marco sends up a single glance.

"Remember I told you on his deathbed I overheard him talking about your family and sister? He was talking about Fawn, not Emilia. All those years, he knew she was alive and out there because he put her out there himself."

"I'm sorry," Marco says tightly.

"If he wasn't dead, I'd kill him myself," Leo grunts, then he moves forward and drags Fawn off of Dante.

Dante is a panting, bleeding mess. His shirt is torn open and blood constantly drools from his lower lip. One eye is swelling shut and his head drifts back and forth.

"You see?" he slurs. "No one's family is perfect, but at least I never sold my own kid."

"You tried to though, didn't you? You were talking about marrying Emilia off before it was too late." Marco starts to pace back and forth in front of his father. "I never did ask who you wanted to marry her to because I was never going to let you. But it was the Ricci's, wasn't it?"

Dante laughs and he sounds like he's drowning.

"Then why me?" I step forward, my heart pounding ferociously beneath my chest. Each step feels like I'm walking on Jello from how hard my legs tremble. "You hid that I was alive. You hid that I had a child. You kept me a prisoner under the guise of safety. Why?"

Dante lifts his head and when we lock eyes, the faint back and forth of his head stops. "You," Dante murmurs. "You were an impossible irritation. A piece I never planned for and in truth I just wanted you dead. But then I saw that baby. And I knew. In my bones I knew who the father was. It was the eyes, you see. I looked at that baby and I saw Marco's eyes."

My skin crawls and I clutch at my elbow to try and stem the sensation across my skin.

"But I couldn't raise a baby." He laughs at the thought. "Setting off the explosives in the safe house was supposed to erase two problems, but Marco survived and with that, you suddenly had use. You could do the raising until the time was right."

"Right for what?" Marco demands sharply.

"You and Leo would kill each other eventually, then I would marry Gianna making *our* daughter legitimate. Then I'd marry Freya off to the Ricci's, let them absorb us and power would be—"

He doesn't get a chance to finish. Marco is on him and there's no stopping him. The fury he unleashes is unlike anything I've seen before, and it matches the flurry in which my mind races.

If Marco had died in that explosion five years ago, Dante would have killed me and taken my baby? And because he didn't, he locked me up to care for her while waiting for Marco and Leo to kill each other off.

When he looked at my daughter, all he saw was something he could use.

I feel sick. My stomach churns in sharp circles as my mind floods with the awful future that was awaiting me, that I was completely oblivious to.

It hurts.

And as I watch Marco beat his father to a pulp, I catch a glimpse of the pleased look in Dante's eye.

"Marco, stop," I say, rushing forward. Marco doesn't hear me, he's so blinded with rage. As his arm flies back to punch Dante once more, I catch it and he freezes. When he looks at me, there's such pain in his eyes that my heart breaks for him.

"Don't," I say softly through the tears building in my eyes. "He's not worth it."

"But he—"

"I know, but he wants this. Look at him. He wants you to break while denying the one person who deserves to take his life."

Marco pants heavily, then we look to Fawn who stares coldly down at Dante.

"What? Not got the balls to finish it?" Dante gurgles behind a smashed jaw.

"Nah," Marco sniffs and he steps back, his shoulders heaving. "It's not up to me."

After a few silent glances, Leo, Marco, and I leave Fawn alone with Dante. We head out of the bakery and gather in the parking lot, giving Fawn the time she needs to put to rest a man who caused her such terrible pain. As we wait, I clean up Marco the best I can, wiping away the blood and trying to clean his busted knuckles.

We're silent until Fawn appears thirty minutes later. She's quiet but there's something lighter about her. She stops nearby and looks at Marco. "Sorry I spent so much time trying to kill you."

Marco chuckles. "Sorry my family fucked you up so much."

"And ours," Leo adds. "Our own father ... Fawn, I'm so sorry."

She rolls one shoulder and sighs. "This is gonna take a shit ton of therapy."

"Will you come home?" Leo asks, taking a step toward his sister.

The hesitation is clear in her eyes. "Maybe. I need to think. Process."

He nods and as they hug, I turn to Marco and cup his face. "Let's go home. Let me take care of you."

A new sadness weighs on Marco as he nods. "Let's go home."

34

MARCO

In my youth, I never would have envisioned giving up the top spot of power. I worked hard to get the Barrone family to where it was, especially from where my father left it. It was my pride and joy and my sole focus in this world. It was, in a way, my baby and the only thing I was proud of when it came to my various accomplishments.

Two weeks after my father's death, I signed the papers merging the Barrone and Simone families and stepped down from power. Many were surprised, and the rumor mill ran rampant with theories and stories about Leo and what he had on me that could force me out of power, but the truth was it was simply the right thing to do.

Anton and Ben, my two most loyal guards, easily accepted the merger because they point-blank refused to leave my side. In their words, it didn't matter where I was, I was still capable of getting into shit and they would be right there to help me out of it. I couldn't say no to that.

Afterward, Leo and I worked with Fawn to wipe out the remaining stragglers from the Ricci family, and we sent a clear message that nothing and no one would be exempt from our wrath if there was even a hint of human trafficking happening in this city. The

Russians sent through a few strongly worded threats when we tore apart their underground ring. Since they weren't Stateside and too scared to confront us in person, those threats remained exactly that, just threats.

Fawn came home. She turned up one night on Leo's doorstep a month or so after the city began to settle and said she was ready to try and rebuild things. With Tara and Cherry by her side, she was a formidable force to have on board and Leonardo was just happy to have his sister back. He was able to piece together some semblance of family.

I was the same. Emilia had been nearing her end when my father died so I kept the news from her for fear it would be the one thing that sent her to the grave. It turns out the news told her for me, and a few weeks later, Emilia was stronger.

She still had life left in those bones.

With the city at peace and a new power maintaining it, I was finally able to turn my full attention to the two people who mattered the most to me: Gianna and Freya.

"You know, if we're late Emilia will kill us," Gianna laughs, touching one hand to the blindfold I carefully secured to her face before driving her out to the country.

"Ah, don't touch," I warn her gently, taking her hand in mine and threading our fingers together. "It will be worth it, I promise. And we won't be late."

"We're always late."

"So she gets a few extra hours playing with her niece. I don't think she'll hold it against us."

Gianna grumbles to herself as she follows me up the winding gravel path, clutching at me each time her heels lose balance on the ground. "Are you going to give me a hint about this surprise?"

"Nope," I say gleefully, lightly squeezing her hand. "But I know you're going to love it."

"How do you know?" she asks. "Maybe my taste in things has dramatically changed overnight and only a hint will serve to get me back on track?"

I bring us to a stop at the foot of some smooth stone steps, and lightly cup her face with my hand. "You're a sneaky one," I say, leaning in close until my lips are an inch from hers. She tilts her head, expecting a kiss but I hold back with a smile. "But I'm sneakier."

"Oh really?" Gianna laughs. "Then what exactly are you—oh my God!"

I remove the blindfold as she speaks and her scolding fades into shock as she gazes up at the gigantic house that is to be our new home. It's an old build with Victorian-style windows and stone pillars lining the steps up to a beautiful oak front door. Around us is a large garden filled with trees, flowers, and every outdoor child's activity I could find when I was ordering.

"What is this?" Gianna gasps, placing one foot on the steps.

"This?" I reply casually, watching her beautiful face light up. "This is our new home. Or it can be if you like it. It's just out of the city so we're far away from those memories, but close enough that we can get to whatever school you choose for Freya and civilization is just over the hill behind us. After our wedding, this can be our new home."

Gianna looks at me with her large, sparkling eyes, then lunges forward and kisses me hard. "It's beautiful!"

"Wanna see inside?" I laugh, gathering her in my arms.

We spend the next hour exploring every room in the new house and Gianna lets her ideas pour. This is the first house she's ever had that's truly hers, and it's a beautiful sight to watch as she points out offices and playrooms, makes excited ramblings about the decor, and even sets aside a few of the rooms for Tara, and Fawn. Even Cherry gets a space, although Gianna is still a tiny bit reluctant there.

Even though Cherry and Tara are on excellent terms under Fawn's wing, Gianna still holds some pain there, and I won't force her to move past it. She will when she's ready.

Our tour ends in the master bedroom, where a large four-poster bed takes up most of the space. It's the only piece of furniture, and Gianna laughs the moment she spots it.

"Really? This whole building is bare but there's a bed?"

"I'm fairly certain it's from the old owners," I smile at her. "Trust me. Our bed will be better than this."

"Aw, so it's leaving?" She darts forward and throws herself onto the mattress, then immediately groans as if she's wounded. "Okay, ow. This is so hard. It's too hard."

Watching her enjoyment throughout this entire trip fills my heart and I can't resist running over and crawling over the top of her with a smirk. "You know what else is hard?"

"Oh God," Gianna laughs, pushing at my shoulders with no real strength. "You'd get turned on by the wind, I swear."

"If you were the one blowing it, sure I would."

We kiss, and my heart floods my chest with a tingling warmth. I am in love. I am happy. There is nothing more in this world that I need. Soft kisses gradually turn more heated and soon Gianna's clothes are on the floor as I nip an enticing path up her body. She clutches at my shoulders, pulls at my hair, and wraps her legs so tightly around my hips that I contemplate letting her take control.

Not yet though. I want to be the one to fuck her in our new house.

Gianna's moans ring through the room, echoing due to the emptiness, and she giggles in between as I kiss her ribs, lavish attention over her breasts, and then thrust inside her with all my lusty determination. She cries out and claws lines of fire down my back with her nails. I start to fuck her, and I fuck her hard. Gianna clings to me like her life depends on it and she digs her heels into the small of my back, her telltale sign to not stop. I have no desire to, and I fuck her as hard as I can on a bed that's surely never seen sex this good.

We climax together, mingling our moans between frantic kisses, and Gianna murmurs an apology for the scratches she left on me. An apology I wave off quickly as I roll to the side and soak up the pain of the sheets pressing to the wounds.

"Always mark me," I pant, taking her hand in mine and bringing her knuckles to my lips. "Always."

"So is now a good time to tell you that the other room across from this one is the perfect room for a nursery?" Gianna pants softly.

I roll my head and look at her. "A nursery?"

She nods quickly and bites her lower lip as my post-orgasm mind struggles through the implication of her question.

A nursery?

For a baby?

I jolt upward. "Gianna, are you saying … ?"

"I'm pregnant," she whispers, her cheeks flushing a dark red. "Is that okay?"

"Gianna, that's amazing!" I tackle her back down onto the bed, kissing her repeatedly, and then I move down to her abdomen. "Our baby?"

Tears sting unexpectedly in the corner of my eyes. I missed so much with Freya and while I love her dearly, I miss the moments I could have had in her early life. Now? Now I get a second chance. As I kiss her abdomen, a sudden thought occurs.

"Wait, what about the wedding? Do you want to postpone it until after the baby?"

"Fuck no," Gianna says and she grasps my chin, dragging me up for another kiss. "There's no way in hell I'm waiting any longer."

35

GIANNA

"Are you nervous?"

It's the simplest question and perhaps the hardest one to answer in this moment. I stand dressed in an elegant wedding dress that is a thousand times prettier than my last one.

The ivory fabric flows over my body like silk, hugging my five-month pregnancy bump. Elegant lace roses stretch across the entire fabric, shimmering so much when they catch the light that there's something almost ethereal about the dress. With a low-cut neckline and a deep plunging back, I feel incredibly beautiful and feminine.

This is amazing, considering my life has become nothing but terrible morning sickness and more with this pregnancy. In comparison, Freya was a delight to carry because my current baby seems intent on making me feel unwell as often as possible. I slide one hand over my bump while Cherry comes into view in the mirror, adding the final few sparkling white mini roses to my curled hair.

Tara, the one who asked the question, looks up from where she's sorting out the zipper on Freya's flower girl dress and repeats, "Are you nervous?"

"I think so," I say, smoothing one hand over my bump. "But not to be married. I'm more nervous that something is going to happen that

I can't control, y'know? Everything has been okay so far, smooth sailing with setting up the house and planning the wedding, so I feel like I'm due some sort of reality check."

"That's it," Tara says sweetly to Freya as she hands her the basket of rose petals, then she stands and takes my hands in her. "Gianna. Nothing is going to happen. I promise. Leonardo has this hotel on lockdown, Fawn will kill anyone who looks at you wrong and we are all here to help you. You are going to get the beautiful day you deserve and it's going to be amazing. I promise you."

As she speaks, my eyes fill with tears and I nod along to her final words. "Then why do I feel so on edge?"

"Because you're about to get married," says Cherry, adjusting my curls with her long fingers. "And that's kind of terrifying."

I clutch at both their hands and squeeze. "Thank you so much for being here. I just … When I think of walking down that aisle toward Marco, I feel so insanely calm. It's just if I consider everything else that I start to get a bit …" Rolling my eyes, I puff air up toward the few soft curls around my forehead.

"Just focus on Marco," Tara instructs. "You will do amazing."

The door behind us opens and in walks Fawn wearing a beautiful emerald dress and carrying a bouquet of blue roses. She waves Tara and Cherry away and they say their goodbyes while escorting Freya out.

"Here," Fawn says as she hands me the flowers. "Your something blue. And this …" Fawn removes a small silver hairpin from her hand and presses it into my own. "Your something borrowed."

"Thank you," I say softly, widening my eyes to try and stop the tears from falling. "This is it. This is really it."

"Yup." Fawn smiles at me. In these past months, she's really come out of her shell. She's still an assassin; she just smiles now, which sometimes can be just as creepy. "Five minutes and we'll be ready."

"Can I have a minute?" I ask as Fawn steps back. "I just need to gather myself."

Fawn clutches my bare shoulder and squeezes. "Take all the time you need." With that, she steps out and I'm left alone in the room.

Turning back to the mirror, I take myself in. It's a battle to stop the tears from ruining my carefully applied makeup, so I focus on the shimmery fabric on my dress and turn slowly back and forth.

I can do this. I want to do this.

I'm just scared of what comes after. Nothing in my life has ever been this good which means it's surely not going to last ... right?

The door squeaks softly and I glance over my shoulder, expecting to see Fawn. Instead, I spot Marco and my hands fly to my dress. "Marco! You're not supposed to see me!"

"Oh please," Marco laughs. "We are far from traditional. I'm sorry, I was so excited I couldn't wait to see you. Holy shit, Gianna." He steps forward, his face completely open in awe. "You look incredible."

"You think so?" I give him a little twirl and laugh, then reach for his outstretched hand. "I think I look alright. "You though ..." I whistle softly as I gaze down at his gorgeous gray suit with a blue shirt and rose that matches my own. "You look so handsome."

"Only for you," he smiles, then his brow knits together. "You're trembling."

"I'm excited," I say softly. "And nervous."

"About the ceremony?"

"No, about what comes after. It all feels too good to be true y'know?" I force a deeper breath. "But it's a wedding, and we're supposed to be nervous."

"True," Marco murmurs and he kisses me delicately on the lips. "I know how to make you less nervous, though."

"Oh?" I say. "Does it involve spoiling my makeup because Cherry might kill you if you do that."

"Nah," Marco smirks. "I have a much better idea."

"Marco, what are you ... ?!" Before I can stop him, my fiancé drops to his knees and slides under my dress while grasping my hips and pressing me back against the wall. My heart immediately starts to race as I stumble beside the mirror and hit the wall. He pins me in place, then grasps one of my legs and hoists it over his shoulder so that I am completely at his mercy.

"Marco!" I whine, seeking his head through my dress but too

much silky fabric is in the way. All I can do is tip my head back and moan as his hot mouth presses against the soft fabric of my panties, and his hands caress my thighs.

Using his teeth, he slides the now damp fabric aside, and his tongue strokes against my pussy with firm determination that sends curls of pleasure spiraling through my body.

He's right. It's a damn good distraction. Suddenly, all the nerves fade as the space inside me is filled with warmth. Each lap of his tongue covers my entire pussy and he adjusts the pressure back and forth, teasing over my clit and back toward my hole. Without anything to hold on to, I slide one hand against the wall and the other cradles the back of his covered head, doing everything I can not to grip the lace despite how I crave something to hold on to.

Marco moans deeply and the sound vibrates against me, sending a sudden burst of pleasure through my gut. I whimper, biting my lip and distantly realizing I'll have to reapply my lipstick. As pleasure builds inside me like a knot forming in my core, Marco presses closer and pushes me up the wall slightly until I'm sitting directly on his face. This new angle allows his tongue to delve inside of me, and as much as I clench my thighs against the curling pleasure, I'm at his mercy. I don't have the leverage to grind against him, nor do I have the strength with the five-month bump keeping me unbalanced.

But Marco is strong and I trust him. He keeps me up, and I finally close my eyes, giving in to the pleasure with a louder moan. Wave upon wave of heat washes over me, sending a flurry of tingles up and down my arms. My abdomen clenches, I sink my teeth into my tongue, and I focus my mind's eye on how deep his tongue reaches inside me and how each outward stroke ends with lengthy attention paid to my clit. Then he slides back inside.

My orgasm hits with the force of a freight train as all that nervous energy builds inside me and releases with the cascade of pleasure Marco pulls from me. I cry out, sobbing behind my fingers as I twitch, whimper and rock in his arms. Marco doesn't move, continuing to lavish me with attention until I'm limp. Only then does he pull back, adjust my underwear, and return to face me.

"Better?" Marco asks, cradling my slightly damp face.

I close my eyes and nod, nuzzling into his palm. "You gonna do that every time I'm nervous?"

"Can do." He kisses the tip of my nose, then he crouches and kisses my bump. "I'll be waiting for you. I love you."

He leaves with a wink, and I have to peel myself off the wall. He's right, my orgasm did make me feel better and my running thoughts are kept at bay through the sheer adoration I feel for that man. Taking a look at my slightly frazzled face in the mirror, I reach for the lipstick just as a familiar musical march drifts through under the door.

It's time.

36

MARCO

I'm getting married.

It's not a joke or for show this time. It's real.

With Gianna's sweetness lingering on my tongue, I hurry to the hotel staging area, where Anton stands at the end of the aisle as my best man, with Ben beside him. They both look slightly worried until they lock eyes with me, and all thoughts of me vanishing disappear from their faces.

"Was worried for a second, boss," Anton hisses softly as he grabs me by the lapels of my jacket and begins adjusting my tie.

"Did you really think I'd run?"

"Nah," replies Ben. "Thought someone made it through Leonardo's security and had run off with you."

"I'd be impressed," I reply softly, tilting my head up as Anton resituates the tie knot. "Leo's got this place locked down like crazy."

And I'm eternally grateful. It's hard to believe that my once nemesis is who I am relying on to keep my wedding safe and secure from prying eyes and old grudges. The man himself sits in the front row right next to an iPad showing Emilia who flashes me a proud smile the moment our eyes meet. I'd been against her attending purely for her own health but with the wonder of technology, she's here in spirit.

I know Gianna would have said yes to getting married in Emilia's room if I'd asked, but it was Emilia's planning that got us this beautiful hotel in the first place.

Then the music starts and my heart leaps up into my throat, pounding like a drum just beneath my collarbone. I only saw Gianna maybe ten minutes ago and suddenly I'm nervous again, like something will have changed in those few minutes. I cast an eye around the hall, taking in everyone we trusted enough to invite. There are a few guards of course, and a few of Leo's men who dealt with the victims we found at the docks, along with the stand-in head of the Barrone family. All people vetted and trusted to carry on my legacy and witness my union.

The music swells and Tara appears in a pink dress, holding on to Freya's hand as they walk down the aisle. Every few feet, Freya tosses out some petals from the basket hanging from her little arm, and emotions threaten to overwhelm me. My daughter. These past few months with her have been *incredible*, learning everything about her. Gianna did a phenomenal job raising her in captivity and now that she has a sibling on the way, Freya has really started to come out of her shell.

"Daddy!" she yells when she spots me, earning laughter from the surrounding people. She waves at me with a fist full of petals and Tara smiles warmly, then guides her toward the bride's section to sit down. Given Gianna's lack of family, it's only right.

Cherry and Fawn are next, flowing down the aisle in beautiful dresses. Cherry wears the same pink as Tara, while Fawn is dressed in green. Gianna asked her to be the maid of honor to thank her for everything she did to keep her and Freya safe. It was a fitting choice.

It may be the first time I saw a real, genuine smile on Fawn's face.

They take their place at the opposite side of the aisle to me, and then my fiancée appears and she is an absolute vision.

She's wearing a glittering veil that covers her face and is adorned with sparkling petals that catch the light as she slowly walks down the aisle. With no one to give her away, Gianna insisted on walking herself and she does so with her head held high. I admire every inch of her, from the delicate nature of her curves enhanced by her dress down to the bump of our unborn child, then down to where the dress pools around her like liquid silk.

Tears sting in my eyes as I clasp one hand against my opposite wrist, trying to control the tidal wave of emotion that threatens to sweep me away. I want to laugh, I want to cry and yell my love from the rooftops until the entire city knows exactly who I am and every detail of why I love this woman.

She finally stops opposite me and through the netting of her veil, I catch the cheeky glint of her eyes.

"Hi," she whispers as the officiate begins his greeting.

"Hi," I whisper back.

"Nervous?" she asks.

Something about her presence instantly calms all nerves inside me, and I slowly shake my head. "Not in the slightest."

She nods and reaches out for my hand, which I grip tightly in my own. The officiate speaks smoothly and carries us through the ceremony with a tailored speech about how we met, with slight adjustments, and the importance of our union.

Then it gets to the vows and at Gianna's request, we wrote our own.

I go first.

"Gianna. When I met you, I was something of a knucklehead. I had one vision and one goal, and I was certain I knew what life was going to turn out like. I was planning every detail and I was in control. It felt like the world was made for me. And then, suddenly, you were in my life and business tangled with pleasure. Before I knew it, all that control I thought I had was just an illusion because you were dismantling everything. And I'm so glad you did. Suddenly, all I could think about was you. How to make you happy, how to make you smile at me in the way that made your eyes crinkle. I was falling for you so fast and just as I realized it, life split us apart. But I knew we were fated to be together because not a single part of me was willing to let you go in death, and I don't ever plan to in life. You've given me a beautiful daughter and are soon to give me another, and I can't express how you've guided me onto a brighter path in life. Just know that I love you, from the bottom of my heart, and from this day forth I will do everything I can to make sure you are loved, protected, and cared for until the end of our days. Days that we will spend together."

By the time I finish, I'm crying and I don't even try to hide it. I can't. It's too raw and honest but I need her to know, I need everyone to know how much I love her.

"Marco," Gianna says, and her voice cracks as she fights to control her emotions. "When you found me, I was a penniless thief. It was fun, in its own way, because I tried to steal from people who deserved it, and boy, when I saw you, you really looked like you deserved it."

A soft murmur of laughter rises up.

"But then, somehow, you took me from that and placed me right into a life that I was certain I'd have to act through. And instead, I fell for you. What I was pretending to be real became something I was desperate *to be* real. And then I was having your baby and suddenly I had this new strength to protect what was mine, this little family that we were growing. We haven't had the smoothest of starts, and so much has gone down that I don't think I'd even recognize myself from all those years ago. But I do know one constant, and it's that my love for you has never faltered. It's been the source of my turmoil when people were telling me different things, and the source of my strength in bringing this family together. Because you've given me what I thought I could never have; a home and a family and a future. So thank you. I love you."

By the time she finishes, her voice trembles violently, and she sniffles constantly as the officiant quickly asks us to exchange rings. We do so as smoothly as we both can, and then he says the words that finally break the hold.

"Now I pronounce you husband and wife, you may kiss the bride."

I sweep Gianna up in my arms and throw the veil back, revealing her beautiful face. Her mascara runs and her eyes sparkle as she looks at me and laughs, then winds her arms around my neck and shoulders.

"Hi," she whispers.

"Hi."

I kiss her as the people around us rise with cheers and clapping, but it's all background to the surge of love that bursts through me like a firework. I cuddle Gianna to me as tightly as I dare, kissing her repeatedly as she clutches at me.

This is true happiness.

"I love you."

∽

"YOU'RE MARRIED!" Emilia cheers a few hours later as by some stroke of luck, she wheels herself into the reception party. Normally I'd be annoyed at her for being so careless with her health but tonight I don't care, I'm just happy to have her here.

"Are you proud?" I ask as she takes my hand to examine the ring.

"So proud. I never thought I'd see the day. It almost seems too normal for someone like you."

"Thanks sis. How are you feeling?"

She prods my side. "I'm fine. Tonight is not about me. Now, where is your beautiful bride?"

"She's right over ..." I scan the sea of dancing people and spot Gianna a few feet away engaged in animated conversation with Tara. She's changed into a blue dress the same shade as her roses and my shirt, and it's much easier for her to move about in. "There. Gianna!"

Gianna looks up immediately, one hand on her belly, and waves at me. Her eyes widen when she spots Emilia. She quickly departs from Tara, who scoops up Freya and begins spinning her around to the music as Gianna hurries over.

"Emilia! Oh my God! What are you doing here?" Gianna clutches at Emilia's hands and kisses her cheek, then clasps my hand and threads our fingers together.

"I couldn't pass up on the chance to see the happy couple," Emilia says with a smile. "And I wanted to give you something."

Gianna and I exchange a curious look. "What is it?" she asks.

Emilia digs under her blanket, then she pulls out a small silver brooch in the shape of a butterfly. It matches the trinket attached to my wallet, and the decorations Emilia used to have in her greenhouse.

"Emilia ... oh my God," Gianna breathes softly, examining the jewelry and then immediately pinning it to her dress.

"Welcome to the family," Emilia smiles.

Gianna throws her arms around her in a tight hug and my heart, which has already taken an emotional beating today, swells further at the sight of my wife and sister being so affectionate.

"Actually," Gianna says as she straightens up. "Can we tell her?" She gazes up at me and I can't say no to that face.

"Sure."

"Tell me what?" Emilia asks.

"Well, since the old estate is in ruins and you've been living at one of the safe houses, Marco and I had a thought. We want the family to be together so we've set up space for you at the house for all your medical equipment and staff, and we're even constructing a greenhouse so you can return to your gardening when you're feeling up for it. We originally planned to tell you once construction was complete but honestly, I think this family has been apart long enough." Gianna clutches her hands together. "What do you think?"

"I think the two of you know better than to get a sick woman excited," Emilia scolds with a tear in her eyes. "You don't need me cramping up your new life."

"I do," I say gently. "Emilia ... all my life, you've been in hiding. I want you to live with us, to be a part of our family and to enjoy your last days, however many there may be, surrounded by people who love you."

"Really?" My sister blinks up at me as a few tears fall, and she hastily wipes them away.

"No more hiding," I say, clutching her hand. "Really."

After thoroughly upsetting Emilia in the best way, we collect Freya and wander the party to say hi to all of the guests. Cherry and Tara dance together, arm in arm and tease that soon we will be nothing more than the dusty parents, in bed by ten. I tell them I welcome a life as peaceful as that. Fawn and Leo are equally happy for us and while there's still *slight* friction between Leo and I, I'm happy to now call him a friend. They congratulate us and Leo reassures me that from here on out, life will be good.

I'm not sure I believe him but it's sentimental all the same.

Then Freya begins to get cranky so we take her out on the patio where the cool night air is enough to soothe her overheated skin and she falls asleep in my arms. As I hold her, rocking back and forth, Gianna jumps suddenly and grabs my hand.

"Marco."

"What? What is it?"

With a wide grin, Gianna moves my hand over her belly where suddenly, I feel little bumps rising across her abdomen.

"The baby's kicking?!" I gasp, lowering down to my haunches and caressing her belly, following the movements. "Oh fuck!"

"Language," Gianna scolds with a laugh. "Our little bean wants to be felt this day too."

"Hey bean," I whisper at her bump, stroking softly. "Mommy and I can't wait to meet you."

"No, we can't," Gianna smiles. She touches my jaw and I rise to my feet, keeping an angle so that Freya doesn't wake up. Gianna kisses me slowly.

"I love you, Mr. Barrone."

"I love you too, Mrs. Barrone."

37

GIANNA

"Darling?" Nudging open the door to the kitchen, I walk through cradling my son, Emil, in my arms. Marco stands near the microwave, gently rocking our other son, Sanzio while waiting for the milk to warm up.

Yes, my second pregnancy had turned out to be twins, and that was a whole new whirlwind of challenges neither of us expected. While I'd struggled with milk when it came to feeding Freya, it was impossible with twin boys, so we'd made the decision to switch to formula, which is why most of our evenings look like this: a queue at the microwave waiting for milk to warm so we can feed our darlings.

"Hey love." Marco smiles at me over the top of Sanzio's head, gently nuzzling into him then he turns back to the microwave, locked in a game of making sure to stop the microwave before the ding. A noise like that will certainly knock the twins out of their slumber and we need them on their best behavior tonight. Because tonight, for the first time in months, we're hosting a dinner party. It's our attempt to feel like people again after months of childcare and I'm so excited I could scream.

I won't though, because babies.

"Aha!" Marco cheers lightly and hits the button, saving us from the too-loud ding. With practiced ease, he removes the two bottles of milk from the microwave and sets them on the counter. I step in, handing Emil to Marco and taking over care of the bottles.

"You look beautiful," Marco says softly, standing with our two tiny sons in his large arms. "Excited?"

"Very," I reply quietly, checking the milk temperature. "I'm ready for adult conversation and no crying children and to hear what everyone else has been up to while we've been stuck in baby land."

"Leo's coming," Marco says. "Did I tell you?"

I shake my head. "No, but it's okay. I included him in the catering so there's space for him."

"He's bringing a plus one."

I pause with milk running down my wrist. "Leo is?"

Marco nods, smirking. "Yup."

"Wow. I feel so out of the loop right now."

"You and me both."

We carefully exchange bottle for baby, and then we settle into the familiar routine of feeding our children. Freya is already tucked up in bed fast asleep as we near nine o'clock at night and with any luck, the twins will go down just as easily after their feed.

Learning I was carrying twins so late in my pregnancy was a huge shock, but having this new home to come back to was amazing. And getting to watch Marco soak up all the aspects of baby care that he missed with Freya has been an extra special gift. The only downside is how fast time moves, and I've missed Tara and the others immensely. They visited from time to time, but baby brain was mostly in control then.

This is the first night I'll get to feel like myself and I'm so excited.

Luckily, Emil and Sanzio drink eagerly and fall asleep within minutes of burping. We set them down in their cribs and rock them into a deeper sleep just as guests start to arrive, and soon the night is in full swing.

"So," Marco says, tilting his wine glass and staring down the table at Leonardo. "How did you two meet?"

Leo reaches across and takes the hand of his date, Carmilla. From their brief introduction, his new girlfriend isn't from our world but she's taken to it pretty easily.

"A book signing," Carmilla replies, smiling sweetly.

"Who was doing the signing?" I ask between mouthfuls of delicious pasta.

"She was," Leo says and a dusting of pink rises over his cheeks.

"Oh?" Marco's brow shoots up. "You're a writer?"

"Is it spicy?" Fawn asks from further down the table, wiggling her eyebrows. "Because I'm in the market for a pick me up."

"Simon didn't pan out then?" I ask, peeking past Tara and Cherry to Fawn.

"Nah," Fawn replies. "Couldn't handle a strong woman."

"Fuck him," Cherry snorts, stealing a roasted potato from Tara's plate. "You deserve a King not a boy."

"Too true," Fawn agrees.

"Anyway," Marco mutters, scolding slightly as he looks back at Carmilla. "You write?"

"I do. Action-adventure novels actually," she replies and her cheeks darken. "It was a hobby that sort of exploded and the next thing I knew, this cute guy was telling me the story was good, but my gun descriptors were off."

"Not in a mean way," Leonardo clarifies. "Just glaring enough that only someone who's fired a gun would notice."

"That's how you flirt?" I ask, pointing at him with my fork. "You point out literary inaccuracies."

"It worked, didn't it?" he smirks. "I got her number and now look at us." Leo's thumb slides over Carmilla's knuckles and she looks at him with such adoration that I'm convinced it's genuine. And I know he must feel the same otherwise he wouldn't have brought her to family dinner.

"So do I need to write?" Fawn pipes up. "Is that how I will find a man?"

"You could always beat someone up and spend six years making them fall in love with you," Cherry remarks with a sly glance at Tara. "Worked for me."

"Maybe I'll try that," Fawn sighs dramatically, then she leans forward. "Speaking of, can we talk business?"

Marco nods. "So long as it's good news because this is the first meal and real conversation I've had since the twins were born and I don't want to hear about some asshole getting too big for his boots."

I laugh with him, diving in to another scoop of pasta and having to wrestle the parmesan away from Tara.

Fawn is making leaps and bounds in charity work, having taken over Marco's role in protecting women in need. With her skills and her contacts, the Russians haven't gained another foothold in the city, and she's been quick to stamp out anyone who sees people as products to be sold. Something that should be obvious to decent people, but it's alarming how many scummy cockroaches creep up, eager to move people like cattle. It's clear she enjoys the work, and the Simone and Barrone names are now spoken with heavy respect. Fawn is someone who is safe to reach out to, and everyone knows it.

Tara and Cherry have become an item and are finding new ground and stability within the Mafia. They are doing what they can to keep the drug money clean and ensure that they aren't killing the market. Given their history, no one would have been surprised for them to eternally hate one another, but their work with Fawn brought them close. Since then, they've been making leaps in the drug trade, and the money pours in.

Leonardo is in an equally big place, with only a few sharks nibbling at the edge of their territories. After the crimes of the Ricci family, Leonardo absorbed a few of the smaller families that were left leaderless after that fiasco. Not everyone is happy about it, but Leo's done a phenomenal job of ensuring everyone knows who's boss.

There hasn't been an explosion in the city since that nightclub so that's a vast improvement.

"And you?" Tara asks as she eyes Marco and me. "What have you two been up to?"

"Other than juggling twins, changing diapers, bottle feeding every four hours and doing everything to make sure Freya doesn't feel left out?" I chuckle softly. "Uh ... snatching sleep when we can and—"

Leonardo stands suddenly, his eyes on his phone and then his head snaps to the door just as Anton rushes in.

"Boss," he says to Marco, then he pauses and glances at Leo. "Other boss."

"What is it?" Marco's hand tightens on mine.

"Perimeter breach."

"Gianna, go to the twins," Marco orders.

He doesn't need to tell me twice. As I hurry from the room, Leonardo and Fawn dart out with Anton, followed swiftly by Marco. Tara and Cherry follow me to the twin's room, where they remain sound asleep; then Cherry slips away to fetch Freya.

"What's happening?" I whisper, trying to keep my voice down as my heart races so fast in my chest that the taste of copper tangs in the back of my throat.

"I don't know," Tara says, clutching my arm. "But we will keep you safe."

I have no doubt about that, but a cold curl of fear settles in the back of my mind. We're away from that life, as far as we can get, but Marco is still Marco Barrone, and we'll never fully be *out* of the life.

Given how involved the rest of our family is, I'm not sure I even want to be given how quickly people swarm to protect us.

Cherry appears with Freya in her arms and I immediately cuddle my daughter to me, standing between the two cribs. Whatever is happening outside I know Marco will handle it.

And yet, says a small voice, what if he doesn't? What if this time will be the last time?

Are we really doing this family a favor by staying on the sidelines? My mind runs with a hundred possibilities, each one worse than the last and my heart continues to race.

"Mommy," Freya whines. "I'm tired."

"I know baby," I soothe her gently, bouncing her on my hip. "We just had a scare, that's all. Daddy's gone to check."

Cherry lingers by the door, keeping her shoulder against it while Tara takes the window and I strain my ears to hear any signs of fighting.

I hear nothing.

The longer the silence drags on, the more anxious I become until finally, Marco comes through the door and makes a beeline for me and Freya.

"Marco, what's going on? What's happened?"

"Cherry, Tara. Fawn needs you. I got this."

They both leave and Marco cups my face, kissing me softly. "It's okay. I promise."

"What happened?"

"Let's get Freya back to bed first."

After she's settled and we've checked on the twins, Marco fills me in as we slowly head downstairs.

"They were after Leo. Some small family wanted a chance at taking down the big dog and heard he was leaving town. They assumed that made him an easy target."

"Oh my God." I place one hand over my still-racing heart. "Is he okay?"

"Absolutely. They didn't stand a chance against Fawn."

"Damn. But everyone's okay?"

Marco takes me in his arms at the bottom of the stairs. "Everyone is fine. Are you okay?" He studies my face. "Did that scare you as much as it scared me?"

"I think so," I laugh softly. "I was wondering what I would have to do to protect our three babies."

"Luckily, we have a trusted family for that now," Marco says. "We're not in this alone."

He kisses me softly and leads the way back to the dining room, where we walk in on Leonardo telling Carmilla how amazing Fawn was at tackling one of the intruders. Spirits are high and the room is brimming with warmth.

Marco is right.

We're safer now than we've ever been.

This is not the life I would have chosen, and it was a painful road to get here, but I have a true family and despite our differences, we all would kill for one another.

Woe to anyone who messes with us.

38

GIANNA

"I knew it was too good to be true," Marco mutters. "We've kept them off these shores for so long I'm honestly surprised it didn't take them longer to try and return."

Marco stands a few feet away from the ladders of the yacht, his gorgeous body glistening in the Mediterranean sun while he deals with whatever important issue Leonardo has called about.

I keep one eye on the conversation the best I can, but the majority of my attention is on my children in the water beside me as another dolphin swims over to investigate the splashing from my eldest, Freya. She's eleven now, with her twelfth birthday on the horizon and she has no idea how turbulent the beginning of her life was. I've done everything in my power to keep our children out of that life, beyond a few basics in the case of disaster.

I don't want them growing up like Marco did, and certainly not like me.

"It kissed me!" Freya squeals. "Mom did you see?! Did you see?!"

"I did!" I laugh as Freya pats the dolphin on the nose. A foot away, the twins Emil and Sanzio are playing with a ridiculous number of inflatables, but they are equally as ecstatic to see dolphins up close. I swim near them, keeping an eye on the dolphin as my two five-year-olds splash hard and laugh.

"Now be careful," I warn Sanzio as his hand splashing comes a little too close to one of the dolphins. "You don't want to scare them."

"Okay!" he replies cheerily and focuses on splashing his brother instead. They dissolve into giggles just as Freya hooks her hand around a dolphin fin and allows herself to be pulled along a few feet.

A holiday in the Mediterranean feels like an impossible dream, but Marco and I strive to give our kids everything they could ever want, within reason. I don't want to spoil them but it's hard. Growing up with nothing, I want my kids to have everything.

As my children have the time of their lives in the water, an alarm beeps from the back of the yacht, signaling that we've all spent enough time in the ocean.

"Alright rascals, play time is over. Back on the boat."

"But *Mom*," rises a chorus of complaints. No one wants to give up their time in the water, but I quickly scoop up Emil before he can swim too far away, and Sanzio follows. I learned pretty quickly that Emil is the more headstrong of the two and right now I'm using that to my advantage.

"I'm sure the dolphins will be back tomorrow," I say, reaching the ladder.

Marco is there with his phone balanced between his ear and his shoulder and he scoops Emil out of the water with one hand. "You heard your mother. The rule was until the alarm and I know you all hear the alarm."

"Fine," Freya groans and she drags herself out of the water with a dramatic flair. "They better be there tomorrow, I'm getting the feeling that I was supposed to be a merperson in another life."

"Oh really?" I chuckle, helping Sanzio back up on deck and closing up the railing. "Well how about tomorrow you use your merfolk powers to bring us a whale. I'd love to see one of those."

"It doesn't work like that *Mom*," Freya sighs. "Land people are so dumb."

"Are they?" calls another voice. Out from the lounge walks Emilia, leaning heavily on her cane. Her health journey has been a tough one, but being free of Dante, free of quiet captivity in a greenhouse, and away from the stresses of Mafia life has done wonders for her.

I swear I saw a new life breathe into her the first time she held the twins.

"Auntie!" they all yell and they charge toward her.

I'd follow but I take one step and Marco sweeps his solid, warm arm around my waist and pulls me close to his broad chest.

"Mm-hmm," he says, still on the phone to Leo even as he dips his face into the crook of my neck and kisses me. "Yep. You got it. Keep me informed, okay?"

"What's happening?" I ask, swiveling in his hold to cup his face as he ends the call. "Do they need us back?"

"Not on your life," he grins, kissing me lazily. "The recent influx of weapons across the East Coast? The Russians. Looks like they're finally brave enough to start infecting our territory again. Leo wanted advice on how to crack down on them."

"You're like a Mafia guru," I chuckle. "Giving advice from beaches and yachts to people a thousand miles away."

"It's a good life," he grins down at me. "Fawn took care of some Triad trouble a few weeks ago and the disturbing family was so alarmed that they gave up the Russians immediately and are seeking peace."

"Wow. A visit from Fawn is enough to scare the balls off even the strongest of them. Do I want to know what she did?"

"Probably not," Marco laughs. "All we need to know is that it worked."

"One at a time," comes Emilia's light laugh. "One at a time!"

The children pile onto her for cuddles, then help her toward one of the sun loungers near the yacht's pool. I watch them for a few moments, never tiring of seeing my family together and happy.

"Oh, and Cherry and Tara have finally secured the top spot on the drug side of things. The Irish bowed out of the race, to an extent. Tara's letting them still do their business, just for a cut. They've dominated the recreational market more than I ever could."

"You know if they break up, we'll have one hell of a lovers tiff on our hands," I point out, lightly running one of my hands over Marco's chest. "We've created two powerful drug lords that happen to be dating, and if they end up falling out then what does that mean for us?"

"Let's hope it doesn't happen before Leo's wedding. He'll be heartbroken not having Tara there to make her famous dip."

I clutch at Marco. "He set a date?!"

"Yup. Carmilla wants a Christmas wedding."

"Oh, that's so romantic," I say with a soft sigh. "I bet she's going to look so beautiful."

"Not as beautiful as you." Marco lightly grasps my chin and tilts my head up, kissing me gently.

"Do you miss it?" I ask in a whisper when he pulls back.

"Miss what?"

"The life. The drugs and the guns and the killing?"

Marco shrugs. "We've had our fair share of scares over the years, so I don't think we'll ever be free. But this is my life now. My focus is on you and our kids. I don't want to miss a second."

He tightens his arms around me, and I kiss him deeply. I close my eyes against the glare of the sun and let the music of the lapping waves and dolphin chirrups wash over me.

"I love you for that," I say against his lips, although it's an unspoken rule that we would be there if things were dire and Leo needed us.

"I love you too," he replies softly. "I'm happy, Gianna. You've given me more than I ever could deserve, and being here in the Mediterranean watching my kids swim with dolphins and seeing Emilia's health glow, and just living this life? It's more than I ever could have asked for."

"God, you're so different now," I tease, kissing his lower lip.

"Is it boring?" he replies with a smirk. "Do you need me to go out and kill someone, come back covered in blood and have my way with you?"

"I would not be opposed." I kiss him again, just as Emil yells and dives into the pool.

"Emil!" Marco pulls back and moves forward. "What did we tell you? You have to shower off the sea water before you dive into the pool water, okay buddy?"

"Sorry Dad!" Emil yells, spluttering as water washes over his face. He makes it to the edge of the pool where Marco scoops him out and spins him around, making him squeal with laughter as he pretends to shake all the water free.

"Come on kids," says Emilia as she stands slowly. "Let's go shower and get some sugar in you after all that swimming."

Marco sets Emil down and we watch him hurry after his brother and sister. As they join up, holding hands and laughing, my heart pulls south as I approach Marco. I cuddle up to his arm and slide one hand over his abdomen, grinding against his hip.

"Hey babe?"

"Yes, darling?"

"Do you think you could handle a fourth kid?"

CRAVING *your next mafia romance fix? Dive into "***Savage Devotion: An Age Gap, Pregnancy, Mafia Romance***," available now on Amazon. Keep the passion and intrigue burning!*

Binge read the entire series here.

Your unwavering support fuels this world of illicit auctions, surprise pregnancies, and perilous love affairs. From the bottom of my heart, grazie mille!

Until we meet again in the dark underbelly of romance...

Keep turning those pages, and remember – in Ajme's mafia realm, secrets are the most valuable currency, and love is the deadliest weapon!

WANT MORE AJME WILLIAMS?

Join my no spam mailing list here.

You'll only be sent emails about my new releases, extended epilogues, deleted scenes and occasional FREE books.

Printed in Great Britain
by Amazon